PRAISE FOR GREGG LOOMIS

"Loomis blends ancient historical legend with contemporary medicine in his lively seventh thriller featuring ex-FBI agent and practicing attorney Lang Reilly (after 2014's *The Cathar Secret*) . . . Loomis smoothly spins a tale of greed and shady political maneuvering while commenting without sermonizing on humankind's capacity for compassion and cruelty."
—*Publishers Weekly*, for *THE POISON SECRET*

"The international setting and fast-paced action grip, and fortunately, Loomis's convincing protagonist possesses the intelligence and emotional depth to carry the reader . . . [Readers] looking to repeat *The Da Vinci Code* experience will be satisfied."
—*Publishers Weekly*, for *THE PEGASUS SECRET*

"More intrigue and suspense than in *The Da Vinci Code!*"
—*Robert J. Randisi*, author of *Blood of Angels*, for *THE PEGASUS SECRET*

"An intelligent, fast-paced, riveting thriller with an explosive ending. A great debut novel."
—*Fresh Fiction*, for *THE PEGASUS SECRET*

"Dan Brown's fans will find *THE JULIAN SECRET* a delight."
—*I LOVE A MYSTERY*, for *THE JULIAN SECRET*

"Another thrilling, action-packed adventure for Lang Reilly!"
—*Fresh Fiction*, for *THE SINAI SECRET*

"Thriller fans will appreciate Gregg Loomis as it is no secret that he provides breathtaking novels."
—*Midwest Book Review*

THE POISON SECRET

THE POISON SECRET

A LANG REILLY THRILLER

GREGG LOOMIS

TURNER

Turner Publishing Company

424 Church Street • Suite 2240
Nashville, Tennessee 37219

445 Park Avenue • 9th Floor
New York, New York 10022

www.turnerpublishing.com

THE POISON SECRET

Cover design: Nellys Liang
Book design: Kym Whitley

Library of Congress Control Number: 2014958498

ISBN 978-1-63026-006-4 (paperback)

Printed in the United States of America
14 15 16 17 18 19 0 9 8 7 6 5 4 3 2 1

This book is for Suzann

THE POISON SECRET

PROLOGUE

King of Pontus, Foe of Rome,
Story of a Hellenistic Empire
by Abiron Theradoplis, PhD
National Museum of Archeology, Athens
Translation by Chara Georopoulos
University of Iowa Press
(Excerpt)

Pergamaman, Anatolla
(Modern-day Western Turkey)
Roman Province of Asia
Spring, 88 B.C.

THE SCREAMS OF THE TERRIFIED, MIXED with the moans of the dying and wounded, could easily be heard from the palace of the recently deceased Roman legate. To the ears of King Mithradates, the song of the lute or lyre could not have been sweeter. All over Anatolla, here in Pergamaman, in the ship-building port of Adramyttion, the commercial center of Ephesus, the hill-surrounded town of Tralles and its neighbor, Nysa, the slaughter of every Roman and Italian man, woman, and child was progressing as planned. Slaves who spoke a language beside Latin were to be spared as were those who revealed any Roman in hiding. Persons giving shelter would be dealt with harshly as would those removing the bodies from where they lay as a feast for the dogs and vultures. The massacre had been carefully and secretly planned for months to ensure it took place simultaneously and without warning.

When the slaughter began at daylight here in Pergamaman, many terrified families of Roman merchants, tax collectors, slave dealers, and money lenders had fled out of the gates to the Temple of Asclepius. By ancient Greek custom, all temples were holy, protected against violence by the gods. Under the right of *asylia*, asylum, anyone, foreigner, citizen, slave, innocent or guilty, could find refuge inside. Pursuers usually dared not commit the sacrilege of violence before the gods. But today there was no mercy shown those huddled around the god of healing. The native-born citizens of the city burst into the sanctuary and shot their foreign neighbors: men, women, children, down with arrows. Those who had not died in the initial assault were hacked to death with swords and daggers.

The Romans may have chosen this city as the capital for their newest province, but most of that province was allied with Mithradates, VI Eupator Dionysus, King of Pontus, victor over the Roman puppet Nicomedes VI and liberator of Anatolia, and ruler in fact of Colchis, western Armenia, Cappadocia, and Galacia. When the day was done, a figure estimated by the historian Appian of Alexandria at 80,000 would be dead, including the Roman Ambassador Marius Aquillius, whose palace the king now enjoyed. The ambassador had died a spectacular if hideous death a few days earlier, suffocated on the molten gold poured down his throat as a symbol of Roman greed.

When the news reached Rome, Cicero, the great orator and statesman, was to observe, "The Roman name is held in loathing and Roman tributes, tithes, and taxes are instruments of death."

At the moment on this sunny spring morning, Mithradates cared little about these facts, only that his plan to free Anatolian soil of the hated Romans and their Italian lackeys seemed to be going well. Violence was common in the ancient world, particularly in the king's experience. As a youth, he remembered too well his father (also Mithradates) lying on the banquet room floor, his silver cup still in his hand. It had been a celebration of the king's birthday at the royal palace in Sinope, capital of Pontus. A whole ox, camel, or donkey (the ensuing chaos had blurred Mithradates's recollection) roasted inside a huge brick oven, Black Sea tuna, eel, and each course served with sweets and a great deal of wine. Magicians from Parthia, snake charmers from India, musicians and poets from Greece, it had all ended suddenly and badly.

The verdict? Poison. Suspects? Laodice, a queen ambitious for her favorite son, a hundred disgruntled subjects, a general conveniently out of the country.

One thing was certain to the young prince: he could well be next. He disappeared. For the next seven years he and his band of companions never once slept under a roof and survived by hunting and fishing.

Yes, violence was on the king's mind as the last shrieks of his Roman victims died on the still air of that spring morning.

CHAPTER 1

THIS COULD WELL BE THE MOST important day of Fatima Aksoy's professional life, and she was in a hurry.

She was a graduate of Emory University School of Medicine, and had done her residency at the prestigious Children's Hospital in Los Angeles. For the last four years, she had been director of the Janet & Jeff Holt Foundation's pediatric hospital here in Trabzon, the only institution specializing in children's health care on Turkey's Black Sea coast.

None of that did her any good at the moment. She and her silver 150cc Dorado Arcon scooter were just as trapped in the traffic of the city's busiest street as the other scooters, motorcycles, and cars. The big black Mercedes in front of her was honking its horn as if it expected the jam to part like the Red Sea at Moses' command.

With nothing else to do but mentally curse the delay, Fatima watched two women on foot pass on the sidewalk. Black hijabs covered their hair. Even here in the world's only true Moslem democracy's more rural areas, Islamic dress for women was losing popularity. Like most professional women, Fatima wore a pantsuit to work. At night, particularly if she and Aydin, her husband, were going to some especially expensive restaurant, the ones frequented more by Greek businessmen than natives, she would wear a dress, even a low-cut one that bared her arms. She had two dresses, both of which she had purchased before leaving California.

Trabzon reminded her of California the way the Pontic Alps fell into the sea. But the mountains here were a lush green, not the dry hills that faced the pacific. She . . .

She forgot the Golden State for the moment as traffic began to inch forward. She shot a glance down a cross street to Meyclan, the center town square, where an open-air market was drawing its usual crowd of bargain-shopping housewives, elderly men bored with the teahouses or otherwise idle, and small children holding onto their mothers' hands or clothes. Then it was past, and she picked up speed. Whatever had caused the delay had inexplicably disappeared.

Within minutes, she was passing through Limoinsuya Yaylasi, a section on the edge of the city with large open spaces between buildings and as many grazing horses as automobiles. She passed the modern five-story Trabzon Kardelen Hotel, a hideous stack of square concrete. As always, she wondered who would choose to stay in a place so ugly and distant from anything else.

Well, almost anything else. The pediatric hospital was only two kilometers down the road. She supposed someone with a child admitted there might stay at the hotel, though the parents of most of her small patients could ill afford to pay for lodging, here or in the less expensive places in town.

Which brought her back to Baris and the reason she was in such a hurry.

Four-year-old Baris had been playing near his village among the ruins of one of the ancient temples that dotted the mountainsides in this part of Turkey. Fatima couldn't remember if it was Greek or Persian, although it hardly mattered. Whatever nation or god or combination thereof, the present residents included what she guessed from the child's description to be a horned viper. Although snakes were much more rare here on the Black Sea coast than, say, along the Iranian border, there was no denying the twin punctures on the back of the child's hand and venom in his bloodstream.

Those were the only things certain. The little boy's parents, ignorant mountain peasants, had noted none of the acute distress, blood, nausea, vomiting, and swelling associated with serpent bites. So, they had ignored the matter for nearly a week, alarmed only when the bite marks refused to heal.

But then what would you expect of a people who believed a pregnant woman's diet determined the sex of the baby? Sweet food produced a boy, spicy meant a girl. Expectant women were not supposed to look at animals such as camels or monkeys but should spend time contemplating the moon. Or that Nazar Beads deflected the evil eye and eating a specially baked bun would make a young girl dream of her future husband.

The venom of the horned viper, Fatima had learned, flowed through the lymphatic system, destroying the blood's ability to coagulate. The snake's smaller prey, mostly mice and rats, literally bled to death internally within minutes. Its larger victims, human or livestock, usually survived even untreated bites, although frequently with the loss of fingers or toes to necrosis from the venom. Fatima could only speculate at the devastation that an untreated bite might wreak on a child as small as Baris who was already little for his age.

Fortunately, she thought, she apparently would never know. Other than the puncture wounds, he showed no ill effects whatsoever.

A miracle?

Perhaps, although as a scientist she tended to discount miracles, leaving them to the Christian tourists who flocked to Turkey's early Biblical sites in ancient Galatia and Cappadocia.

Miracle or not, the explanation defied medical science. At least as Fatima knew it.

Within minutes of Baris's arrival at the hospital early this morning, she had drawn blood, sending it to Emre down in the lab in the building's basement. Because the little boy seemed otherwise asymptomatic, there had seemed to be no rush. Making sure he was resting comfortably and assuring his very nervous parents as best she could, she had made her daily rounds and then left to meet Avdin for lunch at a favorite fish restaurant, one with a hillside view of the Black Sea. She had hardly finished her pilaki, fish sautéed in olive oil with garlic, onions, carrots, and potatoes, when her cell phone rang.

It was Emre and he was clearly agitated.

"Fatima? Come right away!"

"But, what . . .?'

"It's that little boy who came in this morning . . ."

The thought of delayed reaction to the snakebite nearly made her choke. Unlikely, but how likely was it that the venom had had no ascertainable effect in the first place? "Baris? What about him? Is he all right?"

"He's fine."

Fatima felt her cheeks flush with anger. "You called me in a panic to tell me he's fine?"

"I'm not panicked," Emre said defensively. "It's the blood work. You'll have to see it for yourself to believe it."

And so she would very shortly, Fatima thought as she eased the Dorado Arcon into a space in the physicians and staff *otopark*, turned the key in the ignition, and, purse slung over her shoulder, hurried inside. Her first stop was the room Baris shared with another boy.

It had been a real battle to get Baris's parents to agree to leave their seemingly healthy child in the hospital overnight for observation. Only the promise that there would be no charge made them relent. Fatima wasn't sure how she would fulfill this promise. SSK, Turkey's largest government health plan, excluded agricultural workers, which these people were. *Bag-Kur*, the catch-all program, was notoriously difficult to navigate.

She shoved the question of the hospital bill to the back of her mind in much the same way she would have replaced a pair of shoes in her closet after deciding not to wear them today. Even before she reached the open door, she heard the television, the unmistakable sounds of the eternal conflict between Wile E. Coyote and Road Runner. Happily, the "beep-beep" needed no more translation from English than the sound effects of Coyote's latest disaster. Once at the door, she saw both boys engrossed in the American cartoon, one she had enjoyed herself on the rare occasions she had time for diversion from her studies.

Seeing no need to make her presence known, she turned and headed for the stairs. She reached the bottom, her nose twitching with the mixture of chemical smells. She pushed open a door and walked down a white corridor until she reached the lab.

In his usual rumpled lab coat, Doktor Emre Yalmaz was peering at a centrifuge through dandruff-speckled glasses with the intensity of a gambler at the roulette table. At his elbow, a cigarette smoldered among a cemetery of its brothers. Fatima had given up on pointing out the bad example his habit might be for the hospital's young patients.

He must have heard her over the whine of the machine, for he turned and favored her with that shy smile she found so endearing. One of the youngest to graduate from Pamukkale University medical school in Denizli, he had chosen to specialize in hematology, Fatima suspected, because it involved minimal contact with patients. His shyness and the adoration he held for her were common subjects of jokes around the hospital. She routinely denied the latter while secretly flattered by it, even if she recognized puppy-like devotion for a woman ten years Emre's senior.

The centrifuge murmured, sputtered, and went silent.

"You said I should come right away."

The young doctor blushed as he almost always did when she spoke to him. He reached behind him and removed several pieces of paper from a lab table. "Read this, Fatima."

She started to reach for the glasses that hung just inside her blouse. With increasing frequency they were becoming necessary to review documents. This time vanity stayed her hand.

She took the sheaf of papers and held them up to the maximum light the room provided.

Emre produced a magnifying glass. "Perhaps this would help?"

She lowered the papers and glared at him. "What makes you think I need that?"

"The fact you are squinting so hard your eyes are nearly closed."

She considered denying the fact but said, "Why don't you tell me what is in this report?"

He thought a moment as though considering the request. "Very well. First, the child's blood is full of antivenom."

"That's not possible. He was asymptomatic upon arrival. I expressly decided he did not need antivenom. It's in his chart. Who authorized he be given the serum?"

Emre blushed for the second time in as many minutes. "I never said he was given anything."

"But the antitoxin, the antivenom . . .?"

"It appears it was already in his blood."

Fatima looked around, found a lab stool behind her, and sat. "What are you saying, Emre?"

Behind his thick glasses, the hematologist's eyes were exaggerated, giving him a frog-like appearance. He ran a hand through his hair, producing a snowstorm of dandruff. "I'm saying the child's blood already had the antivenom. Did you ask his parents if . . ."

"If he had already been inoculated? Don't be silly. They are simple peasants. Both denied ever being in a hospital before. Besides, if the boy had already been treated, why would they bring him here? It makes no sense."

Emre gave a humorless chuckle. "If you think that makes no sense, wait until you hear the rest."

"Which is?"

"I was curious, so I ran a few more tests."

"And?"

"Among other immunities are those to neurotoxin such as, say, a cobra might have; scorpions; venomous spiders; arsenic; and a number of herbal poisons such as nightshade, hemlock, or wolfsbane. I started to test for immunities to a number of diseases, but that starts to get expensive."

It took Fatima nearly a minute to absorb what she had heard. "Neurotoxin? I don't think there are any cobras in Turkey. And arsenic?"

"A tolerance for arsenic can be acquired by building up an immunity in small doses, which can be easily detected in the blood. Or, for that matter, the hair." He shook his head. "But as to the neurotoxin . . ."

"What you are telling me is quite impossible, you know."

"Perhaps. When I was growing up along the coast here, my family were fishermen. There were stories . . ."

Now Fatima was shaking her head. "Stories? About sea monsters, ghost ships, and giant squid, no doubt."

"Those, too. Fishermen are a superstitious lot. But the tales I had in mind were about a family that lived along the coast here a long time ago, a family that had some sort of immunity."

"Immunity to what?" Fatima demanded.

"Just about everything or, at least, to known poisons."

"And you think this child is one of them?"

"Fatima, I don't know what to think. All I know is the blood of this child is as full of antidotes, antitoxins, and immunities as *kuru fasuly* is of beans. I do know I've never seen anything like it, nor have any of the hematologists I know." He brightened, a broad smile dividing his face. "Perhaps I could write a paper! Yes! A paper for one of the American medical journals, one I can go to present in the United States. Perhaps even meet Mr. Reilly!"

Fatima had met Mr. Reilly only once, in Los Angeles when he had interviewed her for her job here. She had expected more of the head of the worldwide Holt Foundation than the rather ordinary-looking man across the table, an American *avukat*, lawyer. After a few minutes, she had realized there really was little ordinary about him. He had a gaze that seemed to strip her psyche to her very soul, an intensity far greater than she would have guessed was required for a routine hiring of a new doctor in an out-of-the-way hospital nearly halfway around the world and as far from Reilly's culture as the moon. It was only after a few months at the children's hospital that she realized Mr. Reilly had an interest in anything relating to the hospital and, presumably, the Foundation.

He had also seemed to have intuition about people, or at least her. As a first job, she had felt any number of insecurities. Reilly had shown only a calm assurance that she was the right person for the position. She had been surprised before she became accustomed to regular e-mails congratulating her on this or complimenting the way she had handled that.

In spite of only a single meeting, Fatima regarded Mr. Lang Reilly as a friend, although she knew nothing of him other than his connection to the Foundation.

"Fatima?"

Emre was staring at her.

She came back to the present with a jolt. "I was just trying to think of the best way to make your discovery known," she lied.

"Perhaps in America?" he asked hopefully, as though seeking permission.

"Not for me to say, Emre. But I do think you need to translate your report into English and send it to, to . . . What's his name, the Foundation's head of medical operations?"

"Dr. Walsh. I will send him an English version of my report by e-mail immediately. Later today, I'll send him a part of the blood sample by DHL with a hard copy of the e-mail. Do you think he will want me to come there, to America?"

Emre's expression reminded Fatima of a puppy she once adopted, half-Akbash, half-mongrel, who looked that way when his food bowl was empty.

"He might, Emre, he might."

CHAPTER 2

Emory University Hospital
Department of Hematology
1365 Clifton Road
Atlanta, Georgia
Two Days Later

TANYA WAS HAPPY TO HAVE THE job, even if it meant no more than being a glorified maid. The pay was good, the work no harder than pushing a broom and emptying wastebaskets that might contain contaminants, whatever they were. With little Darious outgrowing clothes faster than she could get them from the Goodwill, and Jamal, her baby daddy, insisting on using her EBT card down at the liquor store, there was hardly enough left on it for food, rent, the cell phone bill, or the payments on the flatscreen TV, never mind the money for MARTA to get her from her Section 8 apartment to the Emory campus.

And there sure wasn't no money for that medical tech course she had wanted to start since high school. But then she'd gotten pregnant with Darious, and things just spun out of control.

If Jamal would just get a regular job 'stead of hanging with the homies in the hood . . . He always had some kind of a deal working, but it never seemed to bring in any money. In fact, he had viewed her job as a real opportunity, what with all the expensive equipment just lying around. "Keep your eyes open," he had often said, like he thought she could just slip a BMD 025 analyzer the size of a chest of drawers or a 24-tube centrifuge in her purse and walk out the door unnoticed.

Yep, money was tight, but the joy she got from what she suspected was in her belly kept her mind off it. Too early to be sure, too early to tell Jamal yet, but she was almost certain . . .

She was in one of the labs, empty except for an Asian man in a white lab coat. Usually the lab techs and the docs cleaned up pretty well after themselves, but today someone had left the room with a job in progress. An ice cart used to preserve blood samples was parked next to a high stool. On the counter in front of the stool was a small centrifuge, a microscope, and a stack of papers that she guessed had come from the red and yellow DHL Express envelope next to it.

More from curiosity then criminal intent, she parked her broom against the counter and peered down at the papers. At first, she wasn't certain she was reading the words right. Her second reaction was to remember Jamal's instructions to keep her eyes open for anything valuable. If she was seeing what she thought she was, somebody might pay a lot of money for that information, a whole lot.

She looked around the lab. The Asian lab tech in the white coat had his back to her, staring through a microscope. It wasn't like she was going to steal anything, just borrow a few papers long enough to run them through the Xerox machine down the hall before she brought them right back. They weren't even marked "confidential" or anything. And Jamal would know someone who knew someone who might be interested.

Real interested.

What was the harm in that?

CHAPTER 3

Headquarters of Dystra Pharmaceuticals
Suite 1720
One Atlantic Center
1180 West Peachtree Street
Atlanta, Georgia
The Next Day

WILLIAM GRASSLEY STOOD, HANDS CLASPED BEHIND his back, as he studied Georgia Tech's Bobby Dodd Stadium a few blocks to the southwest from the seventeenth floor.

"Why," he asked no one in particular, "do they go to so much trouble to keep up the grass when the football season is months away?"

"I'd guess it's easier to keep up than start from scratch," someone volunteered.

Grassley turned to treat the other men in the room to a scowl. He had not become CEO of Dystra Pharmaceuticals by guesswork. He believed in keeping your mouth shut if you didn't know the answer. Keep the old lips zipped until you could find the correct solution.

He returned to the purpose of the meeting. "Well?"

"We don't have a lot to lose," observed a black man in a pinstriped suit, Ralph Hassler, CFO. "I mean, if the information is anywhere near accurate, it's worth a hell of a lot more than the five grand the guy wants."

"*If* is the operative word," observed the man next to him, COO Hugh Wright. "I mean no offense, Ralph, but look at the source: a single welfare mother living in Section 8 housing finds something at Emory, and her boyfriend, a small-time dope peddler, wants five grand because it has to do with some kind of medical breakthrough."

Hassler gave him a sideways glance. "You mean a *black* single welfare mother."

Wright sighed. This wasn't the first time the question of race had side-lined an important decision. He knew Hassler had grown up in Atlanta's Vine City, a neighborhood of largely white slumlords and poor blacks sub-sisting in substandard housing. The man had somehow managed not only to thrive in Atlanta's equally substandard public schools, but win one of the first scholarships to Georgia Tech awarded to a black student. He had majored in chemical engineering and, as a minority, found openings in a number of the country's premier firms that, like most of America at that time, were hustling to atone for the past sins of Jim Crow and segrega-tion. When he turned to pharmaceuticals, Pfizer snatched him away from Merck, where he had been with a generous salary, bonus, golden para-chute, and stock options, and brought him back to the city of his birth. Besides a return to Atlanta, the pot had been sweetened with six weeks of paid vacation and free use of the company's multiple European and Car-ribean retreats

He might be one of America's leading drug executives, but he never forgot his origins.

"Black, white, or green," Wright retorted, "the information hardly comes from an impeccable source."

"Just because . . ."

"Gentlemen," Grassley interrupted, "let's look at a few facts. First, if this information is even close to accurate, that someone has discovered anything approaching what this man claims the correspondence says, five grand is nothing. The first company to get FDA approval of such a drug will make Viagra's revenue look like peanuts. Second, as you know, Dys-tra Pharmaceuticals has been limping along the last few years, producing generics once a drug's patent expires along with half a dozen of our com-petitors. Mere crumbs from the big boys' table. If we could get our hands on this serum or whatever it is . . . Well, move over Pfizer, get out of the way, Merck. Hell, this could be as big as aspirin."

"I suppose we owe our stockholders the effort," Hassler said.

"Where is this place?" Wright asked.

"Somewhere in Turkey."

"Turkey?" Wright's eyebrows knotted. "Didn't we do business with some group over there sometime back, back when it looked like the FDA might approve a fat pill?"

Grassley shook his head. "Stupid of us to even think the Feds would okay anything with opium as an ingredient, no matter how small. But, yeah, somebody from, what did they call it?"

"*Gayrimesru*," Hassler supplied. "Mafia world. Turkish mafia. Turks and Kurds. Probably ships more raw opium than anyone else in the world. They're criminals."

Grassley shrugged. "We're not doing anything illegal, just asking a former contact to gather information for us, verify as much as possible of what we think this report we're paying five grand to see has to say."

"If that's all," Hassler asked, "why are we hiring criminals to do it?"

Grassley's mouth was a thin line as he sat down at the head of the conference table. "Because I want that formula, serum, or whatever it may be, and I don't want to go through a lot of international bureaucratic bullshit to get it. Those guys will do whatever it takes. No way we're going to finish second in this race."

"'Whatever it takes' embraces a lot of territory," Wright observed. "I can't speak for you guys, but personally, I have a strong aversion to going to jail."

A sentiment Hassler seconded with a nod.

"Who said anything about jail? Like they say about Vegas, what happens in Turkey stays in Turkey. We pay these *Gayrimesru* out of one of our special offshore accounts, one we use to encourage the local politicos to see things our way. Can't be traced to Dystra."

Hassler shook his head. "I don't know. Those guys would shoot their own mother if the price was right. I'm not sure I want to do business with people like that."

Grassley smiled, though there was little humor in it. "A little late for scruples, isn't it, Ralph?"

There was no answer.

CHAPTER 4

Peachtree Circle and Peachtree Street
Atlanta, Georgia
At About the Same Time

GURT FUCHS WAS LATE. HER SON, Manfred, was about to be released from his first-grade class in less than ten minutes. His school, Westminster, was easily 20 minutes away. That was the problem with one of the city's most prestigious private schools: it was located in one of Atlanta's most prestigious neighborhoods at the far end of West Paces Ferry Road, far from the winding streets of quirky and much older Ansley Park.

At over $19,000 a year, Gurt thought maybe the school might provide bus service, but no such luck. And since she was unaware of any other Ansley Park kids attending Westminster (although most parents here could afford it), there was no carpool, either. At least Lang, Manfred's father, could take the child most mornings, although doing so was a substantial detour from the route to his downtown office.

Her irritation level went up a couple of degrees when the light at the intersection turned red just as she reached it. She sat, glaring at the prominently posted NO TURN ON RED signs.

What she didn't see were the two men stepping off the curb. Each was carrying a bucket of dirty water and a squeegee.

Business had been good so far today for Leon Frisch and his pal D'Andre. Two dollars for swiping the squeegee across some housewife's windshield and demanding two bucks for "cleaning." With his week's beard, six-foot height, stained sweatshirt, pants a size too small, and a not entirely feigned wild look in his eyes, most women acted predictably: they clicked the door lock and proffered the two dollars demanded through the crack at the top of the window.

And why not? These rich bitches in their BMWs and Mercedes would spend more for lunch today than Leon took in in a week. And they didn't have to sit through a hymn and prayer service for a bed at the Salvation Army shelter at night. Wasn't the national mood all about "spreading the wealth"? And wasn't he one of those "hard-working" Americans who needed an even break? After all, the cost of crystal meth kept going up to the point of becoming damn near unaffordable to someone earning an honest living like smearing dirty water across the windshields of expensive SUVs. And the not-so-honest living was getting more and more difficult. At the last convenience store where Leon had planned the old snatch-and-run, the Pakistani man had come out from behind the counter with the butt of a pistol prominently showing above his belt.

Leon hadn't needed the Twinkies and potato chips nearly as badly as he had thought.

He only dimly remembered the pre-meth days when he had a regular paycheck for minimum wages working with a landscaper. His employer had been less than tolerant of absences that increased in direct proportion to the amount of crank Leon ingested, smoked, or snorted. Once unencumbered by a job, he was free to devote his time to worshipping the great god meth. The same faith had compelled him to forge his mother's endorsement on her monthly government assistance check, resulting in her ejecting him from the apartment they had shared.

A job, a roof over his head, regular meals. It all seemed like a half-forgotten dream.

The light changed, and Gurt was about to put her foot down on the Mercedes 320 CDI's accelerator when a face appeared in her windshield. Most of the teeth were missing from the open mouth, hair was gone in random patches, and the skin was dotted with festering sores. At another time in another place, Gurt might have thought she was being assaulted by a leper.

Then she saw the bucket and squeegee.

The driver's window of her 320 CDI whispered down. "No, thanks. I'm in a hurry."

The squeegee was already leaving a greasy trail across the car's windshield. Leon pretended not to hear. He guessed after this and maybe one more car, he could find Ralph down at the St. Luke's soup kitchen and score a teenager, a sixteenth of albino poo, to see him through the night.

Gurt mumbled a few Teutonic curses, snatched her purse from the passenger seat and opened her wallet. It would be quicker to pay this bum than argue with him. Plus, no way she wanted to come within range of his breath. Those sores just might be contagious.

Shist! Only a twenty. Good luck in asking for change.

By now the man had finished, and oily rivulets were running down the Mercedes's windshield. He extended one hand toward the driver's window, the other holding up two filthy fingers — two dollars.

"I told you no," she said through the still open window. "I have no change."

Leon had heard that before. "Lady, I washed your windshield. You owe me two bucks."

Gurt inched the Mercedes forward.

Leon, savvy to all the tricks these women tried to avoid paying, stepped in front of the grill.

In frustration, Gurt leaned on the horn. The man blocking her path didn't move. She glanced at her watch. Manfred would be standing in the foyer of the lower school, wondering what had happened as his schoolmates were picked up.

She got out of the car.

Leon was surprised. The last thing these frightened women did was to leave the protection of their vehicles. And the look on her face somehow made him uneasy. So did her size. Just under six feet. But she was a looker. Long blond hair in a ponytail that reached her shoulders, a figure not even a bulky tracksuit could entirely conceal.

"I need to pick my child up from school," she said. "You must move." And some sort of cute foreign accent. "Oh, yeah?" Leon sneered. "Just who is going to make me?"

Gurt tried not to wrinkle her nose at the stench of body odor, vomit, and smells she didn't even want to try to identify. "If necessary, I shall."

Leon didn't like the assuredness of her tone, but it was too late to back down now. "Sure, lady. Give it a try."

She gave him a shove. Not a hard one, just a little more than a suggestion he should move. Reflexively, Leon pushed back.

He was never quite certain what happened next. He felt two hands on the wrist of the hand he had used to pushed back, two hands a lot stronger than he would expect in a woman. Her foot on his. Then he had an unexpected view of the sky — a sense of flying. D'Andre, his companion — open-mouthed. The landing was less than perfect. He hit the street hard enough to knock the breath out of him, hard enough that a bolt of fear went through him as he vainly tried to suck air into lungs he imagined collapsed by his collision with the ground. There was no imagining the pain that shot along his side with each effort to breathe. He was sure he had broken a rib, maybe two.

The sun was blotted by a form smeared at the edges by his tears. "You will move now? Or will a further lesson in manners be necessary?"

The accent was more menacing now than cute. He shot a quick glance in the direction where he had just glimpsed D'Andre. All that remained were an empty bucket and a squeegee. D'Andre, it seemed, had urgent business elsewhere.

Whatever had happened had to be some sort of accident. Leon didn't have the strength he had before his long and passionate affair with meth, but he sure as hell should be stronger than a woman. Besides, this story would be in every homeless shelter, on the street, under every bridge, in every deserted house, everywhere street folks congregated: Leon's ass being whipped by a woman, and a white woman at that.

He pushed up on all fours, gritting his teeth against the pain in his side. The woman was getting back in her car. With more effort than he had thought he possessed, Leon was on his feet. Groping in his pocket, he found the Swiss Army knife, the one he had lifted from the sporting goods store. The blade attachment wasn't as large as he might have wished, but it sufficed to keep others away from the possessions he carried in the backpack with one strap missing.

And it would serve with that bitch who'd gotten lucky.

He opened the blade and took a step to catch her before she could shut and lock the car's doors.

Instead, she got out of the Mercedes again, a decidedly unanticipated move.

"There is more?"

The question startled Leon as much as her total lack of fear. "You bet there is, woman!"

The smile playing around the corners of her mouth was disconcerting. It was if she relished getting cut.

He waved the blade back and forth the way he had seen knife fighters do on TV. Back before he hocked the set, anyway. She was watching with unconcealed amusement. Leon was aware a small crowd had gathered on the adjacent sidewalk. Better to get this over with before some hero wannabe tried to interfere.

He lunged.

Faster than he could comprehend, a number of things happened, all unpleasant. First, one hand deflected the blade while the heel of the second came crunching down on his wrist. He was certain he heard the top bone, the radius, snap. She still had hold of his arm, using it to snatch him forward into a kick in the groin of which any NFL placekicker would have been proud.

He hardly recognized the shriek of pain as his own as his head smashed into the woman's car. Lying in the fetal position, trying to hold both crotch and damaged wrist, he noted only a very expensive pair of athletic shoes disappearing into the SUV before it drove into the intersection, turned right and disappeared.

But just before it did, he got the tag: GURT. He'd square with GURT later. Maybe when his balls and wrist weren't doubling him over in agony.

CHAPTER 5

Law Offices of Langford Reilly
Peachtree Center
227 Peachtree Street
Atlanta, Georgia
At Approximately the Same Time

LANG REILLY PRETENDED TO STUDY THE papers in front of him. In reality, he was observing the man occupying one of the twin French wing chairs on the other side of the desk. Theodosius Wipp was in his seventies and, in the language of the law, in deep shit.

As with all potential clients, Lang did his homework before taking the case, a task made easy since the Internet's assassination of privacy. He defended white-collar criminals, those who offended society's laws with a pen or computer rather than a gun. Under a 36-count federal indictment of charges including various acts of tax evasion and mail, bank, and wire fraud, Wipp was a good candidate to spend the rest of his days as a guest of the federal government.

The man was about six feet tall, with a pink scalp showing through the remnants of hair that was white but still curly. It was the eyes that drew Lang's attention, permanently half-shut and so reptilian that Lang was almost surprised to see them blink from top to bottom rather than from the bottom up. And the eyes weren't going to be the only problem in front of a jury. The man spoke in the tortured syntax of the Erhard Seminar Training, or EST as its founder preferred, the long and thankfully departed would-be cult of the late seventies.

Electronic research showed it had been a group whose beliefs were ill-defined, and worse, enunciated by members too dull or too embarrassed to admit they had been fleeced. A hodgepodge of philosophical bits and pieces randomly selected from various existential sources of Zen Buddhism, Dr. Phil, and P. T. Barnum.

The requirements for membership — in addition to paying a fee, of course — was to "graduate" from "training." Two consecutive weekends of hours without access to toilet facilities while the "trainers" harangued the paying audience with shouted insults, threats, and obscenities. The only ascertainable benefit to "graduates" seemed to be a tendency to use the third or fourth dictionary preferred definition of words, those defintions, less preferred by Mr. Webster and to speak in jargon, including greeting each other with phrases such as "I got it" for "I understand" and "That was his choice because that's what he chose." Originality of thought was uncommon among members.

Still, from its inception in the late seventies until the last "training" in 1984, over 700,000 paid to attend, proof positive that Barnum was right. Once the supply of the gullible dwindled, a postgraduate course was promptly devised, interrupted only when the cult's founder, Werner Erhard, formerly John Rosenberg, sold the "assets" of EST to his brother, who packaged the same hokum under a new name while Erhard departed for other, hopefully greener, pastures. The faithful bemoaned the fact that now the secret of how Rosenberg/Erhard had transcended from magazine salesman to guru of verbal obfuscation while stuck in traffic on the San Francisco Freeway would never be revealed unto them. The only possible clues were to be found in the man's self-published (and obviously self-edited) autobiography, the more amazing parts including how the author "learned what it was like to die" when he fell from a second-story window as a child.

In the absence of their prophet, the brighter of his disciples ("brighter" being used comparatively) finally figured out that people, like themselves, would actually pay to be verbally abused and become "graduates" too, the only form of success many of them would ever achieve.

The void had finally been filled by Theodosius Wipp, a man who had changed first names in his late sixties and the color of what remained of his curly hair a year or so earlier. A brief review of his occupational history revealed job changes with a frequency that suggested moving on had not been Wipp's idea. In fact, the only consistencies in his life were the number of times he had been sued for failure to live up to contractual promises once he had received his part of the bargain and the unbroken string of firings and business failures.

That and a marriage that had somehow endured 30 years. Mrs. Wipp, Lang thought, must be the marital version of Mother Teresa.

The man appeared to be a professional welcher with a sense of integrity that would make the average politician look trustworthy. At least EST's founder had provided seminars, using the word in its broadest sense. In the last five years, Wipp had used the mail, the Internet, and the telephone to solicit funds for "training" that never took place. Instead, they were "rescheduled" with such regularity as to give support to the government's allegations that he had no intent of ever holding them.

"A misunderstanding," was Wipp's characterization.

Lang cleared his throat, a signal the conversation was about to start. "Explain to me again: why didn't any of these, er . . . seminars take place after people had paid for them?"

Wipp shrugged, a matter beyond the control of mere humans. Or, at least, this particular human. "Actually, several of the trainings *did* take place."

News to Lang. "Oh?"

"Five or six, I think."

"Out of how many?"

Another shrug. "I'm not sure."

"The indictment says 23."

"That's possible."

Not exactly a batting average to be proud of.

Lang hunched forward in his chair, elbows on the desk. "Any facts that would tend to diminish or disprove the government's claim that you never intended to provide the seminars?"

"Training, it's called training."

Lang frowned. "Whatever. Can you show a reason the training didn't take place as advertised?"

Wipp was suddenly fascinated by the design of the Kerman rug that covered most of the dark-planked floor. "The group leaders, the trainers

. . . they just quit showing up." He looked up long enough for Lang to see the anger in his face. "After they had promised to be there, too. Bad karma, breaking your word."

No doubt that was why Wipp was here, bad karma. But Lang asked, "How much were you going to pay them?"

An expression of genuine bewilderment replaced anger. "Pay?"

Lang rubbed the fingers of one hand together, the universal sign for receiving money. Was this guy so stupid as to not understand? Forty years of business failures provided a clue to the answer to that question. "I assume you promised to pay these trainers something."

Lang might as well have slapped the man across the face for the indignation Wipp demonstrated. "EST group leaders don't get paid. They get the experience of being group leaders."

The conners being conned. But Lang said, "Let me get this straight: you were expecting people to donate two weekends of their time when you were the only one getting paid, correct?"

"I did it for Werner," Wipp said sullenly, "but I got to be a group leader."

Forty years of consistent failure had a basis.

"So, what do you think my chances are?" Wipp wanted to know.

Lang took his elbows from the desk and picked up the copy of the indictment, although he was already well acquainted with its contents. "The U.S. Attorney has about a 96 percent conviction rate. I'd say our best shot is to see if we can work out a deal."

"What sort of a deal?"

"A little early to say. First, there's the matter of my fee. I'll need fifty grand."

Wipp looked stricken. "*Fifty thousand?*"

"Payable before I get started."

"Maybe in installments? I mean, I can't afford . . ."

One of the essential things about the law practice, at least a criminal practice, wasn't taught in law school: get paid up front. If the client is convicted, then his lawyer did an inadequate job. If acquitted, well, he was innocent all along and hadn't really needed a lawyer, had he? Taking a promise from a lifetime welcher like Wipp didn't make a whole lot of sense, either.

"You had no trouble paying the bondsman fifty thousand."

Post-law-school lesson number two: if the client can afford bond, he can afford to pay his lawyer. The fifty thousand represented 10 percent of the bond, $500,000. The Feds took serious umbrage at using the mail or phone services for fraudulent purposes. Lang was curious where a loser like this guy got that sort of cash if not from the non-occurring seminars. But he really didn't want to know.

"Yeah," Wipp agreed, "paying the bail bond people sort of tapped me out. I'll have your fee as soon as I can."

Lang stood, indicating the conversation was at an end. He extended his hand. "Soon as the money's in my account, I'll be in touch with the Feds."

Wipp's hand stopped in midair, *handshakus interruptus*. "I told you I'll have the money. I'd hoped you'd get started immediately."

And people in hell hope for ice water. But Lang said, "Office policy. Of course, you are free to seek other counsel."

Assuming you would want one stupid enough to take on a 36-count indictment for free.

"No, no." Wipp shook his head. "You come highly recommended. I'll be back."

It took General MacArthur over three years to keep that promise, Lang thought as he followed Wipp into the reception area and watched him through glass doors as he waited for an elevator in the hall outside.

"Glad he's gone," Sara observed. "The man is just plain slimy."

Lang smiled at his grandmotherly secretary. Sara had been with him since he had opened his practice after leaving the Agency. With the collapse of the Soviet Empire and the so-called "peace dividend," Lang had seen the end of his job in the intelligence community. He had signed on out of college with visions of James Bond dancing through his head: a Walther PPK in one hand and a ravishing woman in the other as he chased his country's enemies from one exotic foreign city to the next.

As is often the case, the reality was somewhat different. Instead of being assigned to Ops, he had drawn Intel, a faceless office in a drab building across the street from Frankfurt's *Hauptbahnhof*, a seedy neighborhood of cheap hotels and greasy cafés that smelled of stale beer and cabbage. Although he had endured the same training as operatives, his duties involved the study of Iron Curtain media for clues as to what the Kremlin might do next.

It was while he was there he met and had a brief affair with Gurt Fuchs, an escapee from East Germany whose knowledge of the German Democratic Republic had made her one of the Agency's most valuable assets. The affair ended when Lang met his wife-to-be, Dawn, and resumed some years after Dawn had succumbed to cancer.

Sara was still shaking her helmet of white hair. "Sometimes I wonder where you get such wretched people."

"Sometimes you forget: we represent accused criminals, not debutantes or priests."

"Speaking of which, you're taking Father Francis to lunch. Why is it you always take him? He take a vow against picking up a check?"

"Sara, in the ten years plus I've known him, he's never lost the flip of a coin for the tab. I suspect divine intervention."

Sara turned back to her computer with a sniff. "Well, I suppose association with Father Francis will do your soul more good than the creep who just left."

Lang turned to go back into his office. "My soul, maybe. The bank account, not so much."

CHAPTER 6

Piedmont Driving Club South
4405 Camp Creek Parkway
Atlanta, Georgia
Forty Minutes Later

MOST OF ATLANTA'S PRIVATE CLUBS BUILT their golf courses north of the city, acquiring farmland in the first decades of the last century, away from today's growing congestion, noise, and crime. Now, a number of these courses border strip centers, gas stations, and heavy traffic. After over a century of existence, the exclusive Driving Club decided to get into the golf business, although any of its members so desiring could have joined existing facilities. The only golf course–sized tract available within a distance not requiring visiting members to carry victuals was south of the city and directly under the arrival/departure pattern of the world's busiest airport, Atlanta's Hartsfield-Jackson International. The price, noise included, was right.

The parking lot in which Lang parked the turbo Porsche was in front of the modest clubhouse. The building housed only a small bar and grill and locker rooms for men and women. Women had been admitted to membership in an unwarranted spasm of political correctness in the nineties after a century of white, male, gentile exclusivity. There was no swimming pool to act as babysitter in the warmer months, no tennis courts for idle housewives, no gym for the health-conscious.

The business of this outpost of Atlanta's socially elite was golf. And catching the bass and bream allegedly stocked in the nine-acre lake.

Lang wasn't surprised to find Francis nursing a tall glass at a table with a view of the golf course and lake and, of course, the undercarriage of large aircraft.

As a Catholic priest, Francis Narumba could hardly afford membership, but, like so many of his profession who had developed a passion for golf, he never lacked for invitations from wealthy members of that religion. He had come to the United States from one of West Africa's worst hellholes to attend seminary and remained to take over a parish consisting largely of immigrants from that area. Oddly, Lang's sister, Janet, had attended that church along with her adopted son, Jeff, Lang's best ten-year-old buddy. When the two had perished in a bomb's fire in Paris, he and Francis had become friends, largely, Lang guessed, by the attraction of opposites.

Today the good father was clad not in the somber weeds of Mother Church, but in fire-engine-red slacks and a white golf shirt. A dazzling white smile split a face the color of midnight.

Lang sat across the table, waited for the building to quit shaking from the blast of a departing jet, and said, *"Vestis viram facit."*

Both men considered themselves victims of a liberal arts education and enjoyed swapping Latin aphorisms.

"Ne supra crepidam sutor judicaret," Francis replied, the smile becoming a grin. "Stick to what you know. It would be difficult to swing a club in my surplice."

Lang glanced around. This was only the second or third time he had driven out here. "You've ventured far from your flock."

"Ah, but not from the Lord."

"God plays golf?"

"Who knows? But I hear him mentioned often on the course."

"I suppose anyone is entitled to a little wasted time."

Francis drained his glass and motioned to the sole waitress. "Wasted? I think not. I cajoled a pledge for a substantial contribution to the church's literacy program from one of my golfing partners this morning. And I broke a hundred for the first time. Am I great or what? Look out, Tiger Woods."

The waitress refilled Francis's glass from a pitcher of tea. Lang held up his glass, "Same, please. And I thought you guys took a pledge of humility."

"The Benedictines, maybe. And I don't see too many of them on the course. Guess those long cassocks get in the way."

There was a pause for another window-rattling roar while both men studied the brief menu. Lang ordered the Cobb salad; Francis, a cheeseburger with fries. The priest's weight never seemed to vary in spite of an appetite that would have quickly put 50 pounds on Lang.

"How do you do it?" Lang asked. "I mean, you stay trim no matter what you eat?"

Francis was munching on the buttered, toasted saltines that were the club's hors d' oeuvres. "Exercise. Like playing golf."

Lang conducted an hour-and-a-half workout three times weekly including weight machines and stationary bikes. "You walk around with a caddy carrying your clubs, hit the ball, walk some more. Don't even tote your own clubs. How is that exercise?"

Francis rubbed his flat belly with one hand while reaching for another cracker. "*Exitus acta probat.*"

"The result validates the means, I know . . ."

A sound, conceivably a tune, interrupted.

"What's that?" Francis asked.

"My iPhone." Lang held it up. "Helluva lot easier to use than the old Blackberry. I understand that an organization that refuses to acknowledge divorce is so stuck in medieval theology that a cell phone might seem extraordinary . . ."

Francis leaned back in his chair. "Ah, my heretical friend, have you not heard? The Holy Father himself texts, tweets, and is on Facebook. If I recall correctly, you do none of the above, relying on outdated means such as e-mail. I meant what was the tune?"

Lang stood. "Tweets? What, that he'd like to sleep in on Sundays? And for your information, the 'tune' was an electronic reproduction of *Chattanooga Choo Choo*. Glenn Miller doesn't translate so well. Electronics haven't progressed enough for one of these devices to sound like the trombone section of his orchestra."

Cell phones were prohibited on club property, a rule observed largely in the breach. Even so, good manners required that Lang not subject his fellow diners to his conversations. It took him only a few steps to be outside.

He recognized Dr. Walsh's number on the screen. "Good afternoon, Doctor."

There was a deafening roar.

As it diminished into the distance, Walsh's voice was raised. "Where the hell are you, at a NASCAR race?" The stock cars would have been a lullaby by comparison.

"Too close to the airport. What's up?"

"I need to see you as soon as possible."

"Can it wait an hour or so? I'm at lunch."

"Got a conference. I'll be here all tomorrow afternoon."

Lang returned to see Francis slathering ketchup on a cheeseburger surrounded by a mountain of French fries. He sighed as he sat down to his Cobb salad. "We were saying?"

"That you should try golf"

"Why not?"

"You'll do it?"

"I'll give it a try."

It was a promise Lang would come to regret.

CHAPTER 7

Trabzon, Turkey
Hasttahane Cocuk (Children's Hospital)
The Next Day (Eight hours ahead of EDT)

FROM NOON FORWARD, FATIMA'S DAY HAD slipped by like one of those film sequences where the actors' images are sped up to give the illusion of the passage of time. Right after lunch, there had been two admissions from the same village, both of whom she initially diagnosed as typhoid. Small wonder, since the populace's drinking water came from upstream where sheep and goats grazed, likely polluting the small creek. The unsanitary conditions were known, but what were the people to do? Digging a well through the hard mountain rock would require more money than the entire settlement would see in a decade.

She had just finished e-mailing a report to the public health authorities in Ankara when a flurry of nurses shouted to her as they passed her open office door. A busload of schoolchildren had run off a narrow mountain road. Casualties were expected to start arriving any moment. Fortunately, almost all the victims were more frightened than seriously injured. Scrapes, bruises, a few broken bones. Incredibly, no fatalities or life-threatening injuries.

She remembered hearing the electronically enhanced voices of the Muezzin from the minarets of two nearby mosques announcing the *Maghrib*, sunset, call to prayer, before the last tear was wiped away, the last bandage applied, the last grateful parent called.

Fatima was not a particularly religious person, but like most residents of Islamic countries, the calls to prayer divided her days into five measurable sections. The early, predawn *Faji*, when she rolled over in bed to hug a sleepy Aydin; *Duhur*, shortly after noon, usually while she was gulping down a hasty lunch at her desk; *Asr*, late afternoon, a reminder to begin afternoon rounds; *Maghrin*, on most days a signal to start wrapping up the day's activities; and *Icha*, historically at bedtime. But in today's life with cinema, TV, and other entertainments, this latter was usually observed, if at all, as most families were finishing dinner.

She looked at her watch. Closer to *Icha* than *Maghrib*. Aydin would be calling her cell phone any minute. It would be too late to cook by the time she got home. No chance Aydin could prepare anything. She smiled, remembering the last time he had tried. He might be a skilled architect, but even boiling water was an invitation to disaster in the kitchen. No, she would call suggesting they go out.

But first, Emre. Had he sent that unexplainable report to Dr. Walsh in the States? She hadn't spoken with Emre in a couple of days, and, based on prior experience, the man might well have forgotten. She reached for the telephone on her desk, then drew back her hand. No, she'd go in person. She stood, looked around her small office, and shut the door as she left.

She paused in front of twin elevator doors before choosing the stairs. Her rubber-soled shoes squeaking on the tiled floor, she walked briskly to the door of the lab, which was uncharacteristically closed.

Her first impression was that Emre had drifted off to sleep. His head rested on a lab table, his face away from her. The inevitable pack of Murad cigarettes were only centimeters away. But what an uncomfortable position, his arms dangling toward the floor rather than cushioning his head.

"Emre?"

Fatima crossed the room and shook a shoulder gently. "Emre?"

No response.

What happened next would be replayed in her nightmares with newsreel clarity for the rest of her life: she shook him again, this time none too gently. Limp as a rag doll, he rolled over onto the floor. Lifeless eyes seemed to look straight through her.

It never occurred to Fatima to scream or do any of the things the women in the cinema did in similar circumstances. Her medical training took over like an aircraft's autopilot. Kneeling, she felt for a pulse and, finding none, placed a hand on the carotid artery. Nothing. The skin, though, was only slightly cooler than normal.

Emre had been alive only a few minutes ago.

But, what . . .?

The hand that had touched the junction of jaw and neck was wet. She stared dumbly at the smear of red, recognizing but not understanding what she was seeing. Slowly, hesitantly, she turned the head to one side. Had she not been looking for it, she would not have noticed the wet spot in the luxurious dark hair. A small hole. Always surprising how little a non-facial head wound bled.

Gently, she lowered Emre's head to the floor and stood. Only the pain made her aware she was biting her lower lip, not to stifle a scream but to staunch the tears that were blurring her vision. She must call the police, of course. Watering eyes searched for the telephone before her addled mind recalled its location.

She took a step toward the plain metal desk and stopped. The file cabinet was open, papers scattered around it. While Emre was less than fastidious about his personal appearance, or, for that matter, his laboratory or office, he was obsessively meticulous when it came to files and records. The file cabinet always displayed a military-like order that bore no relationship to the rest of his life.

Emre had not left this disorder.

Fatima looked around the lab, almost expecting to see an assassin, before approaching the metal, four-drawer cabinet. Yes, she knew she should summon the police. Yes, she knew she might be tampering with a crime scene. But she was drawn to look in the file cabinet by a compulsion as strong as any addict's.

She was never able to explain to herself why she was not surprised that Baris's file containing the hematology report, Emre's notes, and any report he may have sent Dr. Walsh were missing.

She stood by the file cabinet a moment, thinking. She was fully aware that every second she delayed in summoning the authorities gave Emre's killer that much more time to escape. The warmth of the body indicated she might have found the victim while the perpetrator was still in the building.

Still, there was something . . .

Two steps took her to the desk. She pulled open the top left drawer, thumbed through its contents, and closed it. The one below yielded what she was looking for: a stack of red and yellow DHL shipping receipts. The one on top was addressed to a Simon Walsh, care of the Janet and Jeff Holt Foundation. A package. Emre had wasted no time in sending the sample, otherwise he would not have used an express company instead of simply a report that would have been easier to send by e-mail.

She scanned the receipt. Overnight air. Nearly a hundred new Turkish lira. There was only one thing Emre would have sent Dr. Walsh that needed overnight air: bags of ice surrounding a blood sample.

She stuffed the receipt into a pocket of her lab coat and went back to the desk and telephone. By the time she reached it, she could no longer suppress the sobs that convulsed her.

CHAPTER 8

Janet and Jeff Holt Foundation
1527 Clifton Road
Atlanta, Georgia
1:27 P.M. Local Time
The Same Day

DR. SIMON WALSH DRESSED MORE LIKE a businessman than a physician. And justly so, Lang thought as he settled into one of a pair of contemporary chairs. The day-to-day operation of an international multibillion-dollar charity required acumen taught in few business schools and no medical colleges.

Years ago, Lang realized he had neither the time nor the ability to manage the burgeoning Foundation. He had conducted a nationwide search of hospital administrators, officers of eleemosynary institutions, and those who had experience in operating government programs. The Foundation's endowment was increasing faster than he alone could apply the funds, funds supplied annually pursuant to an agreement he had made with one of the world's wealthiest and most secretive organizations as compensation for the death of his sister and adopted nephew.

During the interview, Walsh had been one of only two or three candidates to get the clear, if unspoken, message that the source of the Foundation's funding was not now, nor would it become, of interest to the person who became its COO.

Walsh sat in a hideous ergonomic office chair bristling with levers and buttons. It could well have come from the bridge of the starship Enterprise. In front of him was a matching ergonomic desk. As though to emphasize the doctor's commitment to all things modern, two matching globs of paint hung in their stainless steel frames facing the desk. Lang understood the purported value of comfortable work space furniture, but at the price of a visual assault?

Walsh could have been anywhere between forty and sixty. Salt and pepper hair brushed over ear tops, a face with a perpetual tan, and brilliant white teeth he flashed at every opportunity. The hourglass shape of the jacket of his Italian tailored suit suggested a figure of a man who, as far as Lang could tell, had neither gained nor lost a pound in the five years he had known him. In short, Simon Walsh looked like either a movie star or a politician.

Behind Walsh was the modern glass front of the building through which Lang could see the facade of Emory University Hospital and its main pedestrian entrance that resembled a Roman *palazzo* far more than a medical facility. Atlanta and environs were dotted with Italian facades, most attributable to the city's premier architect, Phillip Shutze, whose early twentieth-century work reflected his admiration for all things Italian. The small, hedge-lined piazza reinforced the impression of the Eternal City. A pity, in many ways, Lang thought, since few entered a hospital through its front doors anymore.

Lang sank into a chair shaped more like a human hand on rollers than furniture.

"I appreciate your coming on such short notice," Walsh said. "I know you stay busy." He favored Lang with a glimpse of pearly whites. "Defending the rich and powerful from otherwise certain justice, no doubt."

Lang nodded in acknowledgement of the hoary line. "Better than the poor and meek. The rich and powerful pay better. But there's nothing more important than the Foundation, Doc. Short of being in court, I can make the time."

Walsh produced an envelope from somewhere. The desk had no drawers. "I received this along with a blood sample from our pediatric hospital in Trabzon."

"Trabzon?"

"Turkey. On the coast of the Black Sea. The Foundation opened there just five or six years ago. You flew to Los Angeles to personally interview the person who is now the director, a Dr. Fatima Aksoy . . ."

Long dark hair surrounding a rather pretty oval face, intelligent brown eyes. The memory came rushing back. Lang had had initial doubts about hiring a female to run a hospital in a Moslem country. He had been more interested in a smooth operation than social justice.

"She is the best qualified?" Gurt had asked the evening he returned from the West Coast.

Lang had admitted she was. "But I'm more interested in providing care for children than sticking my thumb in the eyes of a bunch of Neanderthals who believe women should be confined to having babies and keeping house."

Gurt had put down her sweating glass of Riesling. She preferred her homeland's sweet wine to anything that came out of California. "You remember our trip to Istanbul?"

There was a vague threat in the question, though Lang couldn't see what. "Sure. We went out to Prince's Island and . . ."

"Then, you recall Turkey is not Saudi Arabia. Women drive cars, wear fashionable clothing instead of bedsheets, even work for wages."

Gurt's stand on women's rights would have made Susan B. Anthony seem a reactionary. Lang never understood why. Gurt had never been denied anything because of her sex. In fact, after winning the Agency's women's shooting competition, she insisted she have a chance for the overall trophy, which she won handily from some ego-deflated males. She was tops in women's martial arts, too. Again, she demanded to take on the men. After breaking the arm of her first male opponent, no others stepped forward.

No, there was no real reason for Gurt to be so fierce in her defense of what she perceived as women's rights. But she was. Lang could have justifiably told her that selection of the chief of staff of the Children's Hospital was his duty and his alone. He could have pointed out that he and he alone had the final say in such matters. He could have. He could have spent a week sleeping in the guest room, too.

"Mr. Reilly?"

Lang realized his thoughts had drifted off the center line, what Gurt referred to as "wool gathering." "I'm sorry, Doc. A lot of things on my mind. You were saying you got something from Dr. Aksoy?"

"Not Aksoy, from the hospital's hematologist. A report along with a blood sample." Walsh tendered an envelope across the desk. "I sent the blood sample to the hospital's hematology department since the Foundation doesn't have one."

Nor would it, Lang thought as he took the paper from its envelope. Modern charities, like government, had not been in the business of making money and therefore had grown like Georgia's kudzu, without a thought to cost-effectiveness. Need a post office in a town of 200? Sure, build the sucker. The eleemosynary organization's equipment not as bright and shiny as another's? Modernize now, no matter the old machine worked just fine. Throwing money away, particularly other peoples', could become addictive. Only the cold reality of the economics of the new century's first recession had slowed the trend by eliminating a part of the taxes and contributions that financed extravagance.

Lang glanced at the paper, then leaned back, hands outstretched as though pushing off an invisible wall. "No, no. I can never understand the medical jargon. Tell me what it says in layman's terms."

Walsh shook his head. "I think you can comprehend what you need to understand, Mr. Reilly."

Reluctantly, Lang began to read.

A minute later he put it down. "I'm not familiar with this Emre Yalmaz. Should I be?"

Behind the desk, Dr. Walsh was touching his fingertips as he shrugged. "He's the hematologist Dr. Aksoy hired a year or so ago. Keeping up with the people our individual institution directors hire is my job. In fact, we have an office of two or three people who do just that. Would you like to . . .?"

Lang placed the envelope back on the desk. "Toxicological immunity? That mean what I think it does?"

Walsh shrugged, the answer obvious. "It means the subject appeared to suffer no ill effects from a venomous snakebite."

"Didn't I see something about an immunity to other toxins?"

Walsh sniffed his depreciation for such ideas. "I wouldn't get overly excited about the wilder conclusions of a young doctor. Science knows there is no such thing as a universal immunity. For one thing, I doubt this Yalmaz person had the material at hand to make such a conclusion. It's remarkable enough that the young boy withstood the bite, but that doesn't mean a neurotoxin, like a cobra's, wouldn't be fatal. Or, for that matter, a dose of any number of poisons."

Lang sat back in his chair. "But wouldn't it be great if it were true, that there really was such a thing as universal immunity?"

"Sure. It would be great to find a universal cure for cancer, too. All it takes is time and money, mostly the latter."

Lang recalled his thoughts of a few minutes ago about the waste of money. "You're right, of course. But you called me to come by for some reason."

"This letter is it. I wanted you to see it."

"But, I thought you said there was no such thing as universal immunity."

Walsh smiled again. "I did, but I simply felt you should be informed."

That's what fax machines and e-mailed PDFs are made for, Lang thought grimly. The time visiting here could have been better spent . . .

The buzz of the phone on Walsh's desk did little to diminish Lang's irritation. Simple courtesy would require the man have his calls held.

From his embarrassed expression, Walsh was thinking the same thing. "Excuse me. I told my administrative assistant to hold my calls."

Lang nodded toward the offending instrument. "Then it must be important."

The doctor swept the receiver from its cradle. "I thought I asked my calls be held. What? Yes, put her on."

Lang didn't see him press the speaker button but a woman's voice filled the room. "Dr. Walsh?"

"Yes, Dr. Aksoy, this is Dr. Walsh. Mr. Reilly happens to be here with me. What can I do for you?"

The voice was tense. Lang could detect the anxiety along its edges. "It's Emre, Dr. Yalmaz . . ."

"Yes?" Walsh asked, making no effort to conceal his impatience. "What about him?"

There was an audible intake of breath. Or a sob. "He's dead, murdered."

Lang was out of his chair, leaning over the speaker. "What, what happened? When?"

Another intake of breath. "About an hour ago. I found him in the lab. He had been shot. The police are here now taking statements."

"But why?" Lang asked. He had never met the hematologist, but the idea of someone being shot in a children's hospital, the Foundation's Children's Hospital, was unsettling to say the least. "Anything missing?"

"I . . . I'm not sure," her voice quivered. "His files had been, what do you say? Ransacked, yes, ransacked."

The conversation lasted a few more minutes, ending with Lang's request to be informed before sympathies were extended along with offers of whatever assistance might be needed.

Walsh and Lang were silent for a full minute after the disconnection before the latter said, "Someone doesn't accept what science supposedly knows."

"Beg pardon?"

"That there is no such thing as universal immunity."

Walsh shook his head. "Surely you don't believe . . ."

"From here I can't see any other reason a young doctor in a fairly obscure hospital should be killed and his records stolen."

"But, you don't know . . ."

It was Lang's turn to shake his head. "No, I don't. But I'm damn well going to find out."

CHAPTER 9

Ataturk International Airport
Istanbul, Turkey
12:07 Local Time the Next Day

THE GULFSTREAM 550 USED SLIGHTLY MORE than a third of Runway 17 Left before turning off onto the high speed and awaiting Ground Control's selection of taxiways to the general aviation terminal. It took only minutes for the aircraft to lumber onto the tarmac in front of a modern building and take its place among a Hawker Beechcraft, a Bombardier, and several Citations.

Lang Reilly stood and stretched. It had been a long flight: Atlanta to Karlsruhe/Baden Baden, where the plane had been met by Gurt's father, who gleefully accepted a few days' custody of his grandson, Manfred, now enjoying the temporary liberty of summer vacation. At the small boy's insistence, his constant companion and frequent partner in mischief, Grumps, the family dog, had been allowed to come along.

The arrival at this particular airport, not one of Germany's three official ports of entry, had required some amount of private diplomacy.

But it was the large, long-haired dog with one blue eye and one brown and no discernible specific ancestry that had drawn attention from the khaki-uniformed customs official who had boarded the plane. A presentation of proof of rabies vaccination and an exchange in German between him and Gurt settled whatever issues might have existed. No doubt the toy dogs that had become almost a fashion accessory to the wealthy arriving to gamble in the casino or take the medicinal waters had become commonplace. But 90 pounds of dog that didn't even stop snoring until it was time to trot down the stairs behind his small master?

Then on to Istanbul.

"He will be fine," Gurt said minutes after takeoff.

Lang had been looking at but not really reading a book he had just downloaded. "Huh?"

"Manfred. You were already missing him."

Her ability to read Lang's mind was both astonishing and annoying. He was an open book to her; her thoughts frequently remained her own. "It will do him good to spend time with his *Grossvater*, perhaps even learn a little discipline."

This last was a barb directed at Lang, who was frequently slow to quiet the noisy exuberance of a seven-year-old. In fact, he was just as likely to join in. It was a subject best allowed to die from neglect. He had changed the subject.

Two and a half hours later, they were clearing customs and purchasing visitors' visas in Istanbul before approaching the rent-a-car booths.

"Trabzon does not have an airport?" Gurt asked.

Lang was digging his driver's license and credit card out of his wallet. "It does, but I thought a drive along the Black Sea might be a little vacation for us. We can fly back."

"You mean you do not want to announce our arrival by landing in a Gulfstream."

"That, too."

Although he had no reason to anticipate trouble, experience had taught him the less attention attracted, the better. Google had informed him the Trabzon airport was hardly small, with over a million passengers a year served by half a dozen domestic and international carriers. Still, a private jet the size of the Gulfstream would not go unnoticed.

Besides, he had never driven the Black Sea coast.

There was no reason to notice the swarthy young man in American jeans and a Polo golf shirt who was just one more transient swirling around the rental car booths. Had there been a reason to observe him closely, two things might have seemed odd: first, he had no interest in renting an automobile, and second, he seemed fixated on the American man and the woman as he spoke American-accented English into a cell phone.

"Excuse me!"

Lang shot a look of annoyance at the young American-dressed man who had jostled him just as he was signing the rental contract. "Quite all right."

"Look," the young man said, not disposed to move from the head of the line into which he had broken. "I have no idea about these cars. I mean, this is my first trip outside the U.S., and most of the cars listed here aren't even in the States."

Lang picked up the rental contract and keys, nodding his thanks to the young man behind the counter. "I have no idea what suits your needs, but you might bear in mind gas in Turkey is nearly ten bucks U.S. a gallon."

"In other words, I need an economy."

Lang shrugged. "That's up to you. Now, if you'll excuse me . . ."

Lang and Gurt headed for the rental car lot shuttle only a few minutes before Hertz's bright yellow van pulled up. In minutes, they were passing rows of freshly washed, shiny vehicles. The van stopped.

"Your car," the driver indicated.

Lang and Girt exchanged glances.

Lang sighed as he checked the tag on the keys in his hand against the license plate, hoisted both bags from the van's overhead rack, and stepped to the ground. The Ford Mondeo was a four-door hatchback that would have been unremarkable had it not been a shade of yellow so bright it might have been suggested by a child's crayons.

"It is good we will not be attracting attention," Gurt observed dryly.

CHAPTER 10

Sinop-Istanbul Highway
Between Amasra and Sinop
Three and a Half Hours Later

AFTER HALF AN HOUR OF FOUR lanes, the road from Istanbul shrunk to two as it climbed steadily upward. By the time it reached the Black Sea fishing village of Amasra, only a single narrow lane writhed between mountain peaks where the green of the hills dropped precipitously into the green of the sea, a road far better suited to the occasional flock of sheep that blocked passage than motorized traffic. Periodic raindrops fell from a pewter sky to splatter against the windshield like fat bugs.

Gurt braced herself against the dash and the floor as the Mondeo braked for entry into a blind hairpin. Lang had thought the reaction would have tired her an hour ago. He was wrong.

"What happens if someone's coming the other way?" she wanted to know.

"Hopefully, they will be driving as cautiously as we are."

Her expression indicated she preferred to depend on something a little stronger than hope, but she changed the subject. "The scenery is beautiful. It reminds me of Maine or Northern California. I'm surprised the road is so poor here."

Lang took a hand from the wheel long enough to point skyward. "No sun, no tourists. Almost always cloudy, unlike Bulgaria's Black Sea coast or even Turkey's a little farther east."

She turned to look at him. "I thought you'd never been here before."

The hand was back on the wheel. "Haven't, at least not in person. Amazing how much you can learn from a virtual tour. I . . ."

The narrow road ahead was blocked by a light truck — Toyota, Nissan, something like that. Painted bright blue, it bore the word JANDARMA across the side. From a previous visit to Turkey, Lang knew the *Jandarma Genel Komutanligi* was a branch of the country's military, whose prime duty was to function as civil police in rural areas that had a population insufficient to justify a national police outpost.

"Odd," he murmured.

"What?" Gurt asked.

Lang was studying the men beside the truck. Though long ago, Agency training still alerted him to anomalies, things out of the ordinary: a street person or a junk auto in a upscale neighborhood, a man acting drunk without the smell of alcohol. "The uniforms — dark green pants, light green blouses," he replied.

Gurt looked closely at the three men who were slowly trudging uphill from the truck crosswise in the road. "That is what they are wearing. So?"

"One too small, the other two too big. As if they were wearing someone else's. Plus . . ." Lang squinted. "Plus one doesn't seem to have the collar patches, the red and blue patches that denote rank."

The uniforms, armaments, and various protocols of the military and law enforcement of foreign countries, both allies and enemies, had been a subject the Agency had drilled into its trainees.

Now alerted, Gurt observed, "I don't recall the AK-47 as the standard rifle of any Turkish police or military, either."

Two of the men carried the distinctive Russian assault rifles in the crook of their arms.

"No, it's the German G41 built under license right here in Turkey."

"So . . .?"

The men were close enough now that their facial features were distinct. All three jaws were framed with dark hair, short dark hair that could not have been seen at a distance.

"So, moustaches are okay, but beards strictly forbidden in the military, as I recall," Lang said.

Lang and Gurt exchanged glances. He nodded. They each opened their door a crack.

It did not escape either's notice that the men in uniform split so there was one on each side and one behind the Mondeo. With the road blocked ahead by the truck, they were effectively surrounded.

Not the move of your friendly neighborhood cop on the beat.

The one beside Lang's window made a rolling motion to lower the glass.

He did so, mentally cursing his and Gurt's decision to come unarmed. Although Turkey's restrictive gun laws carried a penalty light in comparison to many other nations, three years' imprisonment plus fine, the risk of having their mission interrupted by being arrested was far greater than any risk to their persons known at the time.

"Anything wrong, officer?" Lang asked innocently.

If the man spoke English, he didn't acknowledge the fact. Instead, he gestured for Lang to get out of the car.

Decision time. Leave the automobile and what little protection it provided or make whatever run for it their predicament allowed.

The instant's hesitation made the man on Lang's side reach for the door handle with the hand not holding the AK-47.

That made the decision easy.

CHAPTER 11

472 Lafayette Drive
Atlanta, Georgia
At About the Same Time
(7 hours difference)

FATHER FRANCIS NARUMBA FELT LIKE A burglar in Lang Reilly's house. Or worse, a prisoner.

There really hadn't been a graceful way to decline his friend's request that he, Francis, take care of the small vegetable garden Gurt insisted on planting every year despite the house's proximity to any number of grocery stores, farmer's markets, and street vendors of fresh tomatoes, corn, beans, and the like.

Francis could understand her need to see her own produce come out of the 50 by 50-foot plot of carefully rotor-tilled, fertilized, and labeled dirt just past the shimmering, cool waters of the pool where the plastic snake writhed with life-like motion as it sucked up an errant leaf. Here squash was anticipated, there carrots planted, and so on. A peace and order among vegetables unobtainable among the humans, especially those of Francis's parish of newly arrived African immigrants, gays, and no small number or parishioners whose attendance was directly related to the free meals served afterward. Having been a child in a country where having enough to eat was considered a luxury, he would have had a home garden himself had not the urban rectory in which he lived had a backyard of concrete.

No, watering the garden, watching the early morning sun turn the hoses' spray into a rainbow, standing here among puddles of shade from towering oaks in their bright green spring garb was a pleasant deviation from his life as an urban priest.

It was going inside the house that made him nervous. Maybe walking around anyone else's empty home would have affected him that way, particularly one where he spent at least an evening every week, playing with Manfred and Grumps, sharing maybe a few too many single malt scotches with Lang. And certainly he ate far too much of Gurt's marvelous cooking, a good part of which she insisted he take home in dishes wrapped in plastic.

She well knew both that Mrs. Adebayo, the rectory cook, was possessed of considerably less than gourmet abilities, and that as the sole support of her Nigerian immigrant family, Francis would eat her tasteless fare indefinitely before replacing her with someone more culinarily endowed.

It wasn't the memories that haunted every room with warmth and friendship. It wasn't the sense of trespassing on his friends' privacy. It was the arcane locks and security devices that made him fear a single misstep would bring the entire Atlanta police force charging in upon him.

There were the concealed steel doors that dropped from the ceiling with the push of a button ("You'd be trapped in here till you starved to death if you pushed that"), not to mention locks that took keys Francis had never seen before, keys with holes rather than notches. He had an impression there were any number of really unfortunate things that could happen to an intruder in this house, all controlled by some panel or series of controls hidden away somewhere.

The priest was willing to accept Lang's assurances that if he only disarmed the alarm and did as Gurt asked ("Water the spider plants and check the ficus. Careful not to overdo the orchids. They only need to be sprayed"), he would be fine. Lang had been mostly right even when Francis had touched an unseen switch or button that dropped steel curtains rattling down each of the den's window frames. That had sent him dashing outside, all too mindful of the starve-to-death remark.

No, it wasn't the gadgets themselves that really bothered Francis. It was the need for panic rooms, locks that couldn't be picked, and God only knew what else.

He knew Lang and, perhaps, Gurt, had a period of their lives that never got discussed, simply skipped over in conversation as though whatever had happened hadn't. He also knew his pal Lang had had problems with some pretty rough people, trouble also never discussed. Maybe it had to do with the man's profession as a white-collar criminal defense lawyer. But Francis found it hard to believe that a whole lot of lawyers had homes with tighter security than Fort Knox.

None of his business, he knew. Still, he found it hurtful his best friend kept not just a few secrets from him but a lifetime of them. As a priest, he was used to the confessions that cleansed the soul. But Lang . . . well, Francis wasn't sure Lang even believed in souls. It was not something they discussed. *Vir sapit qui pauca loqiuitur.* A wise man held his tongue. Francis couldn't be sure his resentment of his friend's silence in certain matters wasn't just a matter of sinful pride, a question he put aside whenever it reared its head.

He caught a glimpse of the face of his watch as he emptied the watering can's last few drops into a pot of African violets sitting in the sun of the window over the kitchen sink. He was careful not to get water on the leaves lest they spot. 8:42. Plenty of time for the short drive from Ansley Park to the Cathedral of Christ the King and his 9:00 monthly meeting with the bishop. He was returning the watering can to its place under the kitchen sink when the doorbell rang.

No one in Ansley Park rang doorbells, at least not during daylight hours. They just walked in and announced themselves. Therefore the bell ringer was not a neighbor. Life in his crime-ridden downtown parish had made Francis wary, if not paranoid.

Putting down the watering can, he passed through the dining room and into the front hall. He could see part of the porch that bordered two-thirds of the house through windows across the front, but he could not see who was ringing the bell. He must be standing squarely in front of the door. A quick squint through the peephole showed an olive-skinned man in a white jumpsuit with some sort of red script across the left breast pocket, the sort of uniform a plumber or electrician might wear. An unmarked white panel truck was parked at the curb behind him.

Odd. Lang hadn't said anything about a repairman coming by.

For once, Lang's security gadgets were more helpful than intimidating.

Father Francis pushed the button on a speaker beside the door. "Can I help you?"

The man on the other side of the door was obviously startled. Because he hadn't seen the speaker or because he had not expected anyone to be home?

"Four-seventy-two Lafayette Drive?"

"Yes?"

"Got a report of an electrical short somewhere."

Something wasn't right here. If Lang and Gurt had expected an electrician, they would have told Francis. Besides, the priest had never seen one that didn't have a collection of tools both hanging from his belt like Christmas tree ornaments and overflowing a handheld toolbox.

By the nature of his calling, Francis was not naturally suspicious. Perhaps the clerical collar he wore induced more candor from the populace at large than would have otherwise been the case, or his profession obviated the necessity for lies and deception. What did a parish priest have that was worth conning him out of? Either way, Francis had a tendency to believe what he was told, with the exception of a small number of people who tended to lie for no other purpose than the enjoyment of mendacity.

But he was no fool, either.

Here he was in a house whose owners felt the need for more security devices than most banks, owners whose pasts perhaps weren't really past, and some apparently unsummoned person was seeking entry.

"Maybe it would be better if you came back in a day or two."

The man shook his head. "A short is a risk of fire."

Francis started to reply when he thought he heard something, something like the back door closing.

That was it, of course. The parish's ancient Toyota was parked in the driveway, a clear indication someone was in the house. The electrician, or whoever he really was, was distracting Francis while a confederate came in the back door.

The revelation came too late.

Just as Francis spun around, a man came from the kitchen, a man with a hood over his head and what looked very much like a gun in his hand.

"Nice and easy, Padre." The voice was all the more menacing coming from inside the hood. "Don't try anything stupid, and you'll be just fine."

In a step he was unlatching the front door and the man in the uniform was inside.

He gave Francis a perfunctory nod. "What about him?"

The man in the hood made a circular motion with the hand not holding the pistol. "Face the wall, priest."

Francis's immediate thought, one so irrelevant it almost made him laugh, was that the bishop would be irritated when he didn't show up.

CHAPTER 12

Sinop-Istanbul Highway
At the Same Time

FORCING HIMSELF TO WAIT UNTIL THE exact moment the man's hand touched the car's door handle took every ounce of training Lang had. Once the adrenaline of anticipated action begins to flow through the bloodstream, inaction, even momentary, is difficult. From the whitening of the knuckles on the hand with which Gurt held the passenger door, he could see she was as tense as he.

The door moved as the man outside grabbed the handle.

"Go!"

As one, both of the Mondeo's front doors flew open, crashing into the man standing beside each with the full weight of Gurt or Lang. As each man staggered backward, arms flailing at empty air to regain balance, Lang and Gurt were on them.

Sweeping a leg against one of her tottering opponent's, Gurt sent him sprawling onto the ground, but not before she had snatched the AK-47 from him. A quick kick in the groin removed what little fight he might have had left in him, leaving him writhing on the rocky ground.

The third man, the one who had been standing in front of the car, had his rifle raised, unable to shoot without a good chance of hitting one or both of his comrades. Gurt had no such problem. Familiar with the weapon, her thumb verified the rifle was on full automatic. A short burst from the hip sent a tree limb just above the man's head crashing to the ground.

It took only a split second for him to consider his options. He turned and fled into the brush to be followed by a companion, still groaning and holding his crotch as he ran.

Gurt turned to where Lang and his antagonist wrestled in the dirt, each struggling for possession of the remaining AK-47.

Pinning his opponent with a knee to the chest, Lang gave the barrel of the gun a yank that failed to dislodge the hands making an equal claim.

He saw Gurt watching idly.

"You might help," he grunted from behind clenched teeth.

"You always get irritable when you think I'm interfering."

"It's never interfering when I might get shot."

"I will try and remember," she replied, placing the muzzle of the rifle she held against the back of the head of the man in uniform. "Freeze!"

He may not have understood the language but the feel of a gun's business end against the back of the skull has a certain significance, transcending words. He raised both his hands in another gesture that needed no translation.

Lang stood, dusting himself off with one hand as he held the AK-47 in the other. "Damn unfriendly locals. Can't say I'd recommend the area on Expedia or Travelocity no matter how swell the hotels."

He used the muzzle of the weapon to prod his former antagonist toward the Mondeo, then shoved him against the car, kicking the man's feet apart before leaning him into the standard search position.

A second later, Lang stepped back. "Nothing, nada, zilch. No wallet, no papers, no keys. He might as well have been born yesterday."

Gurt was hardly surprised. "Could have been worse."

"Oh yeah, how?"

"He could have identification of real *Jandarma*. I do not think the local authorities would be amused."

"Speaking of the local authorities, it's probably best they not be bothered with this little incident."

Gurt's raised eyebrows expressed the question unasked.

Lang gave the AK-47 an underhanded toss that sent it crashing into the brush. "You know how these investigations go: don't leave the area, hours of questioning leading nowhere. No reason to think the Turkish cops are any different from law enforcement all over. They obviously haven't gotten rid of the local bandits any more than the police at home have rid the streets of gangs. I suggest you toss that rifle you're holding and we resume our drive."

Gurt held the weapon up. "And if they come back?"

"Better chance the local *Jandarma* finds it in the car and we get arrested."

"You said 'local bandits.' What makes you so sure?"

"Who else . . .?"

Lang's iPhone chirped Glenn Miller.

He glared at it as he pulled it out of a pants pocket. Nobody paid international roaming charges to dispense good news. His scowl turned to an expression of surprise as he recognized his own home phone number.

"Francis?"

He listened intently. Then, "You okay? Any idea who they were?"

"Francis," he mouthed in answer to Gurt's inquisitive look.

"Any idea what they were after?"

Gurt could hear Francis's voice even though she could not make out the words.

Finally, "No, no point in calling the cops. As long as you're okay, I'd just as soon word of this not get out, not the sort of publicity we want. No, no need. I'd rather clean up myself. I know where things go. Just be sure to turn on the alarm like always."

The keys to the truck were still in the ignition, enabling Lang to move it out of the way. He and Gurt drove past it and rode in silence for a full five minutes.

"Somebody or somebodies posing as electricians jumped Francis while he was in the house," Lang began. "Pretty well ransacked the place."

Gurt absorbed this with considerably less anxiety than Lang had expected.

"What did they take?" she wanted to know.

Lang shook his head. "Francis doesn't know. They put a hood over his head. Sounded like they were looking more for documents of some sort than valuables. I mean, they left the flatscreen TV, but took the computer in my office and left the one upstairs."

"Manfred will be relieved to know his Xbox is safe. You are sure Francis is okay?"

He took his eyes off the serpentine road long enough to look at her.

"'Sure?' He sounded all right. A bit shaken but all right."

They rode in silence for a full minute before Gurt jerked her thumb over her shoulder and asked, "You still think that was a random attack by local bandits back there?"

This time Lang didn't take his eyes from the road. "You think there's a connection?"

"You are the one who does not believe in *koinzidenz*."

When the English word's German counterpart sounded roughly the same, Gurt had a tendency to use her native tongue. Lang wondered if she was aware of the habit.

"Francis says a coincidence is when God wishes to remain anonymous."

Gurt gave the snort that frequently accompanied disagreement. "Actually, it was Einstein. And it was not by chance that they came to the house when Francis had turned off the alarm. To do that means they had been watching, and that means some sort of organization, not some random street bunks."

Gurt's American slang was not quite yet perfect.

"Punks, not bunks. Bunk is a bed. Whoever, God, Francis, or Einstein, you believe there's a connection."

A statement, not a question.

She nodded. "An organization would make that possible, yes. And you think so, too."

Lang slowed for a sharp downhill left. "The question, then, is who and why?"

The answer to that would not soon be forthcoming.

CHAPTER 13

King of Pontus, Foe of Rome,
Story of a Hellenistic Empire
by Abiron Theradoplis, PhD
National Museum of Archeology
Athens
Translation by Chara Georopoulos
University of Iowa Press
(Excerpt)

Exile of the Young Prince

AFTER THE DEATH OF HIS FATHER, Mithradates knew his enemies in the palace might well succeed with the sword where they had failed with poison. The young prince had two choices, neither of them pleasant: remain in Sinope in the royal palace with his treacherous mother and ambitious brother, hoping to thwart their plotting until he was old and powerful enough to seize power. Or he could simply remove himself from her, her spies, and toadies.

There was precedent for the latter course of action. Though we do not know for certain, it is likely young Mithradates read of ancient heroes such as Cyrus of Persia, Alexander, and Mithradates I, the founder of the Pontic Empire. Each had chosen exile for a period in his young life before assuming power. Each had used this period to gather staunch followers who would be critical in gaining popular support later. Mithradates could no doubt identify with the young Cyrus who at thirteen had survived an assassination attempt and fled to Media.

Cyrus' biographer, Xenophon, related how the future king of Persia had gained self-reliance by participating in hunts for lions and elephants armed with little more than his spear. We can understand why Mithradates chose self-exile.

He was not alone. His close friend, Dorylause, son of a general who had served Mithradates' father and who also had been assassinated, had reason to fear for his life, too. Although we cannot be sure what few records remain are complete, Gaius and Diophantus, friends of the young prince, joined the group, as did Gordius, who was to become Mithradates' most trusted advisor in foreign affairs. As noted, the idea of essentially running away from home was not without historical appeal. The young Alexander and his small band had lived on their own in far western Macedonia, meeting the people and raising the support he would need in the future. When word that the king, Alexander's father Phillip, was dead reached them, the young Alexander and his band marched into Pella, Macedonia's capital, without resistance.

Like Mithradates, Alexander's father was also a victim of assassination. Although the actual murder was the act of a single man, a bodyguard during a marriage festival held in the theatre of Aegae, it was widely believed, though never proved, the crime was the result of a conspiracy.

Alexander's early companions became his generals, sharing in spoils from conquests that reached south to Egypt and east to the Hindu Kush. It would not be unreasonable to think Dorylause, Gaius, Diophantus, and Gordius harbored dreams of similar successes.

We know Mithradates was no older than sixteen at the time, and it is reasonable to guess his companions were close to the same age. How these adolescent boys managed to assemble what would have been necessary to survive in the wild we do not know, although Justin's summary of a lost history by Pompeius Trogus gives us a hint.

The royal heir of Pontus "feigned a great passion for the hunt," Justin writes. He and his consorts remained absent from court for increasingly long periods of time. Perhaps the little band secreted weapons and money on each outing. Requisitioning extra horses, bows, spears, and the like would have raised little suspicion.

As Mithradates and his comrades rode out of the palace after a birthday celebration, the young men would have worn dun- or brown-colored cloaks, hats, and tunics and high leather boots, normal hunting attire but also clothing ideal for living and hiding in the forest. Each boy would have been armed with a pair of javelins, bow and arrows, sword, and dagger. Pack horses would have borne bedding, nets for big game, and eating utensils such as cups and plates. Unknown to those who witnessed the departure, each hunter's pouch was crammed with gold coins.

When he returned, it would be as king.

CHAPTER 14

Hotel Kardelen
Trabzon, Turkey
Eight Hours Later

THE HOTEL'S BEST FEATURE WAS A view of the Black Sea some 200 meters below. Six otherwise unimpressive stories jutted out of what Lang guessed was pasture land. For certain, more livestock than people were visible, although a number of small houses dotted the landscape.

"No doubt you have chosen this place because of its location," was Gurt's first observation.

"As a matter of fact, I did. It is the closest to the hospital."

A pair of cows paused munching at a stack of hay long enough to watch the car with bovine curiosity.

"I am relieved to know it is near something. We are going to the hospital?"

Lang was pulling into a small parking lot. "A little later. I'm meeting with Fatima Aksoy, the hospital's administrator, in the morning. Afterward, I'm meeting with the local *Jandarma* captain to see what progress has been made in solving the murder of the hospital's hematologist."

"I do not know why. Even in America, the police move at their own gait. Do you think you can help find the killer?"

Lang eased the Mondeo into one of a number of empty parking places. "Not really. I felt I had to come here to show support not only for Dr. Aksoy, but for the entire hospital staff. Besides, this is one of the few of the Foundation's operations I've never seen."

In minutes, Gurt and Lang were standing in the light wood-paneled lobby, presenting passports to the sole clerk behind the reception desk. Their room, like every part of the hotel Lang had seen, was spotless and neatly furnished in modern furniture distinguishable only for its unattractiveness. Lang opened his suitcase while Gurt went to the window. To his surprise, it slid open.

How long had it been since he had been in a hotel — or other building — where the windows actually opened?

"Lang, come look!"

In a step he was beside her. In the minutes since they had parked the car, a thick fog had rolled in from the sea, lapping over the edge of the cliff like a rising tide. The illusion was that of the hotel itself afloat upon a placid ocean.

The phone rang.

"You are expecting someone?" Gurt asked.

Lang shook his head slowly. "Only Dr. Aksoy, and not until tomorrow morning." He sprawled across the bed to pick the receiver from its cradle. "Hello?"

"Mr. Reilly?" A woman's voice. "I am Fatima Aksoy."

Her voice sounded just a bit higher than he recalled. But then Walsh's speakerphone, the transoceanic transmission, or any number of other factors could have accounted for the difference.

"Yes, Dr. Aksoy. I believe we have an appointment in the morning."

"That is why I am calling. Something has occurred that makes tomorrow difficult. Could you come to the hospital now? It is only a few kilometers from where you are and I need to show you something I found that may help solve Dr. Yalmaz's murder."

"Come there now?" He was looking at Gurt. "We, my wife and I, are beat from the trip . . ."

Gurt mouthed the words, "Go. I want to make a . . ."

"Hold on," Lang said into the phone. "Make a what?"

"*Schlafchen*, nap."

No wonder he couldn't decipher her lip movements. "Excuse me, Dr. Aksoy. I'm back."

"I thought you said you were beaten."

"Beat, tired."

"This will not take long, Mr. Reilly. I promise."

Reluctantly, Lang slid off the bed. "I'm on the way."

Lang guessed the road followed the lip of the cliff. Because of the fog, he could not be sure. In some places it was so thick he had to navigate by following the edge of the pavement. Happily, there was no other traffic, either because of the area's sparse population or because the populous was smart enough not to risk driving in such adverse conditions. Although less than a mile and a half, the trip took a full half-hour. Had it not been for the sign announcing HASTTAHANE COCUK, which he could not understand, along with the international graphic of a cross above a figure in bed, which he could, he would have missed the hospital altogether.

The building was an indistinct blur, the fog smearing both its shape and the lights now on for the evening. Lang walked almost all the way around before finding the entrance. A man in green scrubs was seated behind a desk reading a newspaper.

He looked up as Lang approached. "I'm here to see Dr. Aksoy."

The man in the scrubs looked puzzled. At first Lang thought he was one of the few Turks who did not speak English. This was, after all, a rural area.

The man slid his wheeled office chair over to a computer screen, clicked a few keys, and shook his head. "Today is her day off. She will be in at 0700 tomorrow."

"But I just talked to her," Lang protested. "She was here minutes ago and expecting me."

The man shrugged, perhaps realizing the futility of arguing with someone who is completely and totally wrong. He reached for a phone. "I'll call her office, but . . ."

Lang felt a sinking sensation in his stomach. The woman on the phone hadn't sounded like the voice of Dr. Aksoy, although he had met her only once years ago and talked to her on the phone a single time before tonight. And she had been educated in the States, yet she hadn't understood the slang use of "beat" for tired. Hadn't she originally referred to the murdered hematologist by his first name, Emre?

But why . . .?

Oh, shit! How could he have been so stupid!

"I can call her home," the man behind the desk offered to Lang's swiftly retreating back.

CHAPTER 15

Hotel Kardelen
Twenty-One Minutes Later

LANG HAD KEPT THE MONDEO FLOOR-BOARDED despite virtually driving blind in the fog. He screeched to a stop in front of the hotel, sprung from the car, and dashed through the door, throwing it open so violently he nearly hit an elderly couple about to exit the lobby. Both astonished and angered at his apparent indifference to what could have been a nasty accident, they watched him slam a palm against the elevator button, mutter curses, and sprint for the stairwell.

He climbed four flights of stairs in what, had he thought about it, might have been world record time. Forcing himself to slow down for the sake of stealth, he slid along, back pressed to the corridor's wall, until he reached 410, his room.

For an instant he was still other than gulping air into lungs depleted by his four-story sprint. Then he leaned around the door frame, placing his ear as close as possible to the door.

Nothing.

He reached out and touched the wood.

The door swung open, unlocked.

Lang flung himself inside, squatting to make as small a target as possible.

He need not have bothered. He was the only living creature in the room. Still, he called Gurt's name only to be answered by silence, a terrifying sound.

He stood.

The bed was rumpled as though she had made good on her intent to take a nap. He took a step and something crunched underfoot. Kneeling, he saw shards of glass. A quick glance found a water pitcher and two unbroken glasses on the floor. Where . . .? Oh, yeah, a pitcher and two glasses had been on the dresser. But these shards of glass didn't match. They had come from a small cylindrical object with what appeared to be calibrations on it.

The realization of what he was looking at made his stomach churn.

Beside the dresser, a small, ugly, fabric-covered chair lay on its side.

Now that he knew what he was looking for, small signs of a struggle were everywhere: a lone woman's sandal just this side of the threshold to the bathroom; clothes, perhaps spread out on the bed, now dumped in piles on the floor; a handbag vomiting its contents.

Most telling: a quarter-sized drop of reddish-brown on the tiles of the bath, now going tacky. Someone had shed blood. Not a lot, but blood just the same.

An equal measure of fury and terror washed over Lang, depriving him momentarily of any useful thought. He would personally kill the bastards responsible in the most gruesome manner possible. What if he never saw Gurt again? Worse, would Manfred blame him for not taking Gurt along to the hospital? Or not staying with her?

Then he made a tour of the room and bath, stopping in front of the sink. The mirror above it had been shattered, only a few icicle-like shards remaining in the frame. What, Lang wondered, had caused that? Other than the indicia of a struggle he had already noted, he saw nothing remarkable.

Leaving the room, he took the elevator to the lobby, where he surprised himself at how calmly he had the desk clerk call the authorities.

The man — young boy, actually — with the feathery beginnings of his first moustache, seemed to have a hard time understanding. "Kidnap?"

"Abducted, taken," Lang explained.

"You are sure your wife did not . . .?" He made a vague motion which could have implied anything between simply wandering away and slipping off to keep an assignation.

"I'm quite sure," Lang said evenly. "And every second you ask stupid questions instead of calling the police gives the kidnappers that much more of a lead."

The clerk's open mouth shut with an audible snap and he punched 115, Turkey's 911 equivalent, into the phone's keyboard.

When he had finished a brief conversation, Lang asked in a conversational tone, "What other hotel employees are on duty tonight?"

"On duty?" The young man seemed perplexed by the question, exhaling loudly and sending the sparse hairs on his upper lip fluttering. "The last maid left hours ago. The restaurant staff, cooks, waiters, and such would still be here."

"Other than the main entrance, how do you get in and out of the hotel?"

"There is a service entrance in the basement where food for the restaurant and supplies and laundry are delivered. But it is kept locked when not in use. And there is a fire exit on this floor, also locked. Opening either would set off an alarm."

"The service entrance, how do I get there?"

"The elevator to the basement, but . . ."

Lang was already on his way to the elevator bank.

The basement was shadowed in the half light of space only occasionally used. A pair of hand trucks stood sentry against the far wall, illuminated by widely spaced overhead lightbulbs. A corridor led to a large steel overhead door about 50 feet away. There was the faint smell of overripe fruit that Lang guessed came from a stack of wooden crates piled in a corner.

Lang knelt as he inspected the service door. A simple latching device was the only lock, but it would be effective in denying entry assuming there was no one here to open it. From a panel of numbers a red light blinked. The alarm system was armed. The cement floor was well swept, devoid of any dust that might have captured tracks, either human or automotive.

Back in the elevator, he got out at the lobby, turned his back on the front desk, and followed the signs to the fire exit. Another steel door, this one much smaller. The alarm panel must be located elsewhere, for it wasn't visible, although a sign in English, Turkish, French, and what Lang guessed was Japanese warned of its activation should the door be opened.

Again kneeling, he studied the door. Another simple latching mechanism. A spring at the top would close the door automatically. As with the freight door downstairs, entry would require someone inside. His eyes caught sight of something on the floor, a wad of paper folded multiple times into the size of, say, a U.S. quarter. He picked it up and tried to squeeze it between door and frame. It almost fit, but not quite. If the door had been left barely, almost invisibly cracked open, this bit of paper would have made a doorstop, jamming the door open for entry from outside. And if the alarm were not armed . . .

"You have found something, Mr. Reilly?"

Lang got to his feet facing a man who could have been anywhere between thirty and fifty. He wore khaki slacks and a designer golf shirt under an open windbreaker. Jet-black hair swept back over the ears without a hint of silver. Natural or an expensive dye job?

The man smiled and extended his right hand. "Captain Sadik Kahraman of the local *Jandarma*. You *are* Langford Reilly, whose wife has gone missing?"

The accent was all but imperceptible.

Lang took the hand. "I am."

Kahraman made a gesture indicating himself. "You will please forgive my lack of official uniform. The call came while I was off duty . . ."

"Captain, I wouldn't care if you were dressed like Ronald McDonald. My wife has been taken . . ."

The other man held up a hand. "You believe she was taken."

Typical police reaction the world over: take time to establish a crime really has been committed while the criminals escape.

Lang turned toward the lobby and the elevators. "Come take a look at the room. You can see a scuffle went on."

The captain stood his ground. "And where were you?"

Lang's frustration was growing: Every minute gave the kidnappers a larger lead. "At the Children's Hospital near here. I'm head of the foundation that sponsors it. Now, if you'll . . ."

"What was the nature of your business at the hospital?"

Lang had to make a conscious effort not to grind his teeth. "I came here to find out what I could about the murder of Dr. Yalmaz. I got a call from someone who claimed to be Dr. Aksoy, said she had something I should see."

Kahraman's lips tightened at the mention of the doctor. "Just what interest is this to you?"

Lang sighed audibly. It was clear he was going to have to satisfy the policeman's curiosity before any effort to find Gurt could begin. "The hospital is funded by an international foundation I head. Any time something like this happens, I try to get there as soon as possible, see what I can do."

The captain was looking at him closely. "Do you often have staff murdered?"

"No, of course not. I meant whenever there is a problem. Now, if you'd like to take a look at the room . . ."

"One more thing first, Mr. Reilly. You picked something up from the floor." He extended a hand. "Let me have it, please."

Lang was not happy to give up what might be the only clue as to where Gurt was. "It was only a piece of trash."

Kahraman's smile was frozen, without warmth. His manicured fingers made a beckoning motion. "The object, Mr. Reilly. I need not remind you of the penalties for obstructing an investigation. I am sure your country does not smile on such things."

Reluctantly Lang dug the wad of paper out of his pocket. The Turk took it, tossing it up and down in the palm of his hand. "What do you make of this, Mr. Reilly?"

"You're the policeman. You tell me."

Kahraman shook his head slowly. "Surely you do not believe I would think you would pick up worthless trash? Mr. Reilly, if ill fate has befallen your wife, I would think you would want to cooperate."

Ill fate? Befallen? Where had this guy taken English lessons, the Arthur Conan Doyle School of Writing? Still, Lang had learned to handle the local heat carefully. Whether Atlanta, Rome, or Paris, the fraternity of blue resented anything perceived as an invasion of their turf. To appear to be concealing evidence would start things heading downhill faster than the U.S. Olympic ski team.

Another sigh. "I think it was used as a doorstop to keep that fire door open so the kidnappers could get in and then out without being seen."

The captain nodded in agreement. "But that would require the cooperation of someone in the hotel to keep the alarm unarmed, someone familiar with the system."

The two men exchanged glances before moving as one down the hall toward the lobby. Neither was surprised to see the desk clerk had vanished.

CHAPTER 16

Hotel Kardelen
Room 410

CAPTAIN KAHRAMAN SURVEYED THE ROOM FROM the doorway. "One would not think a woman could put up such a fight."

He obviously didn't know Gurt.

But Lang said, "I'm guessing at least two, maybe three of them."

Kahraman was rubbing his chin. "What is the, er, basis for that?"

Lang knelt and lifted the skirt of the bedspread, revealing the broken glass. "At least one man held her while the other administered, or tried to administer, the contents of a hypodermic."

Kahraman was looking at the American with newfound respect. "I cannot remember the last glass, rather than disposable plastic, syringe I have seen."

Lang stood. "At least let's hope they used a clean needle."

"Mr. Reilly, do you have any idea who might have taken her away and why?"

"I'd hoped you might have that answer."

The Turk held out the wad of paper and began to carefully unfold it. It looked like the bottom half of a printed page.

Kahraman snorted. "Well, we have a good idea as to who the 'who' might be."

"And that would be?"

"The PPK."

"As in, Walther PPK, a pistol?"

"No, as in the Kurdish terrorists, sometimes called the Turkish Mafia."

He noted Lang's blank expression and continued. "This bit of paper used as a doorstop is a, a . . . what would you say, a bulletin? Yes, a bulletin about some event in Lice, a Kurdish town in the southeast part of the country, Diyabakir Provence, from which the separatist terrorists join their brothers to launch attacks into Iraq, Syria, and Iran. Iran is the western part of what is called the Golden Crescent, where brown heroin crosses from Pakistan and Afghanistan. From there it travels, frequently by truck, across Turkey and along the more deserted Balkan highways into Trieste and on into southern Italy, where the Sicilian mob takes over to distribute worldwide. It is how these people finance their campaign of terrorism."

"If you know all this, why can't you stop it?"

Kahraman exhibited perfect white teeth, though there was no humor in the smile. "For the same reason your Drug Enforcement Agency cannot keep drugs out of your country: too few officers, too much money involved."

"Okay, point taken. But what does this have to do with Gurt's kidnapping?"

Kahraman looked over his shoulder and stepped to right the fabric-covered chair. He sat down. "Why don't you tell me, Mr. Reilly, why a band of criminals, terrorists, would choose your wife?"

"Perhaps they saw we were Americans."

The Turk made a steeple of his fingers upon which he rested his chin. "Come now, Mr. Reilly. Why would these Kurds travel hundreds of kilometers from their normal territory to kidnap a single American unless that American — or her husband — were special in some way? I can hardly be of help if you do not . . . what do you say? Level, yes, unless you level with me."

"Okay, I can see that. But shouldn't you be doing something like maybe checking the roads out of town?"

Again the mirthless smile. "That was done before I came here. I am covering every road within 50 kilometers as best I can. I do not have the men to watch every secondary road or sheep path, though." He nodded toward the window where the lights from the hotel's windows played back onto the swirling mist. "It is unlikely the — what is the word for the criminals?"

"Perpetrators?"

This time the smile was genuine. "Ah, yes, perpetrators! It is unlikely the perpetrators will attempt to drive very far. They know we are looking for them, plus this fog not only makes driving dangerous, but the fact they are out in it will draw the attention of my men."

Lang sat on the bed, feeling as weary as if he had hiked here from Istanbul. "What do you suggest we do, then?"

"I suggest you tell me why these people selected the victim they did."

It was clear the Turkish policeman was going to hear the truth before he made any move.

"Okay, then," Lang began. "I'm not sure why we were selected, but this afternoon . . ."

Kahraman was silent for a full minute when Lang finished. Then, "And you did not report the attack to the *Jandarma*?"

"To what point? By that time, they were gone."

The Turk was clearly not satisfied with that answer, but unable to find an objection to it other than, "In Turkey, it is the law that crimes be reported."

Lang was in no mood to split legal hairs. "Looks to me like a real crime has been committed and we sit here doing nothing. Are you going to find the desk clerk? Seems to me he could well be an accessory."

Before Kahraman could answer, the phone rang.

CHAPTER 17

At the Same Time

ALTHOUGH THE ROOM WAS DARK, GURT was pretty certain it had been carved from stone, perhaps the mountainside up which she had been half-carried, half-dragged.

When there was a knock on the door of the hotel room, she had assumed Lang had forgotten something as well as his room key. Violating every rule she had been taught, she didn't ask who was there. Just opened the door, only to have it slammed into her with enough force to snatch the chain lock from the doorframe. She had been knocked down and was getting to her feet when three men in ski masks charged into the room. Two held 9x18mm Makarov pistols. More frightening, the third held a syringe.

The two with pistols pointed at her went to different sides of the room. Standard operating procedure: cover the captive from multiple angles. Their silence was as intimidating as their weapons. On her knees, she retreated toward the only available open space, the bathroom. The man with the syringe approached cautiously, motioning her to extend an arm.

Quick decision: did these men want her alive for some purpose or were they perfectly willing to kill her? She was pretty certain the determination would not be hers to make if she let that man stick her with that needle.

Her back was now against the sink. She had run out of room.

The fact wasn't lost on the man with the hypodermic. He lunged forward, needle extended. The instant he was committed to the move, Gurt threw up both hands, grabbing his belt. Using his momentum and the lower center of gravity being on her knees gave her, she jerked him forward.

There were two satisfying sounds of shattering glass: a tinkle as the syringe shattered on the floor and a crash followed by a shower of glass slivers from the mirror over the sink as her assailant's head hit it.

Something hit the back of her neck, and her vision began to contract. She was aware of reaching for a dagger-shaped piece of the mirror, of its sharp edges biting into her hand, then her side as she slipped it into her blouse just as her world went completely dark.

The next thing she had been aware of was being on the floor of some sort of vehicle, she thought one of the eight- to ten-passenger vans, *dolmus*, that were the backbone of Turkey's public transportation system. Her hands were tied behind her back. Through slitted eyes, she confirmed she was indeed on the floor. Two men were silhouetted against the little bus's lighted instrument panel. She had the sense the third was seated just above where she lay. The next impressions came simultaneously: the back of her head felt as though it separated from the rest of her skull with every motion of the vehicle.

She had no idea how long she had been unconscious nor any means of ascertaining the time. Nonetheless, she succumbed to Agency training, keeping track of the seconds ticking by. The process partially diverted her from the throbbing of her head and would help her calculate the distance covered since coming to. If or why this information might become relevant she could not have said.

The hum of tires on a paved road became the sound of loose gravel pinging off the undercarriage as the vehicle's suspension rattled with each bump, jounces that sent bolts of pain along her already aching head. Once or twice she bit her lower lip to stifle a groan. After four minutes, the motion stopped, and the engine was switched off. A door slammed. Gurt closed her eyes. There was little benefit to alerting her captors that she had revived from both the blow and whatever might have remained in the broken syringe.

A door beside her popped open, and she could feel the night's cool mist on feet she had not realized were bare. Rough hands grabbed her ankles and tugged her across the floorboards. Someone grabbed her shoulders and dragged her uphill. She felt the wet rock on her feet as she was pulled up rough stone stairs, the edges banging painfully into her ankles.

At last she was unceremoniously dumped on a rock-hard floor, her hands were untied, footsteps receded, and a heavy door slammed shut followed by the click of a key in a lock.

Gurt lay perfectly still, listening for any sound that might betray another presence. After five minutes, she reached her hand into her blouse to confirm the sliver of glass mirror was still there. She touched its glazed surface but was careful not to grip it as she had earlier, an effort attested to by the dried blood and pain she could feel along the palm of her right hand. The knowledge she had a weapon gave her some comfort.

Gingerly, she braced herself against the floor and stood unsteadily. The room spun out of control, and only a hand on the wall stopped her from falling. Gradually the dizziness dissipated, and she was able to conduct an inspection of her prison by touch. She had almost completed her circuit when she stumbled over a raised stone. Kneeling, she felt first a line of raised stone (or had it been carved from solid rock like the room?). Above this ridge and perhaps six or seven inches toward the wall, her fingers touched another vertical surface. It took a full minute to ascertain the object was oblong, box-shaped, and about three or four feet high and perhaps just as long.

Remaining on her knees, she ran a hand along the smooth stone until she felt a small indentation, a line. Her fingers traced it. Parallel even lines intersecting parallel even lines at right angles. She sat back on her heels and tried to visualize what the sense of touch had portrayed.

Then she grinned. Not a big grin but a small one, a smile that said she had achieved her first victory over her captors: she had a means of defense and an idea what her prison might be. Not where it was, but what it had been. As a captive, knowledge itself could be a weapon.

CHAPTER 18

Hotel Kardelen
Seconds Later

For an instant, both Kahraman and Lang stared at the ringing phone as though it might speak of its own accord.

On the third ring, Lang reached for it. "Hello?"

Nothing.

At first, Lang thought the caller might have hung up before speaking. Then, "Mr. Reilly?"

"Speaking."

What followed could have been dialogue from a hackneyed crime drama, although Lang was hardly in a mood to notice. "We have your wife. She will be returned to you unharmed if you give us what we want."

Lang swallowed his initial reaction of rage that someone had violently invaded his and Gurt's life, jeopardized her safety, and then made demands, an anger all but eclipsed by fear, terror, actually, that he might never see her again.

He forced himself to speak calmly as he reverted to standard hostage retrieval training. "I'm not discussing anything until I know she's alive and okay."

Silence. Having a demand come from the victim's side of the relationship had apparently not been anticipated.

Then, "Is not possible."

Definitely an accent, though Lang couldn't place it.

"Look," Lang said in the most reasonable tone one could manage through gritted teeth. "You went to a lot of trouble to get whatever it is you want from me. I'm not willing to discuss whatever that may be until I know you haven't harmed her."

He could only hope the apprehension that was clinching his gut wasn't reflected in his voice. Logically, he knew that in the United States, the vast majority of kidnappings were resolved within hours. But this wasn't America, nor was the victim a child taken by a relative, also the overwhelming majority.

Kahraman had been watching him closely, following the part of the conversation he could hear. He got up and went into the bathroom, closing the door behind him as he took a cell phone from his pants pocket.

Lang continued, "It's not an unreasonable request. Just let her say a few words and I'll listen to whatever you have to say."

There was a muffled conversation on the other end of the line, the sound of a discussion while someone had their hand over the phone.

"Is okay, then. Will call you back, you hear her speak. But understand, American: any trick and she dies."

The line went dead.

Kahraman stepped out of the bathroom. "No good. I called the station to have them try to trace, but there were several calls coming into the hotel, one from a cell phone."

Lang leaned across the bed to replace the receiver. "Any luck triangulating on the cell?"

The policeman shook his head. "Mr. Reilly, please try to understand: This is a remote area of Turkey, not a city in America where there are any number of relay stations within miles of each other. Unless that particular cell has a GPS transmitter . . ."

He trailed off, the hopelessness of electronic tracking obvious.

Lang was pacing the room, unaware he was doing do. "For whatever it's worth, they are going to call back."

Two steps forward, two steps back.

Kahraman had his cell out again. "I will see what can be done."

The wait was a short one, less than five minutes.

Lang grasped the receiver with both hands as if by doing so he might touch her. "Gurt? You okay?"

"Lang? I'm fine, hunky-dory, *Kloster Kapelle*. I . . ."

"You've heard enough, Mr. Reilly," the now recognizable voice interrupted. "The woman is, what did she say? Hunky-dory? I'm not familiar with, what, Kloster something?"

"Means the same thing," Lang assured him hurriedly.

"Very well. Now to business: Mr. Reilly, we want the blood sample sent to your foundation from Trabzon."

It took Lang a moment or two to try to make sense of the demand. Dr. Walsh, a contemporary office, a conversation that now seemed distant in both time and geography. "You mean the blood sample from the kid who was bitten by some kind of snake?"

"Precisely."

"Surely you don't think I have it?"

There was a chuckle. Over the phone, Lang could hear little humor in it. "Of course not, Mr. Reilly. But you could obtain it for us."

"That's ridiculous! I can't keep up with every medical test the Foundation performs. Now, if it's money you want . . ."

This time the voice had a dagger edge to it. "Find it, Mr. Reilly. Find it in the next 48 hours, or we start sending back your woman . . . piece by piece."

"But . . ." No use, they had hung up.

Kahraman was shaking his head. "No luck on tracing the cell phone."

Lang smiled for the first time in what seemed like an eternity. "I think I know where she is. Two questions. First: how long will it take you to get together a company of the army?"

He realized the error as soon as the words left his lips. With half a dozen military coups since 1966, plus the revelation of a military plot to overthrow the mildly Islamic government in 2002, the civilian power structure was wary of delegating troops to the army to keep domestic order.

Ignoring the potential political blunder, Kahraman said, "I can have heavily armed police here in an hour perhaps, something like your SWAT teams. But, how do you know where she is?"

"She told me."

"Where?"

"Get your troops assembled first."

CHAPTER 19

At the Same Time

GURT WAS SURPRISED WHEN THE DOOR to her prison rattled open and a man holding an AK-47 motioned her out into the dark dampness of night. Two things immediately told her she was farther above sea level than the hotel from which she had been abducted. First, there had been the steep climb, and now, even in the dark, misty clouds roiled below, shining with a luminescence as though illuminated from within.

The guard shoved from behind, a flashlight playing along a path roughly hewed into stone, a straight drop on one side. A number of buildings lined the pathway, one or two stories, some carved into a rock face, props on a stage like the place she had been confined. Others had been constructed of stones fitted into rocks. Once, perhaps twice, she caught a fleeting view of colors, figures, painted on flat surfaces of structure, forms faded into near oblivion. She intentionally stumbled once, giving her a moment for the beam of the flashlight to confirm what she had already surmised.

The flicker of an old-fashioned lantern from a building just ahead sent impossibly elongated shadows of human forms darting across the path. Inside, two men, one of whom had smashed the bathroom mirror with his face, waited. Although most of his features were swathed in an amateurish attempt at a bandage, there was no mistaking the hatred burning in his eyes.

The other proffered a cell phone. "You will speak to Mr. Reilly," he commanded. "Tell him you are unharmed." He nodded toward the man with the bandage. "Anything more and you will belong to Arin there."

Lang was already on the line. Gurt spoke her few words before the phone was snatched away.

"What means those words, "*Kloster Kapelle*"?

Gurt stared at him with little girl innocence. "I thought you had a command of English. It means I'm hunky-dory, fine." The explanation she and Lang had agreed upon for anything said in German in front of one who likely didn't understand the language.

It was clear that "hunky-dory" might well have been Sanskrit as far as Gurt's captor knew, but she was fairly certain he wasn't going to admit it to his comrades.

The man who had escorted her here exchanged words with the other two. Although the phrases were foreign to her, the furtive looks of the three in her direction didn't bode well. She knew she had served her purpose and keeping her around presented more problem for her jailers than benefit. She touched the glass shard in her blouse.

The man who had brought her here apparently had been ordered to take her back to her prison. There was something different, though, about his attitude, the covert glances, the smirks of the other two.

She was not surprised, then, when he grabbed her by the blouse as soon as they were out of the light generated by the lantern. She managed a convincing whimper as he ripped it from her shoulders and placed a groping hand on her breast. He pushed her up against cold stone, crushing her neck with the forestock of the AK-47 as he fumbled with the fly of his trousers.

Snatching the glass from her shirt, Gurt's arm moved swiftly up as though gutting an animal. A grunt, a gurgle, and the sour smell of a sewer as her assailant took a step backward. His face, what she could see of it in the beam of the flashlight he had dropped, showed puzzlement at the crimson gash that divided both his shirt and stomach into roughly equal vertical halves. The rifle clattered on the stone walkway as he eased down to his knees, as though to offer Christian prayer while his hands frantically tried to hold in his intestines.

There was a weak cry that ended in a gurgle as Gurt whipped the glass shard across his trachea, severing it. He would live for a few more minutes as he futilely gasped for air but would die silently.

Her hands were too slick with blood, hers and the dying man's, to efficiently handle the rifle. She tore a strip from her ruined blouse and used her left hand and teeth to bind up the palm of her right where the glass dagger had sliced her own flesh.

She dared not use the flashlight, so she went on hands and knees to search for the dropped rifle. She could only pray it had not fallen over the ledge into the pit of darkness below.

If only she could find it before the morning star above dimmed and that gray streak in the eastern sky brought the new day's light. In the dark, she had a chance. Dawn would lengthen the odds.

CHAPTER 20

King of Pontus, Foe of Rome,
Story of a Hellenistic Empire
by Abiron Theradoplis, PhD
National Museum of Archeology
Athens
Translation by Chara Georopoulos
University of Iowa Press
(Excerpt)

Aᴌᴛʜᴏᴜɢʜ ᴡᴇ ᴅᴏ ɴᴏᴛ ᴋɴᴏᴡ ᴛʜᴇ precise date, Justin relates an incident that might be illustrative of the working of the mind of Mithradates, supposedly recorded by the young king's best friend among the four, Gordius:

Two of the four brought a boar they had killed into a woodland camp. As the animal was cooking, presumably over an open fire and spit, Mithradates wandered off into the forest. An hour later, Gordius came upon his friend who was busily taking cuttings from a hemlock plant and putting them in a leather pouch he wore around his neck. For whatever reason, he said nothing but returned to camp.

As the boar was prepared, Gordius noted his friend sprinkling the contents of the pouch on his portion of the meat. His youthful curiosity aroused, he observed Mithradates over the next few days, harvesting not only hemlock but belladonna, and other deadly poisons such as henbane and poisonous mushrooms. He knew small portions of some of these poisons brought on states of temporary madness, clairvoyance in which communication with the gods was possible, or stupor, but he observed none of these in the young king, nor did he note the toxic effects of drooling, convulsions, or paralysis.

Gordius said nothing, knowing his lord and soon-to-be king knew best.

CHAPTER 21

On the Road from Trabzon
Thirty Minutes Later

LANG SAT IN THE FRONT SEAT of an FNSS Pars, a Turkish-manufactured 6x6 armored personnel carrier, between the driver and Kahraman, the Turkish cop. Behind them was a surprisingly quickly assembled squad of eight men, uniformed in camouflage under Kevlar body armor. He was less than happy that half carried the *Baba*, 12-gauge shotguns, and the other LMG MP5 submachine guns. Both weapons were more likely to level anything and anyone in sight than help in a surgically precise rescue operation.

The policeman had insisted that Lang, a civilian and a foreign one at that, had no business going on what was essentially a police mission.

Lang had simply shrugged. "Then don't expect me to tell you where she is."

"But, Mr. Reilly," the man had spluttered, "there may be gunfire. These men, if they are Kurds from the south as I would speculate, they may well kill her."

Lang had given the man a stare that could have frozen meat. "I'll get her out myself."

"But, but . . ." the man protested. "You, an unarmed single person against an unknown number of those *hajduk* . . ."

"Those what?"

"Er, bandits, outlaws. You don't know how many. What chance do you stand alone?"

Better than most, Lang thought, although he said, "Tell you what: I'll stay out of your way, even sit here in the truck . . ."

He had no intention of doing so, but standing in front of the hotel arguing wasn't doing Gurt any good.

As the truck and its armed complement pulled out of the hotel parking lot, Kahraman turned to Lang. "Now is the time, Mr. Reilly, for you to share your knowledge of where these people have taken her."

"To the chapel of the nearest monastery."

"Monastery? Chapel? We are an Islamic people, Mr. Reilly. We don't have . . ." He jerked forward in his seat. "Yes! There *is* a monastery nearby, Sumela. Three centuries before the time of the Prophet, peace be upon him, Christians carved it from the face of a cliff nearly 1,200 meters above a forest near here. It became something of a center of Greek learning and culture. After the Ottoman conquest, it was one of the few Christian institutions the sultans allowed to remain open. In 1923, during the forced exchange of population between Greece and Turkey, the monks were forced to leave and the place was abandoned. It has become a popular tourist attraction in Altindere National Park."

"How far?"

The Turkish policeman exhaled through his mouth. "In normal times? Perhaps half an hour. In this fog? One can only guess."

Lang managed to control his impatience as the 6x6's tight suspension found every pothole in the road. It seemed hours, but his watch told him only 40 minutes had elapsed before the APC turned off the main highway and stopped. The men climbed out of the rear as Lang's feet touched a ground carpeted in pine needles. There was the smell, quiet, and feel of a forest. Indeed, as the men set out with Lang trailing, tree trunks were so close together as to make any sort of a path indiscernible.

Suddenly, they were in a clearing. Looking straight up, Lang could see through the parting mist a huge building on a ledge so narrow the impression was that both rock and structure were about to fall. Rows of square windows stared across the valley. To the left was a cluster of smaller structures.

"There are two ways up," the Turkish policeman pointed, speaking to Lang in a whisper. "To the right, there is a road that goes most of the way. On the left, stairs."

He gave a brief, quiet command and the eight uniforms started checking their gear for anything that might give them away: a canteen rattling against a spare clip, a belt buckle clanging against a gun barrel. Lang's anxiety was slightly lessened by the thoroughness of the training evidenced by the precaution. Lang had experienced too many local law enforcement agencies, both in the U.S. and abroad, whose idea of a hostage rescue was to come in shooting, leaving the captives' safety more to luck than skill.

"Your promise, Mr. Reilly," Kahraman said, "was that you would remain in the vehicle. Please return there now."

Rather than argue, Lang turned as if to go, just as the sound of a shot echoed across the deathly still valley, its echo bouncing from the rocky hills in a vortex of sound. Three more in rapid succession preceded a fusillade. Then all was quiet, the only evidence of the disturbance the cries of crows angry at being flushed from the trees into the new day prematurely.

Lang was instantly forgotten. Turning toward the cliff, the small command set off at a trot. Keeping a distance, Lang followed. Within minutes, they were at the base of steep stairs, just wide enough to accommodate a single person at a time. What the ancient monks had built as a defensive measure was still a perfect device for an ambush.

Lang counted the first hundred or so steps, then gave up to concentrate on a climb that was taxing enough without distraction. His shirt was damp and not entirely due to the early morning mist that was now parting like a stage curtain.

It was only when the men paused before a gate even more narrow than the stairs that he realized night's shadows had completely retreated, leaving the dull gray of predawn. Through the gate he saw a scattering of buildings cut into the rock, or made from it. The randomness with which they were placed reminded him of a child abandoning his building blocks. Beyond was the large building he had seen from below. As he followed the group, he saw some walls were decorated with faded stucco paintings. Solemn-faced virgins, halos more memory than visible, held or bent over infants who looked anything but happy, now peered over piles of rubble, structures that had not endured the march of centuries.

The deliberation with which Kahraman's men explored each dark doorway, each building, each pile of rubble was necessary, if maddening. At this rate, searching the monastery would take all day, a day in which

Gurt could well die. He fought back the urge to shout her name, to let her know he was there.

The very stillness was a fingernail across the blackboard of Lang's nerves. He saw a thousand places to hide or from which to launch an attack unseen. There was somebody here. Or had been, as evidenced by the shots.

As one, Lang and the police froze, and one small stone, then another, clicked as it rolled down the stone street. Something, somebody had moved. Gun muzzles came up as men sought the shelter of walls and doorways and glanced at each other uneasily.

Whoever it was, they were approaching.

CHAPTER 22

Sumela Monastery
Forty Minutes Earlier

On HANDS AND KNEES GURT ALTERNATELY searched the area with her finger-tips and glanced at the ever-widening streak of gray that was the eastern horizon. Venus' heralding of the new day was dimming, and it would be full light soon. She was acutely aware that, at some point, the remaining two men would come searching for their comrade, perhaps to join in the sport he had planned to have with her. Certianly if he hadn't returned in an hour or so . . .

Somewhere there was a sound. It was not the spasmodic breeze sigh-ing through the ruins of the monastery; it was not the occasional crack of rock exfoliating as it cooled from the long-past heat of yesterday. Unarmed other than with a glass dagger, she had best hide, hoping Lang could muster a rescue effort that would reach her before the two remaining kid-nappers did.

If there were only two. True, she had only seen the three, now dimin-ished by one. That did not mean there were not others who, for one reason or another, chose to remain unseen.

There it was again, this time the unmistakable crunch of a footstep on the gravel to which the centuries had reduced a large part of the stone. Close, too close. Why had she not heard the previous steps? Because who-ever was approaching felt the need of caution? No matter, she needed a place to hide, something that was not going to be easy in the near dark.

Still on hands and knees, now as a preventative against stumbling, she scrambled up the incline, her eyes futilely probing the last of the night. Centuries of sun had bleached the stones, both rubble and buildings, into a grayish white, making them easier to see than the darker color of the cliff above, but in the predawn, they were little more than a single-dimensional blur. She was desperately trying to distinguish features, to find a crack or cranny in which to hide, when her fingers touched cold steel. It felt like . . . it was . . . the AK-47! At first she could not believe her good luck. The dying man must have tossed the gun toward the upslope. Scree, rubble, something had prevented it from rolling downhill. She would never have found it had she been permitted to continue her search.

Gurt mit Gluck, Lucky Gurt, they had called her at the Agency when she had won the small arms championship. Again with the martial arts competition. She had smiled at the well-intentioned nickname given her by her comrades, smiled the smile of the knowledgeable. Luck had nothing to do with it.

Finding the rifle was another matter. A very lucky matter.

Armed, the requisites of her hidey-hole changed dramatically. Now she needed not only concealment but a vantage point. Slipping an arm through the weapon's sling, she scrambled behind what appeared to be a pile of loose rubble. A nearby building was between the eastern horizon and her hiding place. She should be in shadow for the first few hours of morning.

Minutes ago she was near helpless, able only to hope the night would last a few minutes longer. Now, armed, she was eager for daylight.

Between stones, she was first aware she was able to distinguish color other than gray or black. Then the shapes of buildings a hundred feet or so distant came into focus as though through some cosmic lens. Dawn had arrived.

A shadow moved. No, two shadows. No, not shadows but figures: the man with the bandaged face and the English speaker.

They carried their rifles at the ready as though expecting trouble, heads turning side to side. In a few more feet, they would see their dead comrade.

Gurt intended to act before they were so forewarned.

Careful not to dislodge so much as a pebble, she worked the rifle's barrel through a chink in the pile of stones, resting it in a niche where two met. Not having to hold the wooden forestock would minimize the effect of recoil. She was going to have to account for both targets within seconds or risk a prolonged battle, more than enough time for her opponents to call in any reserves they might have at hand.

She checked the fire selector lever on the right side of the chamber, making sure it was not on automatic. She couldn't take the chance of the gas-operated recoil jamming or firing off ammunition she might need later. This situation called for marksmanship, not massed fire.

The front peg of the open sight rested on the chin of the first man, now less than 50 yards away. He jerked backward in involuntary reaction to the body he now saw on the ground. It was the last move he ever made. The bottom half of his face became a bloody mass before the single shot could echo from the surrounding stone.

The man behind, uncertain of the source, whirled around instead of diving for cover. The move probably prolonged his life for maybe a full second. A shot caught him in the shoulder, spinning him left. Two more followed in rapid succession, both tearing his throat apart and nearly severing his head. He had his weapon on automatic select, for his death grip on the trigger emptied the clip, sending ricochets buzzing like angry bees.

Gurt sat back on her heels, waiting for the ringing in her ears to go away. Then she rose to a crouch, peering through the slit in which her rifle rested. Definitely the sound of more feet, though more distant.

She left her cover, dashing over to where the two dead men lay. She picked up the first's rifle. If the two she had just shot had reinforcements coming, she would need the additional ammunition.

An AK-47 in each hand, she crept over to a small ledge. Ten men, eight armed and in uniform. One in a suit, the other . . . the other . . . she dropped both rifles and, with her hands where they could be clearly seen, picked her way down toward Lang and his rescue force, visible in the new day's light.

CHAPTER 23

Trabzon, Turkey
Hasttahane Cocuk (Children's Hospital)
11:21 A.M. Local Time

KAHRAMAN WATCHED AS DR. AKSOY DEFTLY stitched Gurt's hand. Nearby, Lang inspected the tiles of the ceiling and then the floor, before looking at the photographs on the walls, family pictures he had already memorized.

"I was correct," the policeman said. "The dead men are all Kurds, no doubt PPK."

"The ones you mentioned before?" Lang asked, an additional reason not to watch the silver needle slip in and out of Gurt's open palm. He imagined he could hear it pierce the flesh.

"The same. Kurdish terrorists, call themselves a liberation party. First time to my knowledge they have operated this far from home."

One man's terrorist is another's patriot. Lang kept the thought to himself.

The policeman continued. "Do you have any idea why these people would want . . . what was it?"

"A blood sample."

"Why would they want that?"

Lang shook his head, puzzled but grateful for the distraction from the procedure going on in front of him. "Haven't got a clue. Besides, I don't have it. Far as I know, the sample is in some chem lab back in Atlanta."

"Chem lab?"

Gurt spoke for the first time. "Chemical laboratory."

"Ah! Well, at least we now know these terrorists are the people most likely responsible for the death of Dr. Emre Yalmaz, as well as their motive. Undoubtedly the same three kidnapped Mrs. Reilly."

"Ms. Fuchs," Gurt corrected.

Lang suppressed a smile. People really were more alike than different. In America or Turkey the police were more likely to hang a crime on deceased suspects than continue an investigation. The practice spared time and shoe leather. And, in this case, seemed entirely justified.

Dr. Aksoy pushed her wheeled stool back from Gurt. "There! The stiches are done. We will need to put on a cast to make sure you do not flex your hand and pull the stiches out." She stood, beckoning. "Come."

The three followed her out into a hallway and to a room too small to accommodate all four. Fatima Aksoy turned to the men. "Do you mind? This will only take a few minutes."

"I do not understand why the PPK would involve themselves in attempting to obtain a blood sample," Kahraman said to no one in particular.

"If I had to guess," Lang ventured, "I'd say someone was willing to pay."

"Who?"

Lang smiled. "You're the detective."

The Turk started to say something, but Gurt emerged from the room holding her right arm in front of her. The cast reached halfway to her elbow.

She looked at Lang. "We may go now?"

"As soon as I have a word or two with Dr. Aksoy."

Sitting across the desk from Dr. Aksoy, Lang said, "I want every record of the patient, the little boy with the snakebite, deleted from the computer, any paper record destroyed."

He responded to the question on her face. "Someone is willing to kill for a sample of his blood. As long as he can be identified, he can give another sample, voluntarily or not."

Her eyes widened. "You mean someone might harm . . .?"

"One person is already dead, another kidnapped. What do you think?"

"I think I will see . . . how do you say? Obliterate, yes obliterate. I will see his records are obliterated before I leave here tonight."

Two hours later, the Foundation's Gulfstream 550 screamed off Trabzon's 8,000-plus-foot runway. Gurt lowered her seat back and peered out the window. "Did the doctor have anything to add to what we know?"

Lang was thumbing through yesterday's edition of *Barron's* one of the crew had thoughtfully brought aboard. "Only that the material dealing with the blood work on that little boy was missing. I think we already knew that."

"So, essentially, we came to Turkey for nothing."

"Any time some tragedy hits one of the Foundation's employees, it's good to show the flag, so to speak."

"Great idea, renting a car so as not to attract attention."

"Sarcasm is unbecoming."

"You did not tell the policeman . . ."

"Kahraman."

"You did not tell him our house was invaded."

Lang put the paper down, conceding he wasn't going to get to read it quite yet. "A gentleman always tells the truth; only a fool tells everything he knows."

"Meaning?"

"Meaning God only knows how many plots, conspiracies, et cetera he might have conjured up. He might have kept us there for weeks."

"You don't believe the break-in was related to what those Kurds wanted?"

Lang gave the paper a definitive rattle. "I believe we will soon find out."

The problem, he thought, is we have no choice but to passively wait.

CHAPTER 24

Richard Russell Federal Building
Atlanta, Georgia
Monday, the Next Week

JUDGE WILLIAM SYLVESTER WAS A SENIOR United States District Judge, which meant his caseload was slightly less than that of his younger peers. With a full head of silver hair and a perpetual tan on a face craggy with age, he could have been central casting's response to a request for an actor to portray a federal judge.

A Carter appointee, he personified judicial activism. Zeus-like, he had hurled mandatory injunctions from the Olympus of the Federal Building at the Fulton County sheriff over conditions at the county jail. When the criminals and mentally ill of Castro's cynical 1980 Mariel Boatlift were confined in Atlanta's federal prison, they repaid their new homeland by setting it on fire. The hulking edifice in South Atlanta dated from the first part of the last century and had housed such celebrities as Eugene V. Debs and Al Capone. The former was possibly the only man to run for president while incarcerated. The latter was soon to be sent to other — if not greener — pastures in the newly constructed Alcatraz.

Predictably, the liberal Judge Sylvester found the penitentiary unacceptably crowded and ordered the country's unwanted guests to be dispersed throughout the federal penal system. Unfortunately for Fulton County, it had no place to send its inhabitants. Release of the least violent was the only option, bail or not.

Between acting as the unelected and unappointed supervisor of the two prisons, the judge found some time to handle some of the business of the federal judiciary such as that before him today.

He adjusted his half-moon spectacles, scanned a stack of papers, and looked up at the lawyer in the natty summer khaki suit, blue shirt, and solid blue tie. But he addressed the older man in a wrinkled seersucker suit and white bucks that had gone out of style 30 years earlier.

"Mr. Wipp, did you understand the indictment as read?"

Wipp's response was an unintelligible murmur as he studied the remarkably ugly orange carpet.

"Mr. Reilly, tell your client to speak up!"

Judge Sylvester had as little tolerance for mumblers as he had for prisons without amenities, although he had a different reason: he was too vain to wear a hearing aid.

At the other table, Fred Roberts, the U.S. Assistant Attorney, only half-heartedly tried to suppress a grin as Lang whispered into his client's ear.

"Not guilty," Wipp finally managed.

The judge turned to the U.S. attorney. "Does the government have any reason not to continue Mr. Wipp's bond until trial?"

The prosecutor half stood. "No, your honor," he said reluctantly. Prosecutors hate the concept of an accused felon being on the street. Confinement is more conducive to accepting harsher settlements.

Sylvester was consulting the computer screen, which had become as common on judges' benches as gavels. "Very well, then, gentlemen. I will expect all pre-trial motions filed on or before September one." He frowned, shaking his head. "Make that the Tuesday after Labor Day." He looked up and smiled. "Spending the holiday with my grandchildren at the lake."

Lang and the government lawyer exchanged glances. It was the first hint either had had that the man on the bench had an existence outside the Federal Building. For that matter, it was the first time anyone recalled the man smiling.

"And we will have a telephone pre-trial discussion and commence trial the first Monday in October. Conflicts, gentlemen?"

The U.S. attorney stood, an old-fashioned notebook in one hand. BlackBerries, smartphones, and the like were strictly banned from the Federal Building. "Er, I have to be before the Eleventh Circuit that day, Your Honor."

There is no scowl like that of a federal judge who feels his turf has been invaded. "How many prosecutors are there in the Atlanta Division of the Northern District, Mr. Roberts?"

"I'm not sure, Your Honor."

"Take a guess."

"Maybe a dozen?"

The judge nodded. "I'll accept that. And any one of them can either be here or in the Eleventh Circuit on the first Monday of October. Mr. Reilly?"

Lang had planned to plead for a longer period in which to prepare what little case he had, but his opponent's announcement had changed his mind. No lawyer, whether in private or government practice, feels entirely comfortable handing a case over to someone else. Victory belongs to the lawyer trying it; defeat is too often traced to the initial trial preparation and handling. Add to that the fact he knew the Eleventh Circuit case involved a search and seizure issue that was destined to wind up in the Supreme Court. Being the winning party below or even arguing the case in front of that tribunal had boosted the career of more than one U.S. Assistant Attorney.

In other words, Fred Roberts would be feeling the heat to settle this case.

"First Monday in October it is, Your Honor."

"Anything else, gentlemen?"

With no reply from either side, Judge Sylvester was gone, disappeared behind the bench.

Lang and his client were alone in the elevator when the latter spoke. "I thought you were going to ask for an extension of the trial date. You said that the longer before trial I was free on bond, the better."

"I did," Lang admitted, before explaining his change of mind.

The elevator door hissed open and the two walked toward the bank of doors, past a mural resembling nothing more than a painter's torn dropcloth. Before being mounted on the wall, it had been mistakenly thrown out by the building's janitorial crew, who combined zero sense of contemporary art with a very clear recognition of trash. At the front desk, both retrieved their cell phones.

"Do you think they'll settle, then?" Wipp wanted to know.

Lang shrugged. "Ninety percent of criminal cases do, both state and federal. If either jurisdiction had to try even half the cases, the entire criminal justice system would collapse."

If Wipp was comforted by that factoid, he didn't show it. "Well, I guess it is the beingness of the being."

Lang bit his lip rather than respond to that ESTism. Instead, he pushed open one of a row of glass doors. "Would offer you a ride but it's such a nice day, I walked."

The truth was, he always walked or took a cab. Parking for the Federal Building was not a good idea. The site had once been occupied by Atlanta's Terminal Station, a vaguely Moorish structure built over no less than 20-some railroad tracks. Completed in 1905, the disappearance of rail passenger service, coupled with an attitude toward historical structures inherited from General Sherman, led to the demolition of the building in 1972.

The sleekly dull Federal Building replaced the Terminal but left a subsurface hole known as The Gulch, home to street people who viewed the parking area as a source of opportunity for car break-ins, other petty crime, and panhandling.

No way was Lang going to entrust the Porsche to the Atlanta Police Force's empty promises of patrolling the area.

He had hardly gone a block before a tinny rendition of Glenn Miller came from his iPhone. Modern wonders that such devices are, they are still dismal failures at replicating Miller's trombone. He was surprised to see his secretary Sara's name on the screen. She knew the Federal Court system did not allow any device that took photographs, which, in most cases, included cell phones.

"Yes, Sara?"

"Have you finished your hearing, the pleading of Mr. Wipp?"

Lang tasted bile from the bottom of his stomach. Although he knew the answer, he asked, "Why?"

"The check he gave you yesterday evening . . . The bank wasn't open this morning before you had to leave for the court . . ."

Her tone was indignant.

"You mean the check we couldn't verify until I was already in court? Not your fault, Sara. He swore he'd just gotten the money in time to bring a check before the close of business yesterday, no time to have it certified. It bounced when you presented it to the bank, right?"

"'Fraid so."

Shit!

Bad check or not, judges, particularly those on the federal bench, were loath to release lawyers from representations of clients for whatever reasons for fear it might slow the speed of the all-important dockets. Lawyers, not the courts, were responsible for ensuring that their fees were collected. Taking on the black robes of the judiciary erased memories of the days when they, too, had been mere mortals, toiling for legal fees. Unless Lang could prevail on his client to make good on the check, a lot of his time was going to be unpaid.

And Wipp's history of integrity, or lack thereof, would make a pessimist out of the most dedicated Pollyanna.

Oblivious to a beautiful early summer day, Lang trudged the mile back to his office in the blackest of moods.

CHAPTER 25

472 Lafayette Drive
Atlanta, Georgia
7:26 P.M. That Evening

FATHER FRANCIS WAS ANNOYED HE NO longer felt entirely comfortable in his friends' home. He supposed the all-too-clear memory of having a pistol stuck in one's face could do that to you: make you justifiably nervous.

Everything seemed normal enough: the muted roar of engines as his and Manfred's Formula One cars raced around the video game track, the glass of single malt scotch carefully placed on the low coffee table behind where he and the young boy sat on the floor violently pushing controls, the gently swaying clarinet of Artie Shaw's *Begin the Beguine* from Lang's collection of the big bands of the 30s, 40s, and 50s.

Best of all, the aroma of Gurt's *Rouladen* baking in the oven. Flank steak rolled around onion, pickles, and thick strips of bacon, one of his favorite dishes from her native Germany. The thought of the savory meat washed down by an icy cold beer made him salivate.

Domestic tranquility at its best.

But he still felt just a bit ill at ease.

The red car flashed by a checkered flag waving in front of grandstands bulging with people.

"I win! I win!" Manfred was shouting in the glee only a seven-year-old can muster while pumping arms up and down as though standing in the Super Bowl's end zone.

Grumps, stretched across the doorway to the kitchen, opened one eye long enough to assure himself nothing was amiss before resuming his snoring.

Lang had been observing the contest from the den's leather couch. "Small triumph, Manfred. Your competition's fueled himself with scotch."

Manfred turned to look at his father with the resentment of one deprived of rightful victory. "No fair! I didn't ask him to drink that stuff!"

Grinning, Francis tousled the boy's longish golden hair. "Of course you didn't! Your dad is fooling with you."

"Father Fancy's right," Lang conceded, using the name a younger Manfred, unable to pronounce 'Francis,' had coined. He stood and leaned over to swoop the priest's near-empty glass from the coffee table. "And he and I are making a final pit stop before your mother has dinner ready. As a matter of fact, after today, I may make the most such pit stops ever recorded."

The band's lead-in to Shaw's vocalist, Helen Forrest's version of *All the Things You Are* was background music to the tinkle of ice cubes on glass.

"Tough day?" Francis inquired.

Lang widened his eyes in a baleful stare as he turned to hand his guest a glass of amber liquid and ice cubes. "*Horrible dictum*, believe me."

Francis accepted the proffered glass. "Very well; I'll wait a few more scotches. *In vino veritas.*"

"Why do you do that," Manfred wanted to know, "talk in a foreign language all the time?"

"To shield your tender ears, lad," Lang replied.

Gurt appeared in the doorway. "To show off the uselessness of a liberal arts education, more likely."

"Unfair!" Manfred protested. "It's not fair to say things other people can't understand."

Lang was following Gurt's lead through the kitchen and into the dining room. "I fear, my boy, people saying things that can't be understood is a burden all of us carry through life. If you don't believe me, follow the next election."

Francis put a hand on the child's shoulder. "Your dad doesn't usually start waxing philosophical until later in the evening."

Behind the four humans, Grumps trotted to his place beside Man-fred's chair and lay down. The boy was prohibited from feeding the dog from the table, but if luck caused a scrap to fall to the floor . . .

Lang nodded to Francis. "If you can squeeze the blessing in before dinner gets cold . . ."

Francis was quite aware he was the only one in this household to say anything approaching pre-meal grace, that he was being humored, but he bowed his head and began.

From the sound system the band's solo trumpeter, Billy Butterfield, was playing Stardust.

Dinner over and dishes piled in the sink for the moment, Gurt, Lang, and Francis stretched out in lounges alongside the pool, drinks in hand. They watched the moon rise above the surrounding oaks, eclipsing the few stars bright enough to be seen through the aurora of the city's lights.

Francis broke the companionable silence. "So, how did your trip to Turkey go?"

Lang and Gurt took turns telling him.

"Any idea why those people would want a blood sample from a small boy?"

"It might have something to do with the child's reaction — or lack thereof — to the snakebite."

Francis sat up straight suddenly enough to rattle the ice cubes in his glass. "Where, exactly, were you?"

Lang looked over at his friend, surprised at the sudden interest. "Black Sea coast, little town called Trabzon. Why?"

"Couple of years back, I visited some of Turkey's Biblical sites in Galatia and Cappadocia . . ."

"Where?"

"Galatia and Cappadocia."

Francis noted the ensuing silence. "Galatians is one of the Bible's shortest books, just six chapters. It deals with the early Christians straying from the teachings of St. Paul. Cappadocia was one of the first Christian colonies established by St. Paul. But I'm sure you knew that."

Lang ignored the jibe. "Other than early church history, what does that have to do with someone wanting a blood sample?"

"Maybe nothing."

"You brought it up — the church history, that is."

Francis got up, collected Lang and Gurt's glasses, and went inside to freshen them.

When he returned, he sat and said, "There were about ten of us there in Turkey, all priests."

"I'm surprised there was enough scotch in the country to go around."

Francis ignored him. "We were touring rock churches in Urgup when one of the tour guides got bitten by a spider. Turned out to be a brown recluse. Now, I'm no entomologist, but I do know the brown recluse's bite can cause not only fever and severe lesions but organ damage and, in some cases, death. Far worse than a black widow."

"When did you get into the study of spiders?" Lang wanted to know.

"When you deal daily with a building as old as my church, you learn about all sorts of critters: spiders, mice, even bats."

"Why not let him continue?" Gurt suggested.

Francis gave her a grateful nod. "Anyway, the other tour guide simply shrugged off his comrade being bitten, muttered something like, 'Pontus.'

"That night I noticed the guide who had been bitten felt fine. There was a faint red splotch around the area, but no swelling nor any of the other symptoms you'd expect from a highly venomous bite. I asked him if he was sure the insect involved was a brown recluse. He was, but he either could not or would not explain why he showed no effects of what should have been a pretty toxic experience.

"I was curious, so I asked around to the locals. Seems there is a theory, more a legend, I'd guess, that certain people from a section of the Black Sea coast are virtually immune to venom or poison. The area was an ancient kingdom known as Pontus. Seems one of the region's kings developed some sort of formula or whatever that made him safe from poison, the favorite method of murder in those days. Story has it that some of his descendants in the region carry that trait today."

Lang was sitting up from his lounging position. "And what was the name of this magical king?"

Francis shook his head. "I'm sure they told me, but I don't recall. Didn't seem important at the time. I do recall he was an enemy of the Roman Republic, and Pompey fought him in 66 BC."

"You remembered the date but not the name?"

Francis shrugged. "Odd what sticks to our memory, sort of an arbitrary choice made by the subconscious. Or perhaps a Higher Being."

Lang was tempted to ask if Francis had ever heard of the EST organization.

CHAPTER 26

An Hour Later

GURT EMERGED FROM THE BATHROOM AND noted Lang was missing from his side of the bed, where ordinarily he would already be asleep. In fact, the covers had not even been pulled back. Stepping into the hall, she could see a light from downstairs. She glanced toward Manfred's room, where Grumps's snoring was audible through the open door. She often wondered how the child could come instantly awake at the slightest sound, real or imagined, and yet sleep right through the buzz saw sleeping right next to the bed.

Holding the banister against the chance the stairway might be booby-trapped with one of Manfred's toys, she descended. The light came from under the staircase. Originally a broom closet, Lang had managed to squeeze in an office swivel chair, a file cabinet, a gooseneck lamp, and a small table on which sat a computer monitor and keyboard. With any-one in the chair, there was no room to shut the door, hence the light spilling out.

"Well, who is he?" she asked.

Startled, Lang might have jumped out of the chair had there been space enough to do so. "Who is who?"

"The king Francis was talking about. What else would you be up researching at this hour?"

After years together, Lang was still amazed at the accuracy with which Gurt read his mind. "Mithradates. He ruled an area in what the Romans called the province of Asia, Pontus as well as other parts of what is now Turkey. Was a constant pain the in Republic's ass. He fought two of the Romans' most capable generals, Sulla and Pompey."

"Very interesting," she said in a tone that indicated just the opposite. "It is now after eleven."

Lang sighed and, had there been room, would have pushed back his chair. "Asia, or at least the Romans' province, was basically a Greek culture."

"*Es ist sehr interessant.*"

"You said that and the sarcasm comes across just fine in German, too."

"You coming to bed any time soon? I have no patience for trying to wake you when you have been up late."

He turned the screen so she could see. "There is a man at the Greek archeological museum, Abiron Theradoplis, who wrote a book about Mithradates."

Gurt stuffed a fist into a yawn, using the other hand to click the X in the red box at the upper right of the screen. "Perfect. You can buy it tomorrow."

CHAPTER 27

King of Pontus, Foe of Rome,
Story of a Hellenistic Empire
by Abiron Theradoplis, PhD
National Museum of Archeology
Athens
Translation by Chara Georopoulos
University of Iowa Press
(Excerpt)

THE POWER OF THE QUEEN, MITHRADATES' mother, lay in the city of Sinope and perhaps a few miles around it. His father's friends and allies still controlled the castles and fortifications that guarded the major cities and the strategic cross roads leading to them. Among those cities, most principal was Amasia, home of the Dorylaus family, strong friends of Mithradates' father. Mithradates' small group made the decision to stop there briefly to resupply themselves with such items as arrows, spears, clothing, and other items as they could not find in the forests.

The Greek philosopher and geographer Strabo described the richness and beauty of the area, mentioning the grain, fruit, and rich silver mines in the valley in which the city was located. He also refers to a temple of Zeus on a nearby hill.

We cannot be certain, but it may well be this temple Justin mentions as one where Mithradates had often watched his father, as king of Pontus, perform sacrifices. We do know that, before entering the city, Mithradates and his companions found a wild ass and slaughtered it at some religious site.

It was during this ceremony that either Diophantus or Gaius noticed the long brown centipede climbing up Mithradates' arm. He described it as perhaps two to three *daktylos* (approximately four inches) in length, brown with red antennae waving menacingly. When warned, Mithradates only smiled and continued the ritual. The result is unclear, but we do know he suffered no substantial consequences of a bite because the next day he visited the silver mines. His comrades apparently objected vociferously because the mines were known as death traps where only slaves labored, soon succumbing to the arsenic-laden air. Nonetheless, he went to the mines daily during his stay in Amasia, staying a number of hours each time.

The Dorylaus greeted the three warmly, swearing fealty to the young king and offering to host a banquet in his honor, but Mithradates declined. We can only speculate as to his motives but it seems most likely he did not want to make his whereabouts widely known.

After a period of less than a week, the three travelers returned to the forests.

CHAPTER 28

Headquarters of Dystra Pharmaceuticals
Suite 1720
One Atlantic Center
1180 West Peachtree Street
Atlanta, Georgia
8:27 the Next Morning

HANDS IN THE POCKETS OF HIS tailored wool summer-weight suit, William Grassley stood at his office's floor-to-ceiling window. Below was one of Atlanta's true miracles. Where three high-rise office buildings and a multitude of shops, restaurants, and green spaces were encircled by apartments, town houses, and condos, a steel mill had operated for over half a century. Rather than risk the astronomical cost of remediating an ecological disaster, the plant had stayed open, if not actually operating, until, in the late 1990s, a developer, Jim Jacoby, had come along with a dream for 138 acres of prime Midtown Atlanta real estate, polluted or not.

The mixed-use project opened in October 2003 amid the cheers of many and the doubts of even more.

It had taken special help from the city, county, and state; help that would pay dividends in the increase of tax revenue in years to come.

No such help would be coming Dystra's way, Grassley thought sourly. The company would sink or swim without flotation devices from the government.

There was a rap on the door behind him.

Not waiting for a response, Ralph Hassler entered, looking at his watch. "Where's Wright?"

Grassley checked his diamond-encrusted Rolex, a gift from the company in greener times. "Not quite 8:30. Give him a few . . ."

Past Hassler, Hugh Wright slunk into a seat in one of the pair of wing chairs whose brocade matched the colors of the Chinese export porcelain displayed between leather-bound books in the eighteenth-century *biblotec* opposite the window.

That was the thing, Grassley thought, Wright always seemed to slink, creep, or prowl. There was something downright dishonest in the way the man moved, if that was possible. Like maybe he was avoiding being eaten by something.

"Close the door," Grassley ordered Hassler, remembered the man's prickly disposition and added, "please" before sitting behind an elaborate Louis XIV reproduction table that served as his desk.

There was a moment of anticipatory silence, what years earlier would have been described as a "pregnant pause," before Grassley cleared his throat and begun.

"The operations both here and in Turkey were complete busts. The burglars found nothing, and our people in Turkey had a plan that simply didn't work."

"And that was?" Hassler asked.

"Believe me, you are far better off not knowing."

"Any chance of getting all or some of our money back?" Wright wanted to know.

"About the same success you'd have at your club sending back an empty bottle of wine."

"The funds came from a Cayman account that can't be traced," Hassler said. "Wouldn't be smart to have a record of payments to this Gary . . ."

"*Gayrimesru*," Grassley supplied. "Turkish Mafia."

"Anyone consider the possibility of just making this guy Reilly and his foundation an offer to joint venture or simply buy this blood sample and whatever it implies?" Wright asked.

Grassley was rolling a Bic lighter between his hands, a gesture with which the other two were quite familiar, but of which the CEO was probably unaware. "I'd guess buying a private blood sample is medically unethical."

"Unethical doesn't bother me nearly as much as illegal," Wright said. "As in criminal. Surely this Reilly guy has a price."

Grassley dropped the Bic, grabbing it before it could roll off the table's inlaid top. "Not from what I understand. His foundation seems to mint its own money, spent nearly a hundred mil on research alone last year. Nobody I could find had a clue where the funding comes from. He doesn't solicit contributions, and it's run as a strict nonprofit."

"You can bet he doesn't make that kind of money from the law practice," Wright observed, drawing a glare from his boss who viewed the obvious as the province of fools.

"I take it you have a plan," Hassler said.

The Bic was rolling between palms again. "I do indeed."

"Don't suppose you care to share it," Hassler observed, a statement, not a question.

Grassley put the Bic down. "Trust me, you don't want to know."

CHAPTER 29

472 Lafayette Drive
Atlanta, Georgia
At the Same Time

Lᴀɴɢ sᴘʟɪᴛ ᴛʜᴇ ʀᴇᴍᴀɪɴɪɴɢ ʙʟᴜᴇʙᴇʀʀɪᴇs ʙᴇᴛᴡᴇᴇɴ his and Manfred's bowls of oatmeal as Grumps watched in eager, if unjustified, anticipation from below the table. Then Lang sprinkled brown sugar on both.

"More?" the little boy asked.

From the kitchen counter where Gurt was refilling an oversized coffee mug, she said, "Only a little amount is needed to sweeten. Any more and you might as well be eating pure sugar like those cereals that come in a box."

"Like Sugar Puffs?" Manfred asked. "All my friends at school have Sugar Puffs for breakfast," he added resentfully.

"All your friends will be *dicke*, fat, before they are twelve and be diabetic in their twenties."

"What's 'diabetic'?"

Lang tried not to smile as Gurt explained. In the German custom, *Frustuck*, not breakfast, was the order of the household, a light snack of fruit or cereal with occasional cold cuts and cheeses. Gurt believed anything more substantial tended to make a person, particularly a child, sluggish in the morning, tending toward inattention in school or whatever the day held. She also was determined no one in her home would succumb to the national epidemic of obesity. Oatmeal's supposed cholesterol-lowering abilities had added it to the lighter fare.

Lang had grown up with the mantra that breakfast was the most important meal of the day. Eggs, bacon, grits, biscuits to begin a day southern style. On occasion, the spartan nature of breakfast at home had detoured him to the local International House of Pancakes on his way to the office. It might make him sluggish, but a man couldn't think clearly with his stomach growling, either.

He was not sure what Gurt's reaction would be were his dietary transgressions discovered, and he hoped not to find out.

She ordered Manfred upstairs to brush his teeth, preparatory to his departure for summer day camp, before she sat down, watching Grumps shadow his small master toward the stairs. "You are going to see that man in Greece?"

"Dr. Therodoplis, yes. I'm hoping to learn more about this Mithradates guy and, maybe, why someone is willing to kill over a blood sample."

"You cannot put the trip off? Someone must be here for Manfred's camp pageant. He will be disappointed you are not there."

"Gurt, the house was ransacked while we were in Turkey, and you were kidnapped. Whoever these people are, they are serious. We will be looking over our shoulders until we do something."

"You have spoken to this man who wrote the book you borrowed from Francis, Dr. . . ."

"Theradoplis. Yes, by video conference. Not a very satisfactory conversation. That's why I'm going in person."

"He does not speak English?"

"Only slightly better than I speak Greek."

"You do not speak Greek."

"That's why I'm going."

Gurt contemplated her injured hand, an ugly red scar where the stiches had been removed the day before. "Remember your promise."

Lang didn't need reminding. Shortly after Gurt and Manfred had entered his life for good, she had resigned from the Agency. Lang and Gurt had mutually promised that neither individual would take the risks that dogged their relationship without the other coming along.

"I remember just fine. I'm just seeking information."

She held the palm of her hand before his face. "That is what we said before leaving for Turkey. Surely the trip can wait a few days."

Lang stood and removed his suit jacket from the back of his chair. "You tell me how. Monday I've got a motions hearing in Fulton Superior. Tuesday is an arraignment in the Middle District, Macon Division in the morning and an arraignment that afternoon in . . ."

Gurt waved her hands in a crisscross motion, in football, a referee signaling an incomplete pass. Here, a signal she gave up.

CHAPTER 30

37 Ch. Trikoupi Street
Piraeus, Greece
At the Same Time

ONLY 12 KILOMETERS FROM DOWNTOWN ATHENS, Piraeus has served as the city's port since the mid–sixth-century BC, though there is little evidence of its ancient past among the modern high-rises, narrow streets, and bustling wharves. Its three harbors make it Europe's busiest passenger port and third in container traffic. Its maritime trade has made the Greek shipping magnate almost stereotypical.

Alkandres Kolstas was both. From this intentionally shabby office on the third floor, next door to the city's nautical museum, he had built an empire. Not a visible empire, nor one he would be willing to discuss, but an empire just the same.

Starting with a leaky, coal-burning ship, the *Aphradite*, he had mortgaged everything he could find to buy, he had begun shipping fuel oil to the various Greek Islands. He had barely broken even on each voyage. He paid the crew (almost all of whom were illegal Pakistani immigrants) about half the minimum wage. Ignoring inconvenient maritime safety regulations, he found it far less expensive to pay off the government inspectors.

Evading those regulations had probably been the reason he no longer owned the *Aphradite*. She had turned turtle in a storm, going down with all hands still aboard. By that time, it hardly mattered. Kolstas had a fleet of a dozen or so ships, all taking advantage of a scam peculiar to Greece.

Since the country's main industry was shipping, ship petroleum was, by law, not subject to the taxes placed on, say, automotive or heating fuel. Consequently, when a ship left Piraeus, its cargo could be untaxed and therefore relative cheap shipping oil headed for, say, Crete or Rhodes. Or even a return to the same port from which it had departed. When it arrived, it miraculously held not shipping oil, but fuel to run automobiles or heat homes during the brief Aegean winter. Slightly adulterated, true, but far less expensive than the government-taxed petrol. The oil black market had grown to a three-billion-euro-a-year industry. Paradoxically, Greece imports 99 percent of its petroleum needs but still manages to export more than it imports.

The practice is no secret. Petroleum smuggling is institutionalized at the highest levels, resulting in what one newspaper called (before the government shut it down) a "parliamentary mafiocracy."

The practice was not without its costs.

A majority of the 300 members that constituted the Hellenic Parliament in its former royal palace on Syntagma Square had to be persuaded that spot inspections of tankers' cargo was as bad an idea as repealing the shipping oil tax exemption or placing GPS tracking devices on tankers. Those who didn't have shares in their own shipping companies, anyway. That persuasion could take the form of anything from a week's free use of the villa in the hills of Provence above Cap d'Antibes in France, to a visit from the illegal Pakistani immigrants who controlled Greece's narcotics trade as well as extortion, kidnapping, and other enterprises Kolstas did not want to know about.

It was this latter facet of his business, the Pakistanis, he supposed, that prompted the phone call from the American.

Some years earlier, someone had put him in touch with someone who had introduced him to a man named Grassley, a man who needed a large favor and was willing to pay for it. Seemed Grassley had a pharmaceutical company and was trying to find a country in which to conduct . . . what did he call it? Clinical trials? Yes, that was it, clinical trials.

Many, if not most, big U.S. drug companies conducted tests as far away from the U.S. FDA, tort lawyers, and the press as possible. Because the U.S. had no means of inspecting the test facilities, failed experiments remained secret. India was the country of choice. An existing medical infrastructure, English as the primary language, 40 percent illiteracy, and crushing poverty made the subcontinent near perfect. When someone died from a bad drug, a few hundred dollars bought silence.

But Grassley had been seeking a little more than a place for clinical trials. He wanted guaranteed success in the form of government approval, with or without trials. That, he had said, would move the drug along the . . . quick track? No, *fast* track to U.S. FDA approval.

And he understood Kolstas was not without influence in government.

It was not Kolstas's nature to ask questions. He had provided the influence to approve the drug until subjects started developing an annoying tendency to crave opium. Word got to the Greek press before Kolstas's friends could bring pressure.

"Disaster" would not be a word that exaggerated what followed, including the drug's failure to win approval anywhere in the world that made approval of a drug a prerequisite for sale.

Now Grassley was on the phone. The voice was as clear as though he was in the next room. "Alkandres! How are you?"

"Well," the Greek responded carefully.

He remembered all too clearly "Greek Watergate" in 2004-2005. One hundred mobile phones of the Vodafone Greece network had been compromised, resulting in the tapping of devices of the Prime Minister, the Mayor of Athens, and members of the defense department and parliament. The culprit had never been identified, although the government accused the United States, claiming an over-zealousness in testing the security of the 2004 Olympics.

Kolstas was not so sure it had not been a more sinister effort by Greek law enforcement. Either way, he wasn't inclined to take chances.

"And you are well also?"

"Very," came the reply.

Kolstas waited. In spite of the obsession Americans seemed to have with each other's health as indicated by the greeting, he was fairly sure his was not the reason for the call.

The pause was short.

"I've got a friend coming to Athens tomorrow. His name is Lang Reilly, and he will arrive via private jet at Athens Eleftherios Venizelos. He's staying at the Bretagne."

Kolstas said nothing.

"I was hoping your Pakistanis might sort of take him under their wings, if you get my drift."

Kolstas was not the only party to the conversation wary of electronic snooping. "You have something specific in mind? I mean, what can we do for your friend, Mr. Reilly?"

"When you've picked him up, let me know."

"Treating someone in Athens is expensive."

"The cost is mine. Don't worry."

The line went dead.

CHAPTER 31

The Old Tavern of Psara's
16 Erehtheos & Erotokritouv Str.
Athens, Greece
That Evening

Platka is the old section of Athens, even though few buildings date further back than the Ottoman period. The Acropolis with its multiple crumbling temples is here, where restoration by modern equipment has been going on longer than it took the ancients to build the original Parthenon. There are a number of monuments left by invading Romans, Turks, and others long forgotten. Street markets vie for space to sell largely cheap souvenirs to passing tourists awaiting the departure of cruises to the Greek Islands or those just disembarked and headed for the airport the next day.

Athens is not a city like Paris, Rome, or even London, where visitors tend to linger. They see the nearby sites, perhaps take the long cab ride to the very good archeological museum, and seek other destinations.

The locals, however, do linger, usually at the various *taverna*, restaurants with short menus and few seats, which open mid-evening and serve until the last customer leaves. The establishments are normally small, family-owned, and specialize in the cuisine of their owner's birthplace.

Psara's is all that and much more. Originating over a century ago, the founder's two sons took over the business and their sons after them. The place became so popular it filled the original floor of the building in which it rented space, then the entire structure, followed by the house next door, and then the one across the street. Then the street itself. At dark, the winding street — far too narrow for any vehicle larger than a scooter — is filled with tables, including the steps that traverse the steep hill, as locals and the few visitors lucky enough to hear of the place sip Greek wine (which improves only with volume) poured from glass pitchers and feast on squid the size of footballs stuffed with vegetables, broiled fish, sardines grilled in vine leaves, and other seafood specialties.

By the time at least half the crowd of diners have reached the end of the meal and are sipping ouzo, the oily, licorice-flavored liqueur, a party is in progress.

Near the corner of the street's intersection, two men were not joining in the fun. Both were dark-skinned, perhaps Middle Eastern, though dressed in Western attire of t-shirts and blue jeans. Each had only a fringe of a beard, barely enough to comply with The Prophet's bidding. Both frequently took stock of the surrounding tables as though making sure their conversation was not being overheard. The sole light was the candle on the table flickering from a weak breeze. It was enough to show neither had touched the wine still in its pitcher and that the meal had been largely ignored. Someone might guess the two were here for the cover of the nightly crowd rather than the food.

"He arrives in the morning?" asked the taller of the two in Arabic.

"*In'shalla*, Allah willing."

"And how do we know both this and the place he will stay?"

"It is something called a flight plan that all airlines and private planes entering a country must file. Anyone with a computer may find those of American aircraft in the files of the American government's aviation department, the FAA."

The tall man showed teeth the color of old ivory. "Amazing. The Americans make all public for the sheer sake of doing so. It will be their downfall, Allah willing. But you also know his hotel."

The other man shrugged, a matter of no consequence. "Such places lack real security of their reservations. A skilled computer person may review the lists of incoming guests. There are a limited number of places in Athens where an extremely wealthy American might stay."

The one who had asked the question leaned across the table so that his mouth was only inches from the other's ear. "And the men, you are sure of them?"

"The Prophet, may his name be revered, could not have picked more dependable men."

The conversation paused as the waiter, eyebrow cocked at the full wine pitcher and nearly full plates, sought permission to remove both. He was dismissed with a gesture.

"You are certain the man Reilly suspects nothing?"

"I am sure of nothing. That is the reason I am in need of some of your men."

"They have families. They do not work for free."

The shorter man nodded and stood. He looked around at those enjoying their dinner before removing a fat envelope from a pocket of the jacket he carried, despite the heat which sunset had done little to dissipate. "This is half. The other when you deliver Reilly."

Placing the envelope on the table, he nodded to his companion. Still speaking Arabic, he said, "I would not want men who put no value on their services. May Allah bless our venture."

The other man opened a flap of the envelope, surveying its contents. "And you wish this man Reilly taken alive, yes?"

"He is of no use to me or my friends dead. There will be no further payment for a dead man. Until tomorrow night on the square, then."

Turning, he disappeared down a set of narrow steps while his dinner partner opened the envelope and began thumbing a stack of bills.

CHAPTER 32

Athens Eleftherios Venizelos
(International Airport)
08:36 Local Time
The Next Day

LANG'S EYES FELT AS THOUGH SOMEONE had tossed sand in them. He was never able to sleep on an airplane despite the Gulfstream 550's small but comfortable bedroom. He had spent the first several hours finishing the borrowed Mithradates book, a scholarly, rather stiff translation of what was probably rather scholarly, stiff Greek. The treatise was frustrating in that its focus was the constantly shifting alliances and the endless conflicts with Rome. There was annoyingly little material on the aspect of the Hellenistic king's life in which Lang was interested. He could only hope Dr. Theradoplis knew more on the subject than he had chosen to publish.

Finally, he put the book down. Lang had enjoyed a bottle of Petrus, vintage 2005, from the aircraft's well-stocked wine selection to accompany a juicy filet grilled to his specifications in the tiny but efficient galley. Then he downed a couple of single malt scotches while watching the latest Cliff Eastwood movie on the aircraft's entertainment system.

Sort of a mushy, getting old type of flick, he thought. *The Man with No Name*, *The Outlaw Josey Wales*, and *Dirty Harry* were gone for good.

And still he could only stare at the ceiling.

Looking out of the window as the plane began a steep descent, he tried to forget the thumping pulse behind his eyes or how sleepy he was. Arid brown landscape passed below. Even the green of the olive groves seemed lifeless and dusty. The area would receive little rain now until well into the fall.

The flight attendant, disgustingly cheerful, approached with a tray.

Lang looked up questioningly.

"Coffee and an aspirin, Mr. Reilly."

He gulped both gratefully. "Do I look that bad?"

"No, not at all. It's just that Bordeaux by the bottle tends to bring on a wee bit of discomfort in the morning."

Lang grinned in spite of how lousy he felt. "You are as capable a liar as you are pretty."

She retrieved the tray with a smile. "Thank you, sir. It's always nice to start the day with generous flattery. Now, if you'll fasten your seat belt . . ."

Uniformed representatives from both customs and immigration met the plane at the satellite terminal, swapping passport stamps for multiple copies of general declarations, the papers each aircraft entering a foreign country must present listing information from the pertinent (names and nationalities of passengers and crew) to the absurd (method of disinfecting the aircraft). Lang suspected an international conspiracy of bureaucrats kept the practice alive to ensure that jobs were readily available to store documents that were neither read nor destroyed. The entire Amazon forest could be restored with the trees cut to make the world's supply of general declarations.

From the cab's window, the Hotel Grand Bretagne appeared to have recently been under siege. Sandbags obscured most of the first-floor windows. That indispensable tool of the modern-day social commentator, the aerosol paint can, had decorated the building's façade with graffiti.

Lang did not have to read Greek to get the message: the hotel shared Syntagma Square with the Greek Parliament next door, and, therefore, the rage of a people facing severe cutbacks after decades of government largess. Generous government benefits were on the chopping block due to the government's serial austerity programs.

Greece had learned the truth of Margaret Thatcher's observation that socialism worked fine until you ran out of other people's money. One of the unforeseen consequences of membership in the European Union was an end to a country's ability to print its own currency with which to repay its debts with cheap money. Greece's creditors were pressing for repayment for deficit spending to finance generous pensions, paid vacations, free medical care, and 30-hour work weeks.

The party was over. Either Greece had to demonstrate some effort to stem the hemorrhaging expenses of social programs, or the country would face the direst of consequences.

Santa Claus was dead. Faced with the bleak prospect of government workers actually having to work till age sixty-five rather than sixty-one, massive increases in the national sales tax, severe cuts in both subsidized housing and food programs, the ordinary citizenry was displaying displeasure by rioting in full view of their elected representatives. The political demonstrations had included burning any cars unlucky enough to be handy, breaking windows, and generally destroying any private property at hand.

The law-abiding wealthy had long since departed for the financial asylum on the Costa del Sol, Palm Beach, or the south of France in the face of confiscatory income taxes. Others found it less expensive to pay off tax officials.

Lang had arrived just in time to see the changing of the guard at the parliament building across the square. Not quite Buckingham Palace, but impressive nonetheless. He handed his single bag to the white-gloved, morning-suited bellhop.

He nodded toward the military pageant. "Nice, but you really didn't have to go to the trouble."

The man stared at Lang blankly. Either he had little understanding of English, or less, a sense of humor. With Lang trailing, the bellhop trudged up the stairs and into a columned lobby that could have accommodated a football game. No austerity here: shiny marble, genuine Oriental rugs. Gilded mantel clocks adorned multiple fireplaces between oils of landscapes and near life-size portraits, all lit by ranks of crystal chandeliers. Groupings of what he guessed were reproductions of Second Empire furniture were taste-fully scattered throughout. Louis-Napoleon would have felt right at home.

But he wasn't there. Instead, two men in business suits sipped coffee in the course of animated conversation. Other than them and the uniformed attendant carefully wiping imaginary dust from the furniture, only one other person occupied the lobby area: a dark-skinned man reading a Greek-language newspaper.

His jeans were more worn than fashionably faded, and his sneakers were not even an artful copy of a name brand. He would have been more at home in the mobs on the square outside that Lang had seen on the nightly news.

Years of Agency training set off the alarm in Lang's head. This scruffy guy in the elegant lobby was a wheel-less car up on bricks in a country club parking lot, a guy in a tuxedo at a square dance, an anomaly. And he was either a very slow reader or his attention was focused elsewhere than on the paper he held. He had not turned a page since Lang first noticed him.

Without slowing the registration process at the front desk, Lang made a natural-looking movement so he was facing the news reader, enabling him to keep the man in sight without being obvious. From this angle, he got a partial look at the man's face. Early twenties, a scraggly, goat-like chin beard. With the heat outside at 90 degrees, a concealed weapon was the only reason Lang could think of why he would be wearing the light windbreaker.

As soon as the desk clerk had finished making a photocopy of his passport, Lang returned it to its case in his suitcase and, declining assistance from the bellhop, made his way to the bank of elevators.

If anything, the presidential suite was more elegant than the lobby: 200 square meters of inlaid floors, panel molding, first-cast bronzes, and a fully stocked real, adult, not-mini-sized bar in addition to more elegant furniture and paintings.

None of these were why Lang had chosen this suite.

Not even the much heralded view of the Acropolis, visible and nearly unrecognizable as a tiny white speck in the distance.

He stepped outside onto the wide, brick-paved deck from which one might take in that view. Lang was used to the hot, muggy Atlanta summers, but the heat of Athens was overpowering, like that experienced in Las Vegas, but more so. Dry and oven-like, it clung to the skin like a burning ointment.

Still, the deck was near perfect for his purposes. He measured off its meets and bounds, its proximity to other decks on this floor, satisfying himself that, if needed, he had another exit than the conventional one.

Returning to the oasis of his room's air conditioning, he placed his bag on the king-sized bed and unpacked the scant contents until he reached the bottom, that strip where the roller board is attached to the wheels. He pressed on one end and a section came up. From the shallow cavity, he removed his Glock 40 and held it in his hand for a moment before taking his belt clip holster from the suitcase.

Arrival by private aircraft negated the security procedures suffered by airline passengers. It also made secreting the weapon from prying eyes easy, even in the unlikely event the host country's customs chose to search the plane. The problem was the severe prohibitions against private ownership and possession of handguns in most European countries. It was pure luck his not being armed in Turkey the first time, though, had not been fatal. He would not make that error again.

He checked the clip in the pistol before slamming it back into the butt and pocketing two more fully loaded magazines. Dealing with the local authorities over a gun violation beat the possible consequences of being unarmed.

CHAPTER 33

King of Pontus, Foe of Rome,
Story of a Hellenistic Empire
by Abiron Theradoplis, PhD
National Museum of Archeology
Athens
Translation by Chara Georopoulos
University of Iowa Press
(Excerpt)

WHEN MITHRADATES RETURNED TO PONTUS, he promptly visited his mother and his brother, (Mithradates the Good) at her villa. After an intimate dinner of just the three, they adjourned outside to admire the sunset. Within half an hour, both Laodice and Mithradates the Good complained of a metallic taste on the backs of their tongues. They began to sweat as nausea and stomach cramps bent them double. Their mouths filled with saliva but they could not force it back down throats too swollen to swallow. Later, servants would comment on the strange red tint to their masters' eyes. Drooling and moaning, they clawed at their throats. After an hour of vomiting and diarrhea, the queen and Mithradates' brother and only rival writhed in convulsions. By midnight, both were dead.

But how was this done? All three ate the same dishes. With vigilant servants present, the guest had no opportunity to add poison to the food, and had he somehow managed to bribe a cook or otherwise inject toxic substances into the food before the meal, would he not have died also?

CHAPTER 34

Athens Archeological Museum
28 is Oktovriou 44
Athens
An Hour Later

IN A NEIGHBORHOOD RUNNING FROM NONDESCRIPT to shabby, the Parthenon look-alike sat behind perhaps an acre of green space fronted on the street side by an open air taverna. Ignoring the urge to make a dash from the taxi to the presumably air-conditioned museum, Lang took a seat at an empty table in the little restaurant with a view of the street. He was surprised to see the place was half filled until he remembered it was slightly past noon here. A gap-toothed woman of indeterminable age handed him a greasy menu, waiting, hands akimbo, as he studied, deciding between a Santorini Crazy Donkey pale ale and the Mythos lager. Despite the former's imaginative name, he chose the latter.

His purpose was not refreshment, but to observe. It had not been possible to determine if the cab had been followed in the traffic of Athens — second only to Rome in its suicidal nature. He had taken one cab from the hotel to the Acropolis, entered the museum there only to exit by a side door, and take another taxi here. Still, the appearance of the newspaper reader in the hotel lobby suggested caution was needed.

The beer came, sweating in its green bottle. Lang declined a room-temperature glass and ordered *souflaki*, a Greek kebab, in a pita sandwich with a cucumber-yogurt dressing. By the time he had finished, he had seen no one suspicious and was within minutes of his appointment.

The gray-haired docent at the museum's door invited him in broken English to have a look around while she summoned Dr. Theradoplis. Although Lang could not see any ascertainable historical order to the exhibits of weapons, armor, sculpture, and pottery, two exhibits caught his attention.

One, a golden death mask in a Lucite case, was an artifact he recognized as inspiring part-charlatan, part-amateur-archeologist, Heinrich Schliemann, to claim it to be that of Agamemnon of Homer's *Iliad*. Whether Schliemann actually found the object during his excavation of Mycenae, Agamemnon's capital, or it was one of his many "seedings" of archeological sites with artifacts from elsewhere, has never been decided with certainty.

The other was a life-size bronze of a small boy, an infant, astride a galloping horse. The multi-language caption noted the latter had been retrieved from an ancient shipwreck.

The lady from the front door returned, motioning Lang to follow her to a staircase closed off with a rope. Moments later, they stood in a hallway crowded on both sides with crates, boxes, and odd-shaped figures under canvas. It appeared the Archeological Museum had more exhibits than space.

His guide stopped in front of an open door and motioned him inside before hurrying back toward the stairs.

In front of Lang was quite possibly the first marble-floored office he had ever seen. Like a ship upon a serene sea, a post-modern ebony desk floated on a fluffy, off-white flokati rug that reminded Lang of the fleece lining of a leather flight jacket. Behind the desk rose a short man with a haircut Lang thought had been patented by Albert Einstein. As he approached to take the extended hand, he realized the man was barely five feet tall.

"Mr. Reilly?"

The grip was firm, the shake energetic. "Dr. Theradoplis."

The museum director indicated one of several chairs, each upholstered in either black or white. Only at the last second did Lang realize how heavily the thing was stuffed, designed to swallow, rather than seat, its occupant. The ultra-modern design contrasted sharply with the half-dozen reproductions of scale models of classic Greek statuary lining the walls — Lang recognized the discus thrower, Venus de Milo, and Winged Victory — and the large black-and-white photographs of what Lang guessed were archaeological digs.

From somewhere behind the desk, Dr. Theradoplis produced a thermos and two glasses. "Refrigerated coffee is more refreshing than tea or soda, including your own Coca-Cola."

The man had done his homework. How many Europeans knew Atlanta was the home of Coke? The accent was heavy, but, as is often the case, intelligible in person if not on the phone. It had been a pronunciation, not a language, problem.

Lang accepted the glass and took a long sip of the unsweetened brew, thankful for its coolness, if not its bitterness. It was chilled, but had no ice in it. With some effort, he managed to lean forward in the all-encompassing chair. "Thanks for seeing me on such short notice."

The museum director nodded his acknowledgement. "A pleasure. Not daily does someone come from Atlanta to conference with me. What is your interest in Mithradates, King of Pontus?"

Lang guessed the preliminaries were now over and plunged right in. "I understand he developed a tolerance to poisons."

Theradoplis made no effort to hide his disappointment. "Ah! The man was a major threat to the Roman Republic, the most since Hannibal 150 years before. Yet most histories . . . Make small . . ."

"Minimize?"

"Yes, most histories minimize Mithradates' role in fighting the Romans. He was maybe greatest Hellenistic military figure since Alexander." He paused, looking over the top of his glass. "You know Alexander, the Macedonian?"

"As Alexander the Great, yes."

Lang didn't mention he had been involved in the possible discovery of what might have been Alexander's long-lost tomb while trying to foil an effort by the Chinese to gain a further foothold in the Caribbean, an affair he and Gurt referred to as the "Bonaparte Matter" because of the French emperor's involvement almost 200 years earlier.

"You know of Mithradates as strong leader in Hellenistic world, yet you are only interested in poison."

He seemed indignant at the idea as he continued, "In time when medicine as we know it did not exist, death by eating poorly prepared meat and especially fish was as common as dying by diseases we cure or prevent today. Likes tuberculosis and typhoid. Any time a death left no visible reason, people suspected poison.

"There were no guns to shoot one's self, no bottle of sleep pills. Poison was common means of suicide and murder in the ancient world. Mithradates had at court,. . . what you say, make medicines?"

"Pharmacologist," Lang supplied.

"Yes, Mithradates had Crataeus, pharmacologist who could make potions like poison. Several Roman emperors died under conditions that might have been poison. Nero even organized a school of poisoning run by a woman named Locusta he had hired to kill younger half-brother. One most famous suicides of the ancient world was Socrates, who was made to drink hemlock."

Lang listened politely until he was certain the director had finished. Then, "It wasn't just curiosity that brought me all this way. I have a reason to ask about Mithradates' immunity to poison and venom."

"But not his importance in history of Hellenistic culture?"

Lang could not have cared less if the man had been a fishmonger rather than a king, but he said, "That, too. Let me tell you a story. I am the head of a charitable foundation that operates children's clinics and hospitals worldwide, usually in places where there are none. A few weeks ago, a child came into one of our establishments . . ."

When he finished, Dr. Theradoplis nodded his understanding. "And you believe this, ah, tendency? Yes, tendency to be not harmed by poisons of snakes or plants?"

Lang drained the last of the coffee and set the glass on the edge of the desk. "What I think isn't as important as what the people who are willing to kill believe. Even if they are wrong, the lives of people who work for my foundation are at risk until I can identify and eliminate them. The reason I'm here, Dr. Theradoplis, is I need to know how realistic it is that the immunity you ascribe to Mithradates is a gene, a chromosome, whatever, that can actually be transmitted from generation to generation."

The museum curator shrugged. "I fear I am no geneticist, a word, by the way, that comes from the Greek *genesis*."

One could always count on an academic to supply more information than was needed. That was why scholarly papers had footnotes.

"Geneticist?" Lang knew of the discipline but not the relevance.

"The study of genes and, by necessity, inherited traits. Historical genetics actually began with Hippocrates, who noted that children more than not showed traits of their parents. He theorized these characteristics were carried in the male sperm and sometimes modified in the womb. Aristotle did not . . . how you say? Did not buy the theory, pointing out that if a man lost an arm in battle, his children would still be born with all their limbs. Plus some men had children after what we now know as male pattern baldness, yet their offspring had hair."

It was more information than Lang wanted, and still left the question unanswered. "But can a child inherit an acquired trait such as immunity?"

Again, the shrug. "As I said, I am not a geneticist. You would have to refer to my sometime colleague, Dr. Phoebe Kalonimos."

Realizing he had gotten all the information he was likely to get, Lang was getting restless. "She is here in Athens?"

"She is a professor at the National and Kapodistrian University here, yes. But I don't know if . . ."

He reached for the phone on his desk, tapped the receiver impatiently and spoke in Greek before putting it down.

"I fear Dr. Kalonimos has left the university until the end of August. Perhaps you might contact her then?"

Lang successfully kept the frustration out of his voice. "Dr. Theradoplis, I'm trying to prevent some unknowns who are killing people. I can't wait that long. Is there any way I can reach her now?"

Theradoplis treated Lang to an all-too-familiar look, that expression of the easy-going European for the always-hurried American. "She is at the University of the Aegean this summer, I believe, Rhodes campus."

Rhodes, largest of the Dodecanese Islands, was a little over 250 miles from Athens.

Lang stood, his hand extended. "Thank you so much for your time, Doctor. Could I impose on you to contact your friend . . ."

"Colleague."

"Colleague, then. Could you send her an e-mail that I might be contacting her in the next few days?"

Theradoplis was standing now, too, shaking hands across the desk. "Best give me a way she can contact you, and I'll have her reach you direct."

CHAPTER 35

Syntagma Square
Twenty Minutes Later

THE CAB STOPPED ON AMALIA AVENUE just short of the square. The first thing Lang noticed was the absence of the Evzones, the skirted honor guards at the tomb of Greece's unknown soldier, catty-cornered to the palace King Ludwig of Bavaria had almost completed for his son, Otto, King of Greece. The building originally had 350 rooms and only one bath with running water. After Otto was deposed in 1862, the structure, still unfinished, became the home of the Greek parliament. Presumably, the plumbing had been updated.

Next to Lang's hotel, it faced the square, formerly a royal private garden. Lang didn't notice the blinding white glare of marble from the walkways and benches under a hundred oleander, orange, and cypress trees. All he could see was a surging, roiling, rioting sea of humanity. Police, figures from *Star Wars* with helmet visors down, fired canisters of tear gas from behind handheld shields. They received in exchange rocks, bottles, and the occasional Molotov cocktail. Even with the taxi's windows up and the whisper of the air conditioning, Lang heard the yells of the opposing sides and the crash of things being broken.

The wisdom of the Hotel Grand Bretagne's fortifications became visually obvious. The question was, how was Lang going to get through a violent mob to his hotel immediately adjacent to the object of the mob's rage?

"How long do you suppose this is going to last?" he asked the cabbie.

A shrug was his answer, whether to the question itself or because the man spoke no English, it was unascertainable. One thing was clear: the taxi driver was not going to risk his vehicle joining the several automobiles already burning furiously. Lang could hardly blame him. If he was going to cross that square, he was going to have to do it alone and on foot.

Lang peeled euros from the roll in his pocket. He hardly heard the shriek of smoking tires on pavement as the cab turned around and fled.

Cautiously, he skirted the edge of the barricades surrounding the parliament building, occasionally dodging flying missiles. His target was a contingent of armored police cars directly in front of the Bretagne.

He concentrated on avoiding both being hit by flying bricks, or whatever else happened to be airborne, and the small groups of less-than-peaceful protesters. Had he paid closer attention to his other surroundings, he might have seen two men detach themselves from a group of students shouting slogans and distance themselves from each other to approach him from opposite directions.

The problem with tear gas is that it is impartial as to whom it attacks. A shift in the light wind caused the uniformed police to don gas masks as their own weapon turned upon them, as did the billowing cloud of greasy smoke from the burning cars.

Lang's sight was beginning to blur with tears. Without a gas mask, or at least a bandanna soaked in cider vinegar or lemon juice, he knew his eyes, nose, and mouth would soon be stinging. He would likely experience the purely psychosomatic sensation of choking that had sent a number of his classmates screaming for the exit at "the gas tank," the Agency's training facility that acquainted trainees with both lethal and non-lethal gases.

He was tempted to turn around, retreat to a more peaceful part of the city. Too late. Until washed or cleaned, the gas would cling to his skin and clothes, filling his nose and eyes with fumes. He had to reach the hotel and a shower.

He lowered his head, narrowed his eyes, and plunged onward.

He didn't see the man he bumped into, a man better prepared than Lang. The lower part of his face was covered with a cloth, and the long sleeves of his shirt, despite the heat, would prevent the gas from sticking to his bare skin.

Lang hitched up his shirt to cover the lower part of his face. Poor protection from the gas but the best he could do under the circumstances.

The police contingent was perhaps 50 yards away now, maybe less. If he hurried, Lang might reach them and the relative safety of the hotel before the gas temporarily blinded him with tears.

He bumped into someone else, muttered an apology, and started to back away.

Until he felt the hard metal of a gun barrel in the small of his back.

CHAPTER 36

City of Atlanta Detention Center
254 Peachtree Street
At the Same Time

LEON FRISCH HAD FOUND JESUS. Or, more accurately, Jesus had found him.

Jesus Hernandiz, five foot two, maybe a hundred pounds soaking wet, was hardly a commanding figure. But when he fixed you with those brown eyes and began to speak in his Puerto Rican–accented English, he had the hypnotic power of Kipling's Kaa, the python of *Jungle Book* fame.

Jesus was here in jail just as Peter and Paul had been imprisoned in Rome and, also like the two saints, on a bum rap. But, then, every man here was falsely accused, innocent of all charges and a victim of the "system."

Whatever his history, Jesus believed in forgiveness and redemption. Renounce your sinful ways, repent, make such amends as possible, and be admitted into the Kingdom of Heaven. That simple, simple enough that even Leon's meth-fried mind could get a grip on the concept.

He wasn't exactly sure where the Kingdom was, but the price of admission was reasonable enough. And he was already two-thirds there. During the days since Leon had been arrested for possessing a few crumbs, he had suffered skull-splitting headaches and depression that would have resulted in suicide had not Jesus (the real one, not the Puerto Rican) been right there with him. He had heart-stopping anxieties about nothing (would lunch consist of the four-day-a-week entrees of peanut butter and jelly sandwiches?).

Now, without those crystal rocks, he was back to normal. Or, at least, pre-meth normal. And he was free, standing right here in front of the jail, looking at the Greyhound bus station.

Over 2,800 men packed into a facility meant to house a little more than half that number. Four prisoners in a 12-by-12 cell with a double bunk bed and two mattresses on the floor. A rec room that only a tenth of the inmates could share at the same time. Only 350 at a time could fit into the mess hall, which meant meals were served in shifts. One man might have breakfast at 5:30, lunch at 10:00, and dinner at 4:00, going without food for the next eleven and a half hours.

He'd gotten lucky, a sign Jesus (the one in heaven) looked out for his own. Fears of federal intervention forced the powers that be to reduce the jail's population by releasing as many non-violent offenders as possible to harass the law-abiding population. The result was flooding the city with the homeless, aggressive panhandlers, petty thieves, and various other undesirables.

Okay, he had done the renouncing and repenting, leaving that troubling-making amends part remaining. It's hard to make amends when you're cooped up in a 12-by-12 cell. But now he wasn't real sure exactly how you went about it, either.

There was Old Ben, one of his street buddies, who had found two unattended cell phones on the front seats of a couple of cars in the parking lot. A quick smash of the glass and Ben had the price of all the MD 20-20 he could drink for a week, even if the vintage was within the last 24 hours. But Ben never made it to the ecoATM, the machine that paid cash for old cell phones, to get the money for his bender. Instead, he stuffed them into a coat pocket before sleeping off his last binge. It had been childishly easy for Leon to help himself.

That had kept Leon in crank for a while.

He really should make amends with Ben, but the old man, like most street people, wasn't always easy to find. When you had to walk everywhere you went, a change of locale of a few miles was as distant as another continent.

So, who else should be the recipient of these amends? There was Tyrone, whose face Leon had split with a screwdriver. Couldn't remember what had started the fight, but poor Tyrone was drenched in his own blood by the time a Grady Ambulance appeared.

Hadn't seen Tyrone around since last winter.

There was no shortage of people to whom Leon owed amends, just a dearth of them available.

There was one person, though, who he was pretty sure he could find: the lady he had hassled about washing her windshield and who had left him sore and bleeding in the street. GURT. Yeah, she had gotten the better of him, but the new, reformed Leon knew he'd had it coming for being such a jerk. His wrist had suffered what the jail medic said was a green stick fracture and the bandage was due to come off. He guessed his balls still worked, but, either way, they didn't hurt anymore.

And he had her tag number, had seen it as she drove off. Amends hadn't been his motive as he used all the tricks of jailhouse veterans to get a few precious minutes on the phone to the DMV and run the number.

No, amends hadn't been his motive then, something much darker had been. But now, the new, reformed, about-to-enter-the-Kingdom Leon had at least one person to whom he could make amends, although he wasn't exactly certain how. Jesus (the one in jail) had been turned loose before he could explain. Leon guessed it was sort of like saying you're sorry.

He started walking north, rehearsing what he would say to the white lady when he got to her house.

After that, he'd be on his way to the Kingdom.

CHAPTER 37

Athens
Syntagma Square

At FIRST, LANG THOUGHT, OR HOPED, he had been mistaken by the rioters for someone with whom they had a grievance, like any member of the government.

"Mr. Reilly, come quietly with us."

So much for hope.

Lang held his hands where they would be clearly visible, as someone behind him ran theirs through his pockets and conducted a quick body search. Both his iPhone and Glock were removed.

Perhaps someone might notice what had to look very much like a mugging in a sunlit, open square. Again, disappointment. The police were too busy trying to prevent the rioters from causing further damage, and the rioters were fully occupied with doing just that.

Rough hands spun Lang around to face two men whose lower faces were covered with bandannas, as were those of the bulk of the protesters facing a steady barrage of tear gas. These two were indistinguishable from the mob surging around them.

"Look, guys," Lang was shouting to be heard, "you can have the phone and the gun as well as any cash I've got. Okay?"

Apparently not. Each hooked an arm under one of Lang's shoulders and marched him toward the edge of the square. Beyond, an Opel Vectra waited with a rear door open. A trace of blue oil smoke from the exhaust denoted a running engine. Lang was crammed into it like a bulky bit of luggage. One of the men beside him climbed into the front while the other, keeping Lang's own weapon pointed at him, slid into the back along with Lang. The car lurched away from the curb with all four cylinders rattling as only an underpowered diesel engine can.

Lang was not sufficiently familiar with Athens to know where he was, and his abductors were silent on that and any other subject he chose despite an effort to get a discourse started. It was becoming clear, though, that they were headed out of town. The implications of not being blindfolded were worrisome. These men were not concerned that Lang would be able to direct the authorities to wherever their destination might be. If he were alive, that is. The good news was that they kept the bandannas on.

He avoided looking at his watch, relying on his Agency training to count the seconds, measure the time. He was certain they had not traveled more than 26 minutes before he was aware of the sea nearby. The smell of salt water with an undertone of rotting vegetation and a hint of petroleum products told him there was a commercial harbor nearby. The only one this near Athens would be Piraeus, the city's port.

Shit! Was he about to be taken aboard a ship, its destination unknown?

His fears were slightly diminished when the car turned into a street named Trikoupi and pulled up in front of a row of shabby office buildings, one of which seemed to house some sort of maritime museum. He was hustled out of the car, which was presumably immune to the adjacent sign depicting a car being towed away. The few people on the street studiously ignored what was going on as Lang was shoved into a doorway and through a glass door. People in this neighborhood had apparently learned to mind their own business.

If there was an elevator, Lang didn't see it. Instead, he was pushed up three flights of wooden stairs. At the top was a short hallway of old-fashioned office doors. He was led to one where the upper half was opaque glass with faded gilt Greek letters on it, presumably the name of the office's occupants, across from another door with a window equally opaque with dust. Lang was ushered through the one on the left and into a small sitting area lit by a single brass floor lamp whose tattered shade cast fanciful images on the simple unpainted Sheetrock walls. Four chestnut hand-carved ladder-back chairs with cane seats surrounded a traditional fluffy flokati rug, its woven wool fibers giving the impression of an off-white cloud. On the far side was another wood and opaque glass door, this one blank.

One of Lang's captors thrust him into a chair, confirming it was every bit as uncomfortable as it looked. Another crossed the room, tapped on the glass, and, upon a response, entered.

He returned moments later and motioned his two companions to bring Lang into an even smaller space. Lang's first impression was the sour odor of stale cigarette smoke.

It took a second or two for his eyes to adjust to the dinginess of the room, more shadow than light. To his right and left, streaks of gilt, perhaps picture frames, their contents hidden in the darkness. On the wall behind a desk, a floor-to-ceiling tapestry, its subject matter undefined in the gloom. Once again a hand on his shoulder forced him into the hardness of a cane-seated chair, this time in front of the desk. It had a marble slab for a top. There were two objects on the stone. The first was an ornate brass ashtray from which a blue tendril of smoke wended toward the ceiling.

The second caught Lang's attention: a Tiffany lamp, its hand-blown leaded-glass shade bordered with the "Greek Key" design at the bottom of a field of mottled gold. There was no way to be certain, but Lang would have bet the words TIFFANY STUDIOS NEW YORK were stamped somewhere into the brass base, a series of squares into the lead of the shade. If genuine, he was looking at over half a million dollars. Seeing such a valuable antique in these shabby surroundings was like discovering an original Van Gogh hanging on the walls of a college dorm.

"I assure you, Mr. Reilly, it is quite as it left Louis Tiffany's shop in 1901. One of his better Favrile designs."

Only a faint trace of an accent.

The speaker's face was obscured in shadows, an effect Lang was sure was intentional. What he could see was a man in a dark business suit, the white shirt open and without a tie. The rest was concealed behind the desk.

"Coffee, Mr. Reilly?"

Lang knew coffee played an important social role in Greek life: sharing a cup was a sign of friendship, relaxing over a cup an end to the day. Greek coffee was finely ground, looking like American instant but nothing like it in taste. Brewed three times in a metal cup-like device, a *briki*, and served with the grounds in the cup along with the sugar added during the brewing process.

"You have the advantage: you know who I am, but I don't know you."

A gaily colored ceramic cup appeared, its savory aroma overpowering the stench of the cigarette. "*Glyko*, one of the 49 different degrees of sweetness," the man said, a non sequitur. "I hope it not overly sweet to your taste."

Lang took the cup. "You didn't have to kidnap me to make me drink Greek coffee. I rather like it anyway."

A chuckle. "I question your willingness to leave your hotel with my men voluntarily." In the chiaroscuro of the Tiffany lamp's light and the darkness of the room, the speaker's hands seemed to flutter like wounded birds as he spoke. "And go ahead, enjoy your coffee. If I'd wanted to poison or drug you, there would have been no need to bring you here. Besides, it is necessary you have your facilities for this, er, chat."

So that was it: the guy wanted something he had guessed Lang would be reluctant to give. Stir in a little strong-arm, add plain, old-fashioned fear, and season with a demand. The formula was as old as Hercules' penance and the 12 tasks. The trick was to not appear intimidated. Easier said than done.

Lang took a tentative sip. Good thing he liked his coffee strong. This stuff could have stripped paint. "First, I'd like to know who you are and what, exactly, do we have to chat about?"

The man leaned forward, his face visible for the first time. Short-cropped white hair topped off a weathered face, the visage of a man who had spent perhaps too much time in the Aegean sun. There was nothing worn about the eyes, though. They sparkled as if this whole affair was a source of merriment.

"You can just call me Alex. If you ask around, the people around here will tell you I usually get what I want."

Lang recalled those in the street when he was obviously being forced into this building. They had shown no more interest than had he been the postman going about his rounds. Alex, or whatever his real name was, must be the equivalent of the local godfather.

"Okay, Alex, what is it you want?"

"I think you know, Mr. Reilly."

Lang took a long sip of the super-octane coffee that managed to be both bitter and sweet before he replied. "I'm not fond of guessing games. Why don't you tell me?"

Alex smiled, his teeth the color of old piano keys as he stubbed out whatever was smoldering in the ashtray. "Your foundation has a blood sample we want. I think you know of what I speak. What will it take to get it?"

Blunt enough.

"Who is 'we'?"

The Greek's face retreated back into the shadows. "That really doesn't matter. The question is, how much?"

Lang was suddenly aware the two of them were alone; the three men who had brought him here had slipped away silent as ghosts. He had little doubt, though, they were still close enough to instantly reappear should they be needed.

He sat back, getting as comfortable as the bare wood back of his chair permitted. "If you mean money, the simple answer is, there isn't enough. The Foundation has funding beyond your means, I assure you."

There was the sound of a match striking, a flare of flame illuminating the face, and a puff of smoke. Again, the smell of a cigarette. "Let us not pretend to be naïve, Mr. Reilly. Any offer we make is to you personally."

Again, the plural pronoun with the indefinite antecedent.

"Thanks, but no thanks. And if you were planning on making a monetary offer, the strong-arm display was hardly necessary."

From the darkness on the other side of the desk, Alex tisk-tisked. "Understand, Mr. Reilly: we *will* have that blood sample even if we have to resort to . . . ah . . . less pleasant means."

"Such as?"

A grainy black-and-white photograph floated across the desk, landing upside down in front of Lang. Even so, he had no trouble recognizing Manfred playing with Grumps in the front yard of the Lafayette Drive house. The newly planted row of impatiens in the background told him the picture had been taken in the last day or so.

"The little boy, you must love him dearly. It would be a pity if something happened to him."

Bastard! Lang fought the surge of rage that, if not restrained, might cause him to do something foolish.

"His mother and I take care nothing does. Great care."

The seemingly detached hands made a steeple. "Accidents do happen even to the most careful. In fact, right now in Atlanta, in Ansley Park . . ."

There is a time for apparent acquiescence and a time for immediate, violent opposition. The latter was becoming a more desirable option. Lang thought of the deep laceration in Gurt's hand, the feeling of helplessness when he had returned to an empty hotel room. It might just be time to demonstrate to these people, whoever they were, that the blood sample was not worth the cost.

". . . there are men approaching your house. Lafayette Drive, I believe. Manfred . . . that is his name, is it not? Manfred . . ."

The question went unanswered.

Standing, Lang grabbed the Tiffany lamp and smashed it against the desk, a crash of shattered glass. He paused less than a second, enjoying his antagonist's horror as he realized his near-priceless antique had been reduced to the value of a broken beer bottle.

Lang leapt across the desk, hammering it with the brass base. "Your skull, next, Alex. Not every man gets the chance to die by having his head bashed in by something designed by Louis Comfort Tiffany."

Lang didn't have to hear the door behind him open to know Alex had summoned his crew of uglies; he had anticipated it. Now on the same side of the desk, he slipped the base over the man's head, a hand on each end as it rested across the Greek's throat.

"Come on in, folks. Please note I'm not holding your boss in front of me just for fun. Makes a rather effective shield, don't you think? May as well put those guns down. See the position of the brass bar here? One good pull and the man's neck snaps like a matchstick."

To demonstrate, Alex was snatched upward, his hands fruitlessly tugging at the bar that was choking him while feet kicked empty air like a man just hanged.

"Tell them to go away, Alex," Lang said quietly. "And, oh yeah, I want to see my cell phone and Glock on the desk along with their weapons before they leave."

The three men looked at each other in indecision.

"No, no, guys. Over *here*! Alex, tell Larry, Curly, and Moe there to do as I say."

Lang relaxed the pressure slightly, allowing the Greek to suck air into his lungs. He croaked something in Greek, and the trio started to back toward the door.

Lang gave a sudden pull on the brass base, sending Alex into a paroxysm of gagging and choking sounds. "Naughty, naughty! I clearly said weapons, including mine, on the desk there!"

With glares of hatred, one by one, the three laid down two Glocks, one of them Lang's, a Heckler & Koch P30, and a Colt 1911A .45 automatic. And the iPhone. Sullenly, they filed out of the room.

The lamp base tightly across Alex's throat, Lang marched him around the desk, stopping to shove three pistols into his belt along with his own Glock, a difficult maneuver while keeping pressure on the lamp base.

"We, you and I, are going for a little walk," Lang announced.

His prisoner turned his head as far Lang's grip on the lamp base allowed to give him an apprehensive look.

"Not too far, just far enough that your goons will be out of range."

"You'll pay for this, Reilly," the Greek panted. "You'll pay if it's the last thing I do."

They were at the stairs.

"How smart is it to be making threats in your position?" Lang asked lightly. "And as for the last thing you'll do, try something cute right now. Sorry, but we have to take these steps one at a time."

And so they did, each man stepping down at an angle so that Alex provided a shield for Lang. At the bottom was the door to the street.

"Open it," Lang ordered.

"Open it yourself."

Lang realized his predicament: by reaching to open the door, he would expose a good part of his body to the one or two men outside clearly visible through the glass. Would they risk taking a shot that might well hit Alex? No way to tell.

"And choking me with that lamp doesn't help," Alex gloated. "The second I fall over, you are a target."

CHAPTER 38

472 Lafayette Drive
Atlanta, Georgia
At the Same Time
(12:20 P.M. EDT)

Manfred, home from day camp, was impatiently waiting at the kitchen table for his favorite lunch: peanut butter and jelly sandwiches. Gurt had conceded her campaign of salads and raw veggies. Not even Grumps showed interest in the freshly sliced carrots, radishes, and celery that went untouched on the little boy's plate. The dog did, however, gobble up the slices of hard-boiled egg.

Gurt was at the antique chopping block in the center of the room, making sandwiches. Maybe PB & Js weren't the ideal healthy lunch, but they were low in cholesterol and a good source of the vitamins and protein a growing child needed. And one of only two vegetable sources of protein. And, with the substitution of fruit spread instead of jelly and freshly baked wheat instead of white bread, the calorie and fat content went down. At least, that is what she told herself as she gripped the bread knife and sliced near paper-thin cuts from the loaf.

Anything, almost anything, was better than the candy most of Manfred's contemporaries had for breakfast, frosted this, sugar-coated that. Lunches of hot dogs, low-grade beef and pork by-products with sodium, fat, and nitrates. And enough preservatives to mummify half the pharaohs of Egypt.

Small wonder obesity was rampant in the country. No small wonder so many children became fat adults. Like it or not, Manfred was going to grow up healthy, healthy and . . .

Grumps suddenly awakened from his twenty-three-and-a-half–hour daily nap with an energy not normally seen. Claws scratching for traction against the floor's tiles, he galloped to the front door, barked, turned, and dashed back through the kitchen to the door outside where he waited expectantly, tail a blur of wagging. Other than that exhibited at Manfred's daily return from school when in session, the garbage collectors, and, occasionally, the postman, this was more action than Grumps usually displayed in a week. Even the neighbor's trespassing cat elicited less excitement.

Someone had come to the front door, then walked along the side of the house to the backyard, Gurt guessed. From the kitchen, she would not have been able see the dining room windows, which the visitor would have had to pass.

Had she remembered to lock the door when she and Manfred had come in?

Manfred looked up from his sandwich. "Who the fuck . . .?"

Manfred, like most children, had a hard time remembering to do his homework, but once an expletive fell on his tender ears, it rarely left his vocabulary. This particular vulgarity, acquired in one of Lang's more unguarded moments, had earned him multiple time-outs in his room, a visit to the office of the stern-faced principal of Westminster's Lower School, and a threat that sterner discipline was on the way should "that word" be spread like an infection among his playmates, an almost certain means of ensuring a verbal plague.

This time it would, arguably, save his life.

"Manfred!" Gurt snapped. "You have just earned yourself an afternoon in your room!"

"But Mom . . ." came the inevitable appeal, "Winn Three was coming over to play video games . . ."

"No video, no phone."

Gurt could once again be thankful that at age seven her son was not sufficiently proficient at spelling to begin texting his peers. That, like acne, dating, and driving, were joys she had ahead of her.

She pointed toward the stairs. "Now!"

Head down, as though walking his last mile, Manfred trudged up the back stairs, followed by Grumps. Gurt could have sworn the dog was glaring at her.

She had no time to contemplate the possibility.

The kitchen door slammed open.

Two men were on the threshold. One, his hair hanging below his shoulders in dreads, wore jeans and a light windbreaker despite the season. The other, with cornrows, was similarly dressed. Both were large and threatening. And both had extended magazines in the identical Glocks they were pointing at her.

Proof she had, in fact, not locked the door.

"De kid, where de kid?" Cornrow demanded.

"Not here," was the best answer Gurt could come up with on short notice. "Lady, you lie!" Cornrow asserted. "We seen him in de car when you drove in."

Not only had she carelessly left the door unlocked, she had been oblivious to her surroundings. Men like this would be as obvious in Ansley Park as a grazing dinosaur.

The glance Dreadlocks was giving her body did little to make her feel more at ease. "He be here somewhere." He nodded to Cornrow. "Whyn't you go upstairs an' takes look while I watches Goldilocks here?"

Without reply, his companion headed for the stairs.

"No, really . . ." Gurt began.

Dreadlocks took a step closer, close enough that the muzzle of the Glock touched Gurt's throat. His other hand was on her hip, moving north.

She took a step back, her spine now pressed against the butcher block. Both the pistol and Dreadlocks' body pressed against her. With her left hand, she pushed back against his shoulder while the right searched the worn wood.

"Hello?"

The voice came from the open kitchen door. Over Dreadlocks' shoulder Gurt caught a glimpse of what might have been an Old Testament prophet, except he was black. He had a flowing beard only slightly longer than his hair, and he was thin to the point of emaciation. He was fixed on the scene before him. Gurt had heard of eyes big as saucers, but she'd never believed it until now. But there was something . . . She was sure she had seen him before. But where?

"Ma'am?" Leon's plan for atonement had not anticipated Dreadlocks or Cornrow.

Dreadlocks whirled, the Glock coming to bear on the intruder.

At the same moment, Gurt's fingers closed around the serrated bread knife she had left on the butcher block. Planting it in Dreadlock's back, right under the rib cage, would be her easiest line of attack but not instantly fatal. She could ill afford alerting Cornrow, who had just found Manfred, judging by the little boy's terrified screams from upstairs.

She jumped on his back, left hand full of matted hair, snatching his head back and exposing the throat.

He managed a surprised "Ahhh . . ." before the bread knife's blade sawed into his neck just under the ear and pushed outward, severing the right cervical carotid's sheath, cervical fascia, jugular, and vagus nerve in nanoseconds. He bucked with what strength he had, throwing Gurt to a floor already slick with blood.

Fury or fear or both widening his eyes, he faced her as he slowly sank to his knees, the gun level with her face. She simply pushed it away, and it clattered to the floor as his grip loosened.

She ignored the gasping for breath, the splatter of crimson as his weakening heart futilely pumped blood to the brain. Her sole concern at the moment was that he not cry out to warn Cornrow, an unlikely possibility with a slit throat.

On hands and knees, she skidded across the slippery kitchen tiles to snatch up her victim's Glock.

Weapon in hand, she held onto the chopping block, then the counter to steady her way to that point where back stairs ended just outside the kitchen, pressing against a wall so she was invisible to anyone descending. From the sounds she heard, Manfred was not coming easily, each step accompanied by his screams and growls from Grumps.

Cornrow entered the kitchen, one arm around the little boy's throat, the other holding a Glock to the child's head.

He took a step, his back now to Gurt, and came face to face with Leon. "The fuck . . .?"

Leon the peacemaker, hands extended, moved toward Cornrow. "Man, don't . . ."

He never finished.

Two shots from opposite directions were fired so closely that they could have been one.

Leon spun, his right hand gripping his left shoulder as blood seeped between his fingers.

Cornrow, his weapon slipping from his lowered hand, took two steps forward before his body realized his brain was no longer in command. A good part of it had departed with the back of his head, which had been only inches from the muzzle of the Glock in Gurt's hand.

Manfred, terrified, screamed.

Grumps, uncertain, howled.

Leon, near sure he had been killed, moaned.

Gurt, relieved, put the gun down on the chopping block and reached out to comfort her son. Years with the Agency had prepared her for action, some of which, in the organization's euphemistic jargon, was "wet." But nothing had prepared her for the gore in her own kitchen, the hysterical fear of her child, or how very close the little boy had come to being kidnapped or worse.

She searched through her purse for her phone, noting with objective interest that it took three tries for her hand to quit shaking long enough to input 911.

By that time Manfred had not only calmed down, he was surveying the carnage with fascination.

"Awesome!" he said.

CHAPTER 39

Piraeus

"**B**ACK UP TO YOUR OFFICE," LANG ORDERED.

Alex snorted. "You can't wait my men out forever, you know."

Lang tightened the lamp base against the man's neck. "Let me worry about that."

At the top of the stairs, Lang half-shoved, half-dragged his prisoner to the end of the short hallway.

"There's no other way out," Alex commented. "Sooner or later . . ."

"Alex, a man like you doesn't put himself in a one-exit situation. The question is whether you tell me where the other one is before I lose patience and choke you to death."

For emphasis, Lang curled the lamp base like a dumbbell, sending Alex into a series of gasps and gags.

"Now, let's take another look at your office, shall we?"

Once inside, Lang bolted the door. The lock was a substantial dead bolt that should withstand attack. Not so with the door. It hung from old, partially rusted hinges that would yield to the first body slammed against it. The flimsiness of the arrangement strengthened Lang's suspicions. No way would a criminal like Alex feel secure with a door that would not deter a determined attack and no other way out.

"Okay, Alex, have a seat at your desk, hands behind the chair."

The lamp cord made satisfactory, if temporary, binding.

"I'll get you for this, Reilly."

Lang was running a hand along the wall. "You said that. Maybe I should make sure you're not in a position to."

The Greek's lips curled in a snarl. "You're too chickenshit, Reilly. You could no more kill an unarmed and tied-up man than you could fly. You don't have the balls!"

Lang was examining the tapestry behind the desk. He was close enough now to make out the figures: Flemish, likely fifteenth century. Lords and ladies, horses in pursuit of a stag the size of a cow.

"Don't tempt me, Alex. I . . . hmm, lookie, lookie!"

Lang snatched the fabric from the wall, revealing a small door. It had no knob, needing only a gentle push to swing open.

He patted Alex on the head with the same condescending geniality he might show Grumps. "Well, looks like I'll be seeing you in the old familiar places, Alex."

"You'll regret this, Reilly, believe me. In fact right about now, your family . . ."

Lang pressed the Glock against the man's cheek. "Alex, be real certain that you won't live a week past the date something happens to my family. Now, I really must go."

He was already too far into a low, narrow passage to make out the reply. The way was totally dark and, judging from the cobwebs that brushed his face, unused in recent times. Glock in his right hand, he felt along a wall. Even so, he almost fell when he reached a staircase. Fifteen steps down, a turn to the right. Light was leaking around a door just ahead.

Lang pushed without result. He groped for a handle, a knob, anything he could pull. Following the sliver of light between door and jamb, he saw a bar, a latch. If only it was on this, rather than the other, side of the door . . . He held his breath until his fingers touched a simple sliding bolt.

The door opened.

The smell, the mouth-watering aroma of . . . what? Lamb cooked gyro-style. A quick glance told him he was in the rear of a taverna. A wooden crate overflowed with a leafy vegetable. Two hens, perhaps aware of their fate, clucked forlornly from a wire cage. Stalactites of *loukanio* sausages hung from the ceiling. The smell of fruit beyond its prime competed with gyro.

Ahead, Lang could see where the hall joined the dining area. Perhaps a dozen white-clothed tables jammed a space that could have comfortably accommodated half that many. The twang of recorded bouzouki music drowned out any conversation, had there been any.

He pocketed the Glock, keeping a hand on the grip, and sauntered into the dining area as casually as though he were a customer returning from the men's room. A tavli board was on a table between two old men bent over glasses of ouzo.

The only other occupant was a man behind the counter that ran the length of the room. He looked up as Lang strolled by. A glance from Lang to the rear of the building and back again. A cell phone appeared in his hand.

He held the other up, gesturing stop.

"Just passing through," Lang said genially.

Then he bolted for the door.

Outside, he ducked into an alley. At the end, facing a main thoroughfare, was an open stall selling t-shirts. Lang brushed under a rack bearing English-language maps of various islands and into the street. Amid a blare of horns, he dashed to the other side and into the back seat of a canary yellow cab waiting for the light to turn green.

The driver said something in angry Greek, his hands crossing back and forth, no.

Off duty?

Reaching into his pocket, Lang produced a handful of euro notes. There was a decided change in attitude.

"Acropolis," Lang said.

He certainly wasn't going back to the hotel, the first place Alex and his boys would look, and the milling horde of tourists at the Acropolis, at least those undeterred by burning automobiles, riots, and general civil unrest, would provide some cover.

Now that he was at least temporarily relieved of having to deal with Alex, he took out his iPhone and input the code for the United States and his home number.

Gurt answered on the second ring.

"Gurt, it's me. I've had a little difficulty here."

"Is two of us."

"Huh? What happened?"

She told him, finishing with, ". . . and your difficulty?"

"Never mind. I'll be home tonight or tomorrow, soon as I can get a flight."

A flight. That was the problem. The airport was second only to the hotel as a place Alex would expect him. But maybe not the very port here in Piraeus, a port with day trip and overnight excursions to the Greek Islands leaving several times an hour.

"Driver," he said, making a circling motion with his hand. "Turn around."

CHAPTER 40

Piedmont Driving Club South
Eight Days Later

Lang ARRIVED HOME TWO DAYS LATER by a route only slightly less circuitous than Magellan's: a ferry 200-plus miles to Cyprus, flight from Heraklion's Nikos Kazantzaakis International to Ataturk, Istanbul, to De Gaulle, Paris, and, finally, to Hartsfield-Jackson, Atlanta. No business or first class available.

He didn't dare count the total hours of cramped seating, miserable, if any, food, and uncaring, if not downright rude, flight attendants. Tourist, he decided, was today's steerage class, that inexpensive, cheerless, uncomfortable lower deck of a steamship in which most nineteenth-century emigrants made their way to America.

Yellow crime scene tape still encircled the house like an ugly wound.

Manfred was so eager to recount his and Grumps's part in the affair that he forgot the standard query about the gifts from afar usually distributed upon his dad's return home. Gurt described the security devices she was meticulously and methodically employing. And Leon's pivotal part.

There seemed to be little else that could be done until Lang finished his present court schedule and could contact Dr. Kalonimos on Rhodes. He did ask Detective Franklin Morse of the Atlanta Police Department if the local patrol car could make an extra pass by the house every shift.

Some years ago, the detective had actually asked for a reassignment away from Lang's precinct. He had observed that death and violence were like a stray dog fed once too often: they seemed to habitually follow Lang. The policeman had been less than happy when Lang and Gurt appeared on his newly assigned beat by moving into the house on Lafayette Drive.

"Dunno, Mr. Reilly," the immaculately dressed black cop had said. "Two perps dead. We could direct ever' home invasion your way, the APD could furlough half its officers."

Morse had a perverse sense of humor.

Today, Lang's immediate court obligations were completed, he had taken two golf lessons, and was ready to demonstrate his newfound skills to Francis. For convenience sake, they began on the ninth tee, the one immediately behind the clubhouse, one of two fairways along the lake.

There was a swish as Lang's driver split the air, the crack of contact, the splash as it hooked into the lake. "Your mulligan," Francis said, not being particularly successful in suppressing a grin.

What Lang had to say was mercifully blotted out by a departing 777.

"I'm glad I didn't hear that," Francis said.

Lang was teeing up another ball. "Me, too."

"Try keeping your head down," Francis suggested.

"That's what the pro said. Problem is, I can't see the ball that way. Fact of the matter is, I don't see the whole damn game. You play for the lowest score instead of the highest, if you're right-handed, you play left-handed, and you use implements ill-suited to the purpose."

Francis was teeing up his ball. "*Vanitas vanitatum, omnis vanitas.*"

"All may be fruitless, but I've got a fortune invested in these new clubs."

"*Vilius argentum est auro, virtubus aurum.*"

"I doubt Horace ever played this game. I see damn little virtue in it."

Lang watched Francis's drive. The ball ascended a gentle arc, sliced right, hit a pine tree, and bounced onto the fairway 150 yards away.

"Why do I have the feeling I'm not playing against just you?"

Francis said nothing as he picked up the stump of his tee, grinning again.

"No comment? Not even a *Deus vult?*"

The priest was handing his driver to the young caddy. "The battle cry of the Crusaders, 'God wills it?' That would be a bit egotistic, wouldn't it, thinking God wills the flight of one's golf ball?"

"No more than the so-called 'Divine Right of Kings.'"

"Which, as I recall, died some time ago."

Lang was teeing up his second, post-mulligan, shot. He tried to avoid discussing religion with his friend. Although he, personally, supposed he conceded the possibility of a Higher Being, he was fairly certain that Being was not the benign, loving entity Francis espoused. Lang had seen too much of the real world to accept that anything with good intentions ruled it.

He didn't answer. Instead, he hit his ball and tried to conceal his delight when it hit squarely in the fairway and rolled a dozen feet past Francis's. Perhaps the Ruler of the Universe had a beneficent side after all.

The two men were walking across the lush grass of a manicured course to an even smoother green followed by the caddies when Francis asked, "Did you ever find out who those thugs were?"

The roar of jet engines low overhead contrasted with the serenity of the golf course on a weekday afternoon. It also prevented Lang from being sure of what Francis had said. "Say again?"

"Those men who broke into your house while you were in Greece, the ones Gurt, er, took care of."

"I'll say. What about them?"

"Ever find out who they were?"

Lang shook his head. "Not yet. I think the police know. I've threatened to file a Freedom of Information request."

Francis squatted, frowning, either at his putting possibilities or what came next. "I'm afraid to ask why you want to know."

"Then don't," Lang snapped, then regretted the edge on his reply. "Look, Francis, I can't just sit by and hope the problem will go away. First, Gurt gets kidnapped in Turkey, then I'm abducted in Athens and threatened at about the same time there's an attempt to take Manfred. These people, whoever they are, want the Foundation to give up what might be the greatest medical discovery since penicillin."

"Is it worth human life?"

"Depends on whose."

He saw the expression on his friend's face. "Francis, we may be on the verge of a universal antidote, not just for poisons but all sorts of reptile and insect venom. Think of the lives to be saved! If I can find out the names of those bastards who tried to snatch Manfred, I might be able to find who hired them."

Francis got up and inspected his lie from the other side of the green. "What makes you think they were hired?"

"Didn't you hear me? There has been a series of attempts to abduct me and my family. That's not coincidence."

Francis looked at Lang. "If you find who is behind these attempts, promise me you'll let the authorities handle it."

Lang's caddy handed him his putter. "That I can't do. I can only promise these attempts will end."

A departing 767 spared Lang the reply.

CHAPTER 41

Boardroom of Dystra Pharmaceuticals
The Same Day

WILLIAM GRASSLEY WISHED HE WERE ON the golf course. Or at home. Or anywhere but here and with just about anyone but the company's chief financial officer and chief operating officer.

The CFO, Ralph Hassler, was reviewing a statement from a bank on Grand Cayman. A statement that had no duplicate, either electronically or hard copy. There was no such thing as an electronic file, bank account or no, that could not be hacked into, given sufficient time and skill. The company didn't need for an offshore account to be made public, particularly one used for business best kept here in this boardroom

Hassler peered over half-moon glasses. "I thought we weren't paying the Greek unless we got results."

Grassley whipped the *puchette* from the breast pocket of his suit jacket and started to wipe the beads of sweat from his forehead. The candy-ass little piece of silk was Hermes, a gift from his wife, he remembered at the last minute. Probably cost as much as his tailored suit. "For show, not for blow," she had said as he had managed to show far more enthusiasm for the gift than he felt.

No reason to be perspiring, anyway. The damn suite of offices was kept at a constant 70 degrees year round. He replaced the scrap of silk and picked up one of the paper napkins beside the coffee urn. It came away from his face soaked.

Ralph Hassler was still waiting for an answer.

"He did. He was to draft the account."

"Did what?" Hassler persisted. "Best I can tell, all he did was kidnap Reilly from the street. Lot of good that did us."

"My call," Grassley defended. "Those aren't the kind of people you want to piss off. Besides, he has connections with a national black gang here, maybe part of the Bloods or Crips or something like that. He laid out his own money to have them snatch Reilly's kid."

"'Them' consisting of two dead gangbangers," Hugh Wright, the COO, spoke for the first time. "Fuck lot of good that did us."

Grassley reached for another napkin. "The hell was I supposed to know Reilly's wife was some kind of Wonder Woman? Account in the papers said she handled both of those punks alone."

"Maybe we should give up on forcing Reilly to come up with the blood sample, quit while we're ahead."

Grassley glared at his chief operating officer. "Ahead? How do you figure that?"

"We're not in jail."

"Goddammit, Wright, if you don't have the guts for this, resign."

The room was quiet while Wright seemed to consider the option.

Grassley broke the silence. "Another bit of bad news: Our lawyers have received a cease and desist letter from Johnson & Johnson's legal department. They're claiming we're infringing their patent for that heart drug, ReoPro."

Wright shook his head. "Prevents cardiac complications. They patented the fucking drug six years before it went on the market, a common practice, as you know. They didn't extend, so the drug could legally go generic February a year ago. Tell 'em to shove it."

"Not quite so easy," Grassley said. "You're right, but the cost of litigating could put us out of business even if we win, and those people know it."

"But we're already producing the generic," Wright protested. "It's our most profitable product."

Ralph Hassler cleared his throat, and the other two looked his way. "If we can't produce our generic of ReoPro, we'll be out of business unless . . ."

Grassley was reaching for another napkin. "Unless what?"

"Unless we get what we need from Reilly and can use it to patent the universal antidote, or something damn close to it."

"Any ideas as to how we go about dealing with Reilly?" Grassley asked. "He and that wife of his aren't people easily intimidated."

"Award of the year for most masterful understatement," Hassler observed dryly.

"I'd sure like to figure a legal way," Wright interjected.

"I'll settle for any way we can," Hassler said. "Surely someone in this room can figure a way."

"Maybe we should just stay here until we do," Grassley said.

"Anyone consider the possibility of getting our own sample?" Hassler asked. "I mean, getting a sample from that kid in Turkey has got to be a fuck of a lot easier than dealing with Reilly and his superhero wife."

Grassley shook his head. "Would have been a great idea a few weeks ago. The name of the donor, the kid who got bitten by the snake, disappeared."

"Disappeared?" Wright asked. "What do you mean, disappeared?"

Grassley's temper was getting shorter by the moment, and he made no effort to conceal the fact. "What don't you understand about 'disappeared'? Presumably, the name and pertinent data were in the hospital's computer system like any other patient's. When our guys in Turkey botched snatching the woman, I bribed an employee to hack into that system. There was no mention of a snakebite victim, immunity, or anything related to it. Obviously, Reilly or someone guessed whoever was after the sample might harm the kid, so they deleted it."

"Deleted data can always be retrieved," Wright volunteered.

Grassley gave him a scowl that spoke volumes of what he thought of the man, none of it pleasant. "Brilliant! You want to go to some place in the middle of Turkey and try to retrieve data you can't even read, *via con dios, amigo.*"

"You said you hired someone to look for it," Wright defended.

"And just how do we make sure whoever the fuck, the employee we hired, doesn't decide to contact the authorities this time? There's at least an unsolved murder and a kidnapping the Turks still have on the books, remember?"

"What about the people we already hired?" Hassler wanted to know.

"The *Gayrimesru*, Turkish Mafia? They aren't sophisticated enough. Besides, after the fiasco of trying to kidnap the woman, I'd just as soon not risk any further contact. I'd bet the Turkish police, army, somebody has infiltrated them by now."

All three men were planning on a long evening.

CHAPTER 42

763 Juniper Street
Atlanta, Georgia
Later That Day

A DECADE EARLIER, THE POWERS THAT governed the city of Atlanta realized that crime (other than that normally associated with politicians) did not occur at City Hall or other government complexes. It occurred in neighborhoods both residential and commercial. This was particularly true of property crimes such as burglary, auto theft, and auto break-ins. The politicians figured out that a police presence in the area might even reduce the activity of the miscreants.

The solution was a dispersal of the force, the creation of neighborhood precincts. Shopping centers, storefronts, even former single-family residences now serve this purpose.

Specifically, the precinct closest to Ansley Park was a single-story brick building whose stingy windows and lack of inspired architecture suggested its origins as a 1950s office suite, perhaps for a sales or distribution force. The worn linoleum tile floor, the intuitional pale yellow walls, and the buzz of long-outdated fluorescent overhead lighting confirmed Lang Reilly's guess as to the age of the structure.

A bulletin board bristled with memoranda and wanted posters, many of the latter yellowed with age.

A bored officer looked up from the *Journal-Constitution* crossword. "Hepya?"

"I'm here to see Detective Franklin Morse."

"Expecting you?" the cop asked suspiciously.

Lang nodded. "I spoke with him on the phone less than an hour ago. He said he'd be here."

Without taking his eyes off Lang, the policeman picked up a phone and punched the keyboard. "You got a visitor. Name of . . ." He looked up at Lang.

"Reilly, Lang Reilly."

Lang looked around for a seat, found none. Apparently visitors to the cop shop weren't supposed to be made comfortable.

"Mr. Reilly?"

Morse stood in the entrance to a hallway. Half a head taller than Lang, he wore the pants to a seersucker suit, a white button-down, and rep tie. Spotless white bucks peeked out from below razor-creased trousers. Lang pushed away the mental image of the policeman with a gaily ribboned straw boater on his head.

Morse gave a half-turn, half-bow. "This way, Mr. Reilly."

Once in the hallway, Lang could hear the buzz of electronics, the clicking of keyboards. From somewhere came the metallic tone of a voice filtered through a radio.

Morse stood aside, indicating an open door about halfway down the hall.

Inside, a metallic desk was against the wall below the window framing a view of a parking lot jammed with police vehicles, most marked, some not. Next to the window, a chair matched the desk in utilitarian ugliness and faced outward. Beside the chair, its twin faced the desk, the only difference being a worn cushion. The desk bore a silver-framed photograph of an attractive black woman and two teenage boys. It and a pair of cheaply framed certificates on the wall were the only personal items Lang saw in the entire cramped space.

Morse pointed to the outward facing chair. "Do have a seat, Mr. Reilly."

Land sat gingerly, nodding toward the desk. "Nice-looking family, Detective."

Morse slid into his chair with a sigh. "Thanks. Older boy, Adam, starts Tech come August. Full scholarship. Wants a degree in computer science."

"And the other?"

"Still time to change his mind. Wants to be a lawyer."

Was that the ghost of a smile Lang saw float across the policeman's face?

"We certainly wouldn't want that," Lang said.

Yes, definitely a smile. It vanished with certainty.

"Well, Mr. Reilly, I 'spect we done 'xhausted the pleasantries. Shall we get down to business?"

Over the years, Lang had noted Morse's speech varied from the simply ungrammatical, to Southern Black dialect, to perfect English, depending on the circumstances. He guessed the affectation was used to conceal a truly bright mind.

"Okay, Detective, what do you have?"

Morse extracted two files from a stack beneath his chair and opened the one on top. Lang caught a flash of a mug shot stapled to the inside. "You wanted to know about the two homies who broke into your house. Both perps have raps going back over ten years: larceny, grand larceny, assault on a teacher when one was only nine, auto theft, sexual assault, battery with a deadly weapon, attempted murder. And that ain't even gettin' to the distribution of controlled-substance charges. You name it. Since they were juvies, they been in jail more'n out. They members of the YM's, Young Money, Bankhead-area gang related to the Bloods outta LA. Couple of real sweethearts. Gang isn't what you'd call organized beyond coordinating a robbery or break-in. You can bet somebody else was paying them to try to snatch your son."

"Believe me, we didn't choose who was going to try to kidnap Manfred."

The policeman nodded agreement. "I'm sure. Fact of the matter, you — or Ms. Fuchs — pro'lly saved the taxpayers a fortune in prosecution and incarceration costs."

"So, what's the problem with giving me a look at their files?"

"Mayhem, Mr. Reilly, mayhem. You and I know I been the detective on the beat when someone jumped from your condo on Peachtree Street. What was it, 24 floors? I was called in after someone tried to kill you by blowing up said condo, endangering the lives of the other hundred or so residents. It was on my beat when you chased down a car all the way to Charlie Brown Airport and trashed a million-dollar-plus-aircraft. Need I go on?"

"And your point would be?"

"Mr. Reilly, you and I both know you ain't asking for this info so you can put flowers on these punks' graves. They dead, they most likely gonna stay that way. Only thing you wants to know is who sent 'em. To get that information, you gonna track down whoever you have to. My experience is whoever you find not gonna say, 'Oh yeah, sure. Lemme tell you 'bout the recently deceased.' They have anything to do with you, good chance I got another set of vics, dead vics. You unnerstan' what I'm sayin'?"

Lang shrugged, hands palms up, the quintessence of innocence. "All I want is information: from those guys' friends and families, and from you, to which I'm entitled, by the way."

Morse handed over the files. "Not gonna do you a lot of good. Both lived with they womans out to the Bankhead Courts."

"Which aren't there anymore."

In 1936 Atlanta opened Techwood Homes, the nation's first public housing, a much-heralded event attended by then-President Franklin Roosevelt. By 2009 it had become obvious that the projects were breeding grounds for poverty, crime, and violence. Some less-than-perspicacious soul figured out that dispersing the residents would solve the problem, so the projects came under the wrecking ball to be replaced by housing vouchers, federal Section 8 subsidies, and requiring "affordable housing" units of developers of multi-family residential projects. The result was as predictable as it was ill-thought-out: like quarantining a plague by dispersing its victims.

Said poverty, crime, and violence were now equitably distributed throughout the city. Homeowners of both the mansions of Buckhead to the north and the shotgun cottages of Cabbage Town, a former mill village, on the south side now equally shared the joy of neighbors whose dubious occupations, if any, included dealing narcotics, mugging, and prostitution.

"Which ain't there," Morse repeated. "Don't see as how you gonna get ennythin' outta whoever you find. Why not let the police do the job we paid for?"

"Detective, do you really believe you or anyone from the APD is going to take the time to run down friends and relatives of those two, just to try to find out why they wanted my son or who sent them?"

Morse sighed, shook his head, and shoved the files toward Lang. "You right. The book on them two perps permanently closed. We got enough live ones keep us busy. Plus, knowin' you, Mr. Reilly, you knows damn well who sent those guys and pro'lly the reason why. Just one thing, Mr. Reilly: I'd soon arrest you as anyone else who thinks they sort of a vigilante. Whoever you find, they be friends or relatives of the deceased, they ain't gonna likely to be the sort you see at your club's annual ball. But that no excuse to take the law into your own hands. We unnerstanin' each other?"

They did, far better than either would admit. Lang didn't doubt stepping across the line between self-defense and murder would land him in jail. And Morse was correct: Lang knew perfectly well who had sent the would-be kidnappers. He simply needed to be sure before he carried out his promise to the Greek.

CHAPTER 43

472 Lafayette Drive
Atlanta, Georgia
That Evening

LANG REILLY HAD A SURPRISE WAITING for him when he got home.

Having Manfred climb out of the pool to embrace him, leaving his suit jacket somewhere between damp and soaked, wasn't it. Nor was Grumps awakening from his nap. The *Beetenbartsch*, beet root soup with sour cream, or *Konigsberger Klopse*, meatballs in a white sauce, in the kitchen only suggested Francis was due for dinner, since they were among the priest's favorites.

Truth be told, just about any of Gurt's native German dishes so qualified, as did meals by any of his parishioners. That he was to be a dinner guest was far from surprising.

The surprise was the tall black man with his left arm in a sling. In the kitchen, he seemed to be getting in Gurt's way more than helping.

She was bent over, peering into the oven. Lang gave her rear a loving pat. "Who's . . .?"

"Name's Leon Frisch." The disembodied voice came from somewhere inside the oven. "He's just out of jail, hasn't got anywhere else to go."

Lang eyed the stranger with renewed interest. "We've started running a halfway house?"

Gurt's upper body appeared as though by magic. "He's the one I had the, er . . ." She moved her fists in a circular motion as though boxing. "*Auseinandersetzung, Schlagerei*. He wanted to wash my windshield."

"You mean the bum you had an altercation with on the way to pick up Manfred?"

Gurt set a tray of freshly baked bread on the counter. The aroma almost made Lang forget what they were talking about.

But not quite. He looked at Leon with distaste. "You said he was on meth or something."

"I was," Leon volunteered. "And I want to atone for the trouble I caused this lady."

Lang shook his head. "Look, Leon, or whatever your name is, we're not in the turn-the-other-cheek business."

"But I am."

No one had seen Francis come in. "And just to whom are we turning that cheek?"

Lang pointed to Leon, who certainly looked less than worthy of redemption: pink flip-flops, no doubt a souvenir of his stay at the taxpayer's expense; just enough beard stubble to be the result of laziness rather than a desire to re-grow his beard; a shirt that had put in time between washes, as evidenced by whiffs of body odor; and that sling for his left arm, a dirty piece of cloth holding an arm with an equally dirty bandage.

"Good question, Padre," Lang said. "Even better, just why is he here?"

Gurt took off a pair of oven mitts and used her hands to push back a few strands of hair that had escaped the tight chignon, then gently slap Lang's probing fingers away from the freshly baked bread. She stared at Lang for a moment. "Did I not say . . .?"

"No, you neglected that part."

Her hands fluttered from her head to be clasped before her. "Mr. Frisch here, Leon, took a bullet meant for me."

Lang stared at the stranger, then at Gurt, then back again.

Gurt reached out and touched his jaw. "You should not leave your mouth open so, Lang. It is most unattractive."

"You mean when those two men . . .?"

"*Ja.*" Gurt nodded emphatically. "Were it not for Leon . . ."

There was a chuckle from Father Francis, a deep sound of merriment like the crackle of a fireplace. "Sounds like Leon is going to be around for a while. Other than saving fair maidens, Leon, can you do anything useful?"

"Before I succumbed to the devil, I worked for a landscaping company. Started when I dropped outta high school. Anything to get outs Bankhead Courts."

Succumbed to the devil? People like Leon didn't "succumb," Lang thought. Or submit or yield, for that matter. They were possessed or taken over. Leon was parroting what he had heard.

Francis picked up on it, too. "And just how long did this succumbing last?"

Leon studied the ceiling as though the answer might be written there. "I, I'm not sure. I started doing recreational meth, then I was missing work at the landscaping company. There are some big gaps in my memory, Father. Next I knew, I was on the street. That's been . . . oh, been at least two years ago."

Lang looked at Francis questioningly. "You're the only expert on addiction I know. Sound reasonable?"

Francis shook his head sadly. "All too reasonable. Every time I do my homeless shelter ministry, I hear pretty much the same story."

"Yeah, Father," Leon interjected. "But I'm clean now."

"So were 99 percent of the people I see. Problem is staying that way."

"What are the odds of that?" Lang wanted to know.

"No better than 10 percent."

Gurt gently slapped Lang's second attempt for the bread before turning on Francis. "Shame on you! You and your church preach forgiveness and redemption, yet you are against giving Leon a chance at both."

The priest raised a defensive hand. "Whoa! I never said I was against anything."

"Well, I am," Lang said. "No matter what good deed Leon here did, you heard Francis: there's a 90 percent chance of him going back to whatever fucked him up in the first place. You want to take that risk with Manfred around, not to mention whatever we may have of value in the house?"

Leon was following the discussion, head turning from speaker to speaker as though watching a tennis match.

As was so often the case, Lang had lost the war before being given a chance to muster his forces. He might get the last word of the argument, only to later realize those words were the beginning of a new argument.

"Why don't you and Francis go into the library and have a drink before dinner?" she suggested sweetly. "Leon will be getting settled in the guest room in the pool house. We can use some landscaping around here."

Recognizing defeat, Lang led Francis into the library, a room where overflowing bookcases were built into three of the paneled walls with a window looking onto the pool in the fourth. A flatscreen TV and old-fashioned record turntable stacked with vinyl 78s shared space with books.

From beneath the screen's blank stare, Lang knelt and opened the doors of a cabinet. "Same old?"

Francis nodded.

Lang took out a Lalique decanter of Macallan scotch and poured into two Baccarat highball glasses, tinkled in some ice, and handed a glass to his guest. As he stood, the distinctive bravura trumpet of Harry James began the opening notes of *Little Things Mean a Lot*. Kitty Kalan was in full soprano voice by the time he crossed the room to sink into the leather club chair across from the one occupied by Francis.

Neither man spoke in deference to the single malt. In unison, both nodded approval before Lang shook his head. "Don't know what Gurt had in mind, taking in a street person and a dope addict at that."

Francis smiled. "All God's children, Lang. Here, this one has a better chance than most."

"And an even better chance to rip off everything in the house soon as he gets back on whatever shit was running his life. Let's face it: the man has reached rock bottom and has started to dig."

Francis tut-tutted between sips of scotch. "There's a little bit of good in the worst of us, Lang. He may work out fine. I mean, a street person, probably grew up in the projects . . ."

Black. Bankhead Courts.

There was an idea sniffing around the perimeter of Lang's mind like an animal just outside the light of a campfire. From experience, he knew, sooner or later, it would step into the light.

CHAPTER 44

472 Lafayette Drive
The Next Morning

LANG WAS TUGGING THE KNOT IN his tie when he heard his son's voice from downstairs: "Not fair! None of the other kids have their mothers come to the park with them!"

'The park' referred to Winn Park, one of several neighborhood green spots encircled by Ansley Park's wandering streets and towering hardwoods. Part botanical garden, part playground, this one was literally across the street from the house. Since no major thoroughfares need be crossed, children enjoyed the facility without the presence of parents so humiliating to the young.

Lang was descending the stairs as Gurt replied, "The bad men, the ones who grabbed you by the arm, tried to take you away. They are still there."

"Are not!" Manfred contradicted, a rare occurrence. "They're dead!"

How many seven-year-olds even understood death, let alone witnessed it in its more violent form? Lang felt a surge of irrational guilt. Nothing he had done had brought this violence down upon him and his family. The fact made him feel not one whit better.

"I'm afraid there may be more." Gurt was trying to reason with a seven-year-old, rarely a good idea.

"Grumps will chew 'em up," Manfred asserted, based more on imagination than experience.

"Why don't you have your friends come over here to play in our yard? You can even have hot dogs out by the pool for lunch."

Bargaining was even worse.

"I want to go to the park."

Lang had no doubt where his son's stubbornness had come from. Except when referring to Gurt's, he called it "tenacity."

No more bargaining or reasoning. "You'll stay right here."

"Not fair!"

"Fair or not, you can invite your friends over or not as you wish, but you will not leave the yard."

"It's not fair!"

"Neither is life."

Lang was wondering how a small child might deal with this all-too-true observation as he entered the kitchen. Manfred, just out of a high chair — what, only a few years ago — was seated at the kitchen table, the usual bowl of oatmeal dotted with blueberries before him. Lang noted his son's mother had made a special dispensation of wheat toast and fruit jelly sweetened with its natural pectin.

The bribe obviously hadn't worked. Manfred's expression was stormy. Grumps, ever the optimist, sat under his small master's chair in anticipation of whatever might fall his way. Breakfast went silently and quickly. Manfred excused himself and retreated to his room, anger in the sound of his footsteps punctuated with the slam of his bedroom door.

"He has a point," Lang observed, helping himself to the Mr. Coffee.

"You wish to risk him being knapsacked?"

Although Gurt had spent the best part of the last decade in the United States, the American vernacular occasionally eluded her.

"Kidnapped. Knapsack is *ein Proviantbeutel.*"

"Either way, is he not taken?"

"Whatever. We need to bring this matter to a conclusion. I assume all the security devices are working."

"The house has been on full alert since we returned from Turkey."

Lang tried to conjure up the vision of the two-story shingle home girding its loins for battle. The image wouldn't come. It was sufficient, he supposed, that the house had tighter security than most banks.

"And the car?"

"Manfred complains I will not let him lower the windows."

Doing so would vitiate any protection from the specially installed bulletproof glass.

"I imagine Grumps is less than happy not to be able to get his head out and ears in the airstream."

She shrugged.

"And you don't leave the house unarmed?"

"It is difficult to fit the Glock into a pair of shorts, but I do so even to water the lawn."

Lang grinned. Over the years, he had noted a sudden increase in yard work by his male neighbors whenever Gurt donned shorts and t-shirt to do pruning, weeding, or sweeping.

"Well, your new pal Leon can take care of that. Matter of fact, he may be able to help us find out who's after that blood sample."

Gurt's spoon stopped halfway between her mouth and the bowl of blueberries in lowfat milk. "And how is that?"

"I'm not totally sure." He glanced at his watch. "Gotta go!"

And he was out of the door. His haste was not for the court hearing an hour and a half from now. It was to make sure he had time to get a real breakfast at the IHOP, away from Gurt's health-conscious gaze.

By 9:30, Lang was entering the chambers of Susan Kopenski, United States Magistrate. In the Federal judicial system, a magistrate is a "tweener," somewhere between a judge and a clerk but not really either. In districts with serious overload problems, such as the Northern District of Georgia, magistrates take on fact-finding missions, resolution of discovery disputes, and such other pre-trial controversies between lawyers as might otherwise require judicial intervention, thereby in governmentspeak, "conserving valuable judicial resources."

Lang had filed a motion to exclude recordings of certain telephone conversations conducted by his unwanted client, Theodosius Wipp. Ms. Kopenski would hear brief testimony dealing with the circumstances under which the FBI had tapped the man's phone, and the legality, or lack thereof, of such action. She would also read the briefs submitted by both Lang and the government. At some point before trial, she would make a recommendation to the judge who, more than likely, would issue a ruling along the suggested lines.

Or he might indulge in that rarity of legal activity known as independent thinking.

Either way, Lang was never comfortable with his case resting on the judgment of what was no more than a bureaucrat, particularly one who was becoming increasingly uncomfortable with Wipp's stares at the place the top button of her blouse strained to keep an ample bosom in check.

Wipp, it seemed, was a lecher as well as a welcher and scammer. Your all-around sleazeball.

"Morning, Mr. Reilly!"

Wipp's tone was as happy as if he were greeting a fellow parishioner in church.

Lang growled a reply.

Wipp's eyebrows arched. "My, aren't we in a foul mood this morning."

Lang sat, turning the chair to face his client. "I'm not accustomed to representing people who pay fees with stiff checks. If I could, I'd withdraw."

"But you can't," Wipp replied cheerfully. "And your ethics compel you to do your best in my defense anyway. Wonderful things, ethics."

Spoken like a man unburdened with such trivial matters.

Any retort was silenced by the magistrate's announcement. "All right, let's proceed. Mr. Reilly, I understand you have moved to quash certain evidence, specifically six telephone conversations between Mr. Wipp here and people he was trying to convince to send him money for a course that never took place."

"And the basis of the motion is those conversations commenced just minutes before the order allowing the phone tap was entered according to the timestamp. How am I doing so far?"

Lang stood. "Right on, Your Honor."

As a magistrate, Ms. Kopenski was not entitled to the honorific, but no lawyer in his right mind was going to risk her displeasure by omitting it.

She turned to the U.S. Attorney's table. "And what says the government?"

For the first time, Lang noted the adjacent table was occupied not by the senior staff member who would try the case, but a man young enough to be a very recent law school grad. That telegraphed the lack of interest the prosecution had in this hearing. Kids still wet behind the ears took little part in felony cases. Or, at least, in important phases of them.

Lang's intuition was right: the kid stood, nervously adjusting his tie. "A mere technicality, Your Honor. But the United States is not willing to risk a possible reversal. We will concede Mr. Reilly's point."

The judge glanced at Wipp before shifting her gaze to the prosecution's table. "You are aware that without the phone tap, all six counts are subject to dismissal?"

The kid nodded. "Yes, Your Honor. The United States feels comfortable with the remaining 30."

This last part was directed more at Lang then the magistrate.

Minutes later, the appropriate order dictated, Wipp stood beside Lang, waiting for an elevator.

The old man said, "Nice job, Mr. Reilly. Believe me, I really will pay for your services."

How long at prison wages would that take?

But Lang said dryly, "As you observed, I'm ethically bound to give you the best representation I can."

Wipp put a hand on Lang's shoulder, a gesture that Lang started to shrug off. "Mr. Reilly, you are a credit to the space you occupy."

Compliment or insult? Lang was certain of only one thing: he wasn't going to get paid.

CHAPTER 45

472 Lafayette Drive
That Evening

THE FIRST THING LANG NOTICED WHEN he nosed the Porsche into his driveway was that the grass had been cut and lined with boxwoods that hadn't been there this morning. As if confirming his memory, neat piles of red Georgia clay evidenced recent planting.

Gurt, in t-shirt and shorts, was following Leon who, favoring his healing wound, pushed a wheelbarrow into the garage with Manfred and Grumps close behind. Gurt was crusted with a patina of sweat and clay while Leon exhibited little evidence of whatever labor had occupied him that day.

She used the back of a very grimy gloved hand to push back an errant strand of hair that dangled before her eyes. "Hi, Lang! Leon and I were just finishing up."

"And Leon showed me a new game to play in the pool," Manfred announced.

That explained the misdistribution of grime: Gurt had installed the shrubbery while Leon played with Manfred. The man might have had experience at landscaping, but his first day on the job had been spent entertaining a small boy. He mentally shrugged. Gurt would take the observation as an unappreciated "I told you so."

"Plying your landscaping skills, Leon?" Lang asked, easing the car into its space beside Gurt's.

"Do what?"

Lang could not help but note the covetous stare the man was giving the Porsche. No doubt calculating the amount of meth it might bring.

"Your landscaping experience. It came in handy today, right?"

Leon grinned, showing large gaps between the remaining teeth. "Not hardly. I hepped load an' unload them there bushes. Then, Manfred n' me got to playin' in the pool an' Gurt, she say, 'Stay there. Too early to exercise that arm.' Nex' thing I know, she done all the plantin'."

At least the man was honest.

That night was one of the rare occasions when Gurt allowed Lang and Manfred to order in pizza. She was simply too tired to cook, and it was too late to begin anyway. Manfred, Leon, and Lang sat at the kitchen table as Grumps, ever the optimist, patrolled the area under the table. Gurt had satisfied whatever appetite she had with a pair of bananas perhaps past their prime and was studying a dozen or so eight-by-ten cards from her recipe collection spread out on the granite countertop.

Leon swallowed a bite of pepperoni with a gulp and was reaching for a tall glass of iced tea. "Man!" he managed between swigs. "This here pizza reminds me of the time I tried working deliverin' pizzas."

"You drive around with one of those little signs on top of your car?" Manfred wanted to know.

Leon put down the glass to renew his attack on the pizza. "Naw, didn't have no car. Stayed over to the Bankhead Courts an' there was a Domino's 'cross the street. I'd deliver in the project. Over a thousand folks there an' . . ."

Lang put down his slice of pizza. "Bankhead Courts? Public housing? The ones torn down in 2009?"

Leon looked puzzled. "Don' know nothin' about torn down but, yeah, lived there with my mother till I dropped outta school, started doing sh . . ."

A reproachful glare from Gurt reminded him to mind his vocabulary around the child and prevented the sentence's completion.

"Ever know fellows about your age named Ladustine Weaver or Justinian Holt?"

Leon nodded slowly. "Called Smoof an' Little Boy. Gangbangers, they hang. Las' I hear, they both in jail."

Gurt looked up from her recipes. "Weaver and Holt? Weren't those the names Detective Morse gave you, the names of the two . . . ?"

"Morse didn't 'give' me anything. I had to threaten him with a Freedom of Information request. There was no ongoing investigation to hide behind. He had to share the file with me."

Once again, Leon's head swiveled as he followed the exchange. "What them two homies done now?"

Lang ignored the question. "You said they were gang members?"

Leon nodded. "Uh-huh."

"What gang?"

"BMF."

Black Mafia Family. Unlike most inner city gangs, such as the various divisions and subdivisions of the nationally known Bloods and Crips (which were little more than leaderless, unorganized groups acting largely as opportunity presented itself), BMF was— or had been— a tightly coordinated, family-led clique for the distribution of cocaine. Founded in Detroit by the Flenary brothers, the enterprise moved largely to Atlanta about the turn of the present century. Like so many successful illegitimate businesses, it had expanded into other endeavors, including the legitimate and growing hip-hop music trend, as well as darker pursuits such as murder of rivals, kidnapping, gambling, and other sundry undertakings of a criminal nature. By the time the federal government wrapped up the BMFs around 2009, there was no longer any real certainty in law enforcement as to exactly which pies the family had its fingers in.

Once the business was too large to be handled solely by family members, recruits, mostly from neighborhood gangs, were employed to do the heavy lifting of violent crimes. The new soldiers of this army, however, did not forswear seizing the opportunity for robbery, burglary, or car theft. Sidelines of prostitution, hired killing, and narcotics were common, as was the elimination of anyone brave enough to drop the dime on gang members.

Leon's lips were pursed as he tried to concentrate. "They not part of the family."

"The Flenarys?"

Leon nodded again. "But they either in the gang or hang with members."

"Where do they hang since the gang's been busted up?"

"Hard to say. They not in jail, Mechanicsville neighborhood mostly."

The area across I-75-85 from Turner Field just south of the interchange with I-20.

"Mechanicsville's a large area."

Leon shrugged. "Ain't seen them a lot since I went on the street." He gave a self-deprecating snort. "Not a lot of bling to be stole from a street person."

Bored with not being included in the conversation, Manfred began, "Momma . . ."

Gurt shushed him with a wave of the hand that reminded him he was not to interrupt grownups. "Could you recognize the gang members Smoof and Little Boy hang with?"

Lang gave her look that said her mind was on the same track as his.

Leon's expression said he wanted no part of whatever they had in mind. "Man, those are seriously bad dudes. You don't want to f . . ." He glanced at Gurt. "You don't want to mess wid dem."

Lang stood. "Come on, Leon. We're going to take a ride."

"Lang," Gurt began. "Surely you're not . . ."

"Unless you have a better idea how to stop whoever kidnapped you and tried to take me and then Manfred, you bet I am."

CHAPTER 46

Rosa Burney Park
477 Windsor Street
Mechanicsville
Atlanta, Georgia
Ninety Minutes Later

THE NOISE FROM TURNER FIELD EBBED and flowed like an audible tide against the steady hum of traffic on the nearby interstate. Lang had had to rent the Mustang convertible at the airport, all other car rental offices being closed at this hour. He had easily come to the conclusion this was not the area of town in which to prowl in the Porsche, an automobile whose price exceeded by double most of the cottages and bungalows that made up the bulk of the neighborhood. He had chosen the ragtop to visually distance himself from anything the police might drive.

At first, Gurt had protested his idea, but she came around quickly enough when she was unable to come up with a better one.

"But, why not go tomorrow, in the daylight? I can go with you then."

Lang was undecided if Gurt's main motive was to not miss out on the action or to be there to have his back. A little of both, probably. He had shaken his head. "These are nocturnal creatures, Gurt. Unless we knew exactly who we were looking for and where they were, we'd never find them."

"I can make arrangements to let Manfred spend the night with a friend tomorrow night."

"And what friend does he have whose home and family will give him the protection you and this house can?"

There was, of course, no answer.

Cruising by the park, Lang noted most of the street lights were dark, shot or burned out. The few remaining showed a gazebo in the center of an open space. Lang thought, but was not sure, he saw tables and benches, perhaps room for 40 people. Cigarettes glowed like eyes in the shadows cast by the sloping roof.

He parked the Mustang and got out. Leon remained in the passenger seat.

"Come on, Leon. I didn't bring you here just for your company."

"Man, them the baddest-ass niggas you gonna see."

"Those are the ones I'm looking for. Now, come on! And remember how we play this."

Lang and Leon circled the gazebo to approach from the side with the most light. Lang didn't want anyone surprised. The closer he got, the stronger became the odor of marijuana. As his eyes became accustomed to the gray darkness, he could make out five or six men lounging on picnic tables and benches. Although he couldn't see well enough to be sure, he could all but feel all eyes on him.

When they were less than ten feet from the structure, Lang prodded Leon.

"Ho, man, wassup?" Leon began.

"Jus' hustlin'. You good, dawg?"

The words were friendly enough, but the tone suspicious.

"Yeah, man," Leon responded. "I lookin' for Smoof an' Little Boy."

The group went silent until one of the group, a tall silhouette with a backward baseball cap, detached himself from the group and made a point of slowly circling the newcomers. "What fo' you lookin'?"

"Got a job fo' em."

"What kinda job?"

"'Tween us an' Smoof an' Little Boy."

The man kept circling. "You dunno some white ho done busted a cap on dem?"

Leon did a credible job of being surprised, most likely because he was. Lang hadn't told him of the demise of the two would-be kidnappers.

"No shit? They dead?"

Baseball Cap stopped circling. "Meybbe you tell us what you want wid 'em, we can hep."

Leon was turning out to be quite the performer. "No, dawg, we ain' red arrowing this here. Smoof an' Little Boy serious bad asses what we need."

Another man left the anonymity of the gazebo to join the first. "Smoof an' Little Boy ain' the only bad asses. Paper be enough, I find you somebody." He looked Lang up and down. "'Less you be po-po."

"Paper?" Lang asked. "Po-po?"

The poor light prevented him from being sure but he thought he saw the man roll his eyes.

"Money," Leon translated, "police."

Lang raised his arms to shoulder level to show he had no concealed weapon. Not in a shoulder holster anyway. "I'm not the cops. What kind of heat would come down here and solicit someone to do a job and then arrest him for it? You gentlemen ever hear of entrapment?"

"Whee!" came an unidentified voice. "Don't he talk funny!"

The recent addition to Lang, Leon, and Baseball Cap outside the gazebo spoke over his shoulder to the group under the roof. "Tell th' mu'fucker shut his mouth!" He turned back to Leon and Lang. "You wants a special job? Meybbe you come back here tomorrow when it be light, know what I mean?"

Leon said, "The man wants to do business tonight."

"Keep it real, bro! Ain't nobody do no business some white-bread dude he never seen before. All I know, the bushes be full of the man, jus' waitin' to make a bust. You be back here, say 3:00."

As if to emphasize the finality of the offer, he spun on his heels, his form merging into the others in the gazebo.

CHAPTER 47

Rosa Burney Park
6:26 A.M.
The Next Morning

THE ANGRY RED STREAK IN THE eastern sky, the zipper between light and dark, was widening as the gray began to chase night's shadows into their daytime hiding places. The patches of grass were turning from blotches into islands of white as the infant day reflected from a heavy dew. Other than a couple of homeless men snoring peacefully on the picnic tables under the roof of the gazebo, the park was deserted. Loose wrappers from fast food, borne by a gentle morning breeze, skittered across mostly bare clay. The sounds of an awakening city included the grinding gears of an approaching garbage truck.

The surrounding homes, mostly cottages, showed substantial deferred maintenance: rashes of bare wood spotted painted surfaces; front steps were frequently less than aligned, leaning drunkenly to one side or the other; plastic sheeting was almost as common as glass in windows. Some roofs displayed patches of varying colors. A few flowers valiantly struggled in yards of hard-packed clay that seemed to mostly grow oil puddles and disabled or vintage automobiles. The most common element was the bars: a barred door in front of every entrance, burglar bars on every window. Lang had little doubt the residents had not only fortified their homes but were prepared to defend them. It was not a community a burglar would make his first choice.

The neighborhood had the appearance of defiance in defeat, a stubbornness against hopelessness.

The good news was that no one was stirring other than the sanitation department.

Lang had timed his arrival perfectly: there was just now sufficient light to see what he was doing, but it was far too early for there to be anyone around to notice him.

In the parking lot of the City View Apartments across the street, the garbage truck's lift whined a dumpster overhead, banging it noisily. Lang ducked behind a scraggly plant that had somehow survived years of the park department's less-than-benign neglect. He waited until the truck's crew was back on board and the vehicle grumbled out of sight.

He stood, searching. A squirrel, the only animal he had seen this morning, scolded him from an oak that seemed to be flourishing.

"I don't suppose you have any ideas?"

In the predawn solitude, speaking to an animal seemed a perfectly normal thing to do. He addressed Grumps all the time.

With an indignant flip of his brush, the squirrel disappeared up the tree trunk and into a clump of foliage. He emerged seconds later, dashing along a limb and making a dive an Olympian might have envied onto the lip of a trash barrel behind a bench. With another flick of its tail, it disappeared inside.

The trash barrel. Of course.

Lang took a final look around to make sure he was unobserved before walking over to it.

That afternoon at 2:30, the park was alive with the noise of children at play, music, and passing cars with tuned exhausts. Somewhere a kids baseball game was in progress, judging by the sound of an aluminum bat. The gazebo was filled with the fragrant smoke of barbecue and people in a festive mood.

It was as though the park of the early morning hours might have existed on a distant planet.

In the direction of the ball game, a man sat on a bench reading a newspaper. The jacket he wore belied the warmth of an afternoon in late spring.

His eyes, barely visible under a hat, were on the gazebo, not his paper. Two others stood on the edge of a path in a conversation not intense enough to prevent them watching Lang and Leon's approach. Their pants were low enough to expose underwear had it not been for concealing shirttails that could also have hidden a weapon. A fourth sat in an old Lincoln Town Car with mirror-shiny wheels. The vehicle seemed to vibrate with the blasts of hip-hop from a sound system that would have done credit to an opera house.

Leon's gaze followed Lang's. "We early. He be here after he sure we alone."

Confirming the observation, the man with the newspaper produced a cell phone, spoke briefly, and returned to his vigil.

Whether through caution or just tardiness, it was well after the half hour before a black BMW 760Li glided to the curb. Its tinted windows made it impossible to ascertain who or how many were inside. Two men got out. One, short and stocky, was the driver. The other could have been the one who had joined Baseball Cap outside the gazebo last night. It had been too dark to be sure.

The afternoon sun glinted off his shaved scalp, already beading with sweat from the warmth of the day. Even though reflective sunglasses hid most of the upper face, Lang guessed him to be in his mid-thirties. His most noticeable characteristic was the diamond embedded in a gold incisor, an adornment that sparkled when he smiled, which he did often, though there was neither warmth nor humor in it. He wore an expensive golf shirt and slacks that could have been tailored. Some species of lizard had died to cover the otherwise bare feet. He moved with assurance, the near-swagger of one in total control of his environment.

The man in the sunglasses surveyed the scene as two more men climbed out of the back seat. Bodyguards, certainly. Big men whose heads were shaved and whose faces were hidden behind mirrored eyewear. Tattoos on the arms had been done with a crudeness that could only have been the work of a prison artist. Lang saw no replication of the artistic dentistry.

Lang sensed Leon tensing as the man approached flanked by his bodyguards. "Be cool, man!"

"You know who that is, dude?" Leon whispered.

"Haven't had the pleasure."

"Hoarus 'Scoop' Meadows. He Big Meech's main man."

Big Meech was — or had been — Demetrious Flenary, in another crime organization's lexicon, the BMF's *capo di tutti capo*. He was now merely another number on the Feds' guest list. Meadows was, Lang guessed, playing Nitti to Flenary's Capone.

The two men from the backseat approached, one signaling Lang to raise his arms.

The man Leon had identified as Meadows worked a toothpick from one side of his mouth to the other as he watched Lang being roughly frisked. "Hope you don't mind."

"Oh, no. Happens every day."

Again, the humorless smile. "No problem, dude, 'less you strapped or wired."

"He mean carryin' or wearin' a wire," Leon explained, submitting to the same procedure by the other bodyguard.

As far as Lang could tell, no one in the park seemed to notice.

"He's clean," the man searching Lang announced.

"So's mine," the other said.

"Well, now," Meadows said, "we can get down to business. 'Xactly what did you have in mind for Smoof an' Little Boy?"

Lang made a show of glancing around. "Something I'd as soon keep private. Let's you and me take a walk."

Meadows nodded approval to his bodyguards. "Which way?"

Lang took a second or so to reply, a man making an inconsequential decision. "Over toward the oak?"

He paused long enough for Meadows to catch up before walking along the path. A few irregularly spaced dogwoods had survived a few feet from the pavement. The corpses of more were a monument to the City Parks Department's less-than-successful efforts to line the path with white or pink blossoms in spring.

The two moved in silence until Lang stopped and looked over his shoulder. "Guess this is far enough." He indicated a park bench just out of reach of the branches of the oak. "Why don't we have a sit?"

Meadows sat. "Okay, dude, what you want wit' Smoof an' Little Boy?"

Lang sprawled beside him, arms draped over the back of the bench. "'Spose I wanted somebody snatched, kidnapped?"

Meadows expelled a breath loudly. "That be a federal rap. Mighty risky."

Lang shrugged and started to get up. "Okay, I won't waste any more of your time."

A hand grasped his wrist. "Chill, dude. No need to bail. Didn't say I couldn't."

Lang let himself be pulled back down on the bench, again, arms along the back. "I'm listening."

"Takes a dude with some juice, pull something like that off. Smoof an' Little Boy assed out, they tried it."

"You telling me that's how they got killed, trying to kidnap someone?"

Meadows nodded. "That's what I . . ."

He stopped in mid-sentence. His head didn't move but his eyes did, "What th' fuck . . . ?"

"What you feel against the back of your head," Lang said calmly, "is exactly what you think: a .40 caliber Glock. You so much as wiggle your ears and your brains will be on the path there."

"But you frisked clean . . ."

"Your guys didn't frisk the trash barrel. I'd fire the incompetent bastards, I was you. If I lived long enough to, that is."

"You crazy? My guys . . ."

"I could empty the clip in your ear before the first one could get off a shot. You'd be dead before they had a clue. They can't see the gun from where they're standing."

Meadows seemed to relax. Or go limp. "Okay, dude, you bad ass. What you want?"

"The name of the person who wanted you to kidnap the little boy."

"How the hell would I know who sent Smoof an' Little Boy?"

Lang pressed the muzzle of the gun into the man's skull a little harder. "Don't fuck with me, Meadows! Those two wouldn't order in pizza, you didn't tell 'em what topping. You don't want to make your last mistake thinking I won't kill you."

Meadows cut his eyes even further toward Lang. They suddenly widened with recognition. "Shit! You . . ."

"Good guess. It was my son those two goons were going to snatch. I'm making sure it doesn't happen again. I could begin the process by whacking you. Or I could go after whoever had you send those two. Your choice. Just make it quick."

"How do I know you won't do me if I tell you?"

"Same way I figure you won't try to harm me or my family again: You're a businessman, Meadows, not a revenge killer. There's no profit in risking coming after me or my family unless you're paid to do it. Whoever had you send those two guys to take my son won't be around to pay you again, I promise. On the other hand, you don't tell me, there's not a reason in the world to make sure you don't complete the job. Follow me?"

Meadows nodded slowly. "Yeah, I gets you. Truth is, I don't know the man's real name. Big Meech done some deals wit' him when we started gettin' into smack, heroin. He had some ships . . ."

"You're doing fine, Meadows, but I need a name, a location, something."

"I tell the truth, man. This Greek . . ."

"You sure he was Greek?"

"S'what Big Meech called him, the Greek."

"The name Alex mean anything to you?"

"Yeah. That was the name I heard Big Meech use once when they talked on the phone. You satisfied?"

"You done good. Now, one more thing: Can you count to a hundred?"

" Course I can! How dumb you think I am?"

"You really don't want to know. You can start now. Just don't move, don't even turn your head till you get to a hundred, understand?"

"But why . . . ?"

Lang jabbed him with gun's muzzle. "Just do it!"

By the time Meadows finished counting, Lang and Leon were gone.

CHAPTER 48

472 Lafayette Drive
That Evening

SHOUTS OF GLEE AND MOANS OF despair were clear over engines at high rpm coming from the library as Manfred battled Leon on the world's fastest road course, *Le Mans*, through the magic of a video game. On the actual track, nearly eight and a half miles with few *chicanes*, or turns, speeds had reached 250 mph until both engine power and track configuration had been modified to slightly reduce the lethal speed. There were no such limitations placed on the virtual competitors.

The kitchen featured a much duller scene: Lang and Gurt loading the washer with the dinner dishes. Months ago, Lang had insisted Manfred be given a share of the duties, but small hands had proven far more adept at the joystick of a video game than handling breakable china and glassware.

"You think he'll be safe at the farm?" Lang asked for at least the third time.

Gurt was placing plates in the machine's rack. "Larry saved our lives, remember? He and Darleen can take care of Manfred."

The conversation concerned acreage Lang owned about an hour south of Atlanta, "the farm." Four or five years earlier, Lang and Gurt had retreated there after an abortive attempt on Lang's life. The then would-be assassins had attacked the small two-room farmhouse to be met with shotguns from the next-door neighbor, Larry Henderson, and his tenant, who had mistaken the criminals for poachers of their well-hidden marijuana crop.

Lang had reciprocated by getting the drug charges against Larry dismissed on an evidentiary technicality. Since then, Larry and his wife Darleen had become friends as well as guardians of Lang's property.

It had been Larry who had taught Manfred the joy of catching (if not cleaning) the bass and bream that populated the six-acre pond. For reasons Lang would never understand, the child was happier sharing the seat of Larry's 5E John Deere as he plowed fields prior to planting soybeans than riding in his father's turbo Porsche. Grumps viewed the noisy green tractor with suspicion if not open hostility, pacing and whining pitifully until his young master returned sweaty, dusty, and laughing. Lang suspected canine jealousy.

"What about Leon?"

Gurt was wiping her hands with a dish towel. "What about him?"

"I'm not sure I'm comfortable leaving him with Manfred. The guy is— was — a meth head, after all."

Gurt folded the towel, sat at the kitchen table, and intertwined her fingers, a sure sign she had given the matter thought. "First, Manfred will be with Larry and Darleen. They could not be more protective than his own *Grosseltern.* Perhaps more so when you consider what Larry and his man, Jerranito, can do with their shoot guns . . ."

"Shotguns."

"Shotguns." She held up two fingers. "Second, Leon has been off the drugs for some time, and who knows where he could get it in Lamar County."

Lang wasn't sure the few days Leon had become a member of the family equated "some time," and he was certain Gurt had no idea of the pervasiveness of the homemade drug.

"Third," she held up three fingers, "you are not going without someone to cover your backside." The fingers now became the palm of her hand, divided by the ugly scar from Turkey. "Besides, I am — how you say? Invested, yes, invested in getting this matter settled."

The crux of the discussion.

Lang placed the last glass in the dishwasher, shut it, and pushed the start button. "If we're going to go, we may as well move."

Gurt glanced out of the window at the late spring dusk. "It is better to wait until dark. I am not certain your BMF friends will be quick to forgive and forget that you have hissed them."

"Dissed. I disrespected their leader. But I'm sure they have better things to do than retaliate."

"Hissed, dissed. Amounts to same. People like that do not take insults lightly."

"That guy Meadows is a businessman. Revenge is a waste of his time."

Lang was rarely as mistaken as he was now.

CHAPTER 49

I-75 South
Fifty Minutes Later

MANFRED AND LEON OCCUPIED THE MIDDLE seats of the Mercedes ML 320 CDI, a Genesis portable game player between them. Grumps snored softly between suitcases and toys in the rear.

Lang slowed and glided onto an off-ramp.

"We are not an hour from the house," Gurt observed. "We need no fuel. Surely you do not already need to go to the toilet."

She could see him shake his head, a silhouette against the lights of the dashboard. "There's a car behind us. It's been there since a block from our driveway."

"You are sure?"

"Impossible to be sure at night, but let's see if it follows us into that McDonald's parking lot ahead. It would be too much of a coincidence if they wanted a Big Mac just as we pull in."

Gurt reached up to pull down the vanity mirror on the passenger side sun visor. Long ago Agency counter-surveillance techniques told her not to telegraph awareness of the car behind by turning around in her seat.

Lang almost passed the golden arches before making a sudden and unsignalled left turn into the drive-through lane. The pair of headlights in his mirror mimicked his move.

There were three cars ahead, four counting the one with the driver shouting his order into the microphone embedded in the oversized menu.

Lang slowed as if to stop before floor-boarding the accelerator. Although hardly nimble and less than speedy, the three-liter diesel engine actually squealed rubber as the SUV darted for the exit, barely missing a pile of curbing stones piled to one side of what Lang guessed was a street-widening job in progress.

Had there been any doubt as to the following car's intent, it would have dissipated as the auto swerved to speed around a car exiting the parking lot.

"What's up, dude?" Leon's voice came from the back seat. "We suddenly in a rush?"

"There's a car following us," Lang answered as the tires protested the sharpness of the turn onto the on-ramp.

"So, call the cops on your cell."

"And tell them what?" Gurt interjected. "That we are being followed?"

"No time anyway," Lang said between gritted teeth. "Here they come."

It was not until the following car pulled into the left lane that Lang recognized it as a dark-colored, large BMW, quite possibly the one in which Meadows had arrived at this afternoon's meeting. Whether it was or not, the light from the fast-receding McDonald's reflected off the weapon extending from the front passenger window.

"Manfred, tighten your seat belt."

"It's already tight."

"Suck in your breath and get it tighter. NOW!"

The instant the command left his lips, Lang's side mirror showed the BMW's headlights pull even with the Mercedes's left rear fender. He snatched the wheel to the left.

Sheet metal screamed as the BMW reeled sideways drunkenly. The heavier Mercedes shuddered but did not lose traction.

Manfred shrieked in fear.

"The fuck . . .?" Leon gasped.

Grumps was no longer snoring.

Lang lifted his eyes to the mirror, watching the headlights momentarily fade before growing again. "Here they come!"

He felt nearly helpless as the BMW pulled into the left lane again. This time, there was no effort to pull even. Instead, Lang could see a figure almost half out of the front passenger's window. His hands clasped something with a long, curved clip.

Lang slammed on the brakes.

The BMW tried to emulate but was a fraction of a second too late. Lang could see the terror in the shooter's eyes as he realized what Lang was about to do.

Sharply cutting the wheel to the left again, the man's upper torso was momentarily caught between the two vehicles. His scream as he was crushed almost drowned out the sound of metal on metal.

The BMW slowed, and Lang pulled away.

"A businessman, eh?" Gurt murmured. "Too busy for revenge, is it?"

"Save your sarcasm until we're out of this. They're coming on again."

Gurt reached down and picked up her purse, drawing out her Glock. "Perhaps . . ."

Lang took a hand from the wheel long enough to push it aside. "No telling how many are in that car or how many of what weapons they have. Our best chance is to not give them another opportunity."

"You have a plan?"

"I do. Listen up, Leon."

"Man, now is the time to call the cops!" he protested.

"And how long for the local law to get here? Think our friends in the BMW are going to wait?"

As he spoke, Lang took the next exit ramp, crossed the overpass, and headed back in the direction from which they had come. Just as he reached the bottom and pulled onto the interstate, he saw the battered BMW going the other way. It slammed on the brakes hard enough for the nose to dip and tires to smoke but made the exit ramp.

Their pursuers were not gaining as fast as before. Perhaps the two collisions had damaged the Beemer's suspension, Lang thought. Or having a man smashed between two cars had made them a little more cautious. Whatever, Lang's foot was hard against the floor as he headed up the next ramp and for the McDonald's.

He jolted to a stop at the edge of the parking lot's exit, threw off his seat belt, and almost rolled onto the ground in his haste to make a place for Gurt at the steering wheel. "C'mon, Leon. We don't have all day!"

The two men reached the curb just as the Mercedes's taillights vanished down the same entrance ramp it had used only minutes before. Lang and Leon flattened themselves behind the small pile of curbing stones as the

BMW flashed by perhaps a full minute later.

Lang grabbed one of the heavy stones, grunting with the effort. "Let's go, Leon. We only get one chance!"

With the pain in his shoulder forcing Leon to stop and go under the weight of the rock he was carrying, it seemed to take forever for each man to lug his stone to the overpass and lift it to the top of the wall running along the edge. They had just succeeded when Leon yelled, "There they are!"

To their left, headed north again, the Mercedes was speeding toward the off-ramp. Behind, the BMW followed. Sparks came from somewhere underneath. One or both impacts had knocked something loose. That was why the car wasn't quite as fast. Both cars would have to pass under the overpass bridge to reach the circular exit ramp, pass just below where Lang and Leon now stood.

The Mercedes slipped beneath their feet on the road below.

"Okay," Lang said as calmly as possible. "On my count."

The BMW was clearly visible from above. Even through a cracked windshield, Lang could see figures inside illuminated by the instrument panel.

"On three. One . . ."

The BMW was maybe 50 yards from the bridge now. Hitting a target moving at nearly a hundred miles an hour was not exactly shooting fish in a barrel.

"Two . . ."

At least there was no windage problem. The stones were far too heavy for any light spring breeze to alter the trajectory that would be straight down. Trajectory . . . Don't overthink a job already difficult.

"Three! Drop!"

The first stone struck the pavement no more than five feet in front of the BMW's grill. Before Lang could absorb the fact of a miss, the car braked hard, the reason the second rock scored a direct hit.

The bridge's lights showed a windshield dissolved into a translucency of spiderwebbing quickly turning crimson. The driver had not fared well. The automobile spun to its right, the front fender smashing into the concrete of the overpass's abutment in a shower of sparks. The scene below seemed to magically go to slow motion as the vehicle's bodywork folded up like an accordion. A tendril of smoke drifted lazily upward from somewhere underneath, followed by a whooshing sound that sucked the air from Lang's lungs and turned the BMW into a raging fireball, the heat from which scorched Lang's face.

He was transfixed for a second. Perhaps longer had Gurt's voice not come from behind him. "I do not think we have time for backside patting."

He turned to see the Mercedes, passenger door open. "Back. Back patting."

"Either way, the police will soon be here."

CHAPTER 50

Lamar County, Georgia
State Route 18
Half an Hour Later

THE ENTRANCE WOULD HAVE BEEN NEARLY invisible to anyone unaware of its existence. The height of the grass between the twin dirt tracks told Lang no one had been this way lately. A startled doe, eyes orange in the headlights, sprinted into the shadows followed by her spindly legged fawn.

If he saw her, Grumps showed little interest. He had learned his abilities did not equal the speed of the local whitetail deer. In fact, a number of his encounters with the local fauna had ended badly; notably, with a porcupine that had resulted in painful trip to the veterinarian in Barnesville. Harassment of a skunk had ended with Grumps being ostracized from his family, kept out of the house for nearly a week, and being given half a dozen baths.

Limiting his canine duties to mere barking seemed the better part of valor.

Lang had gone to some trouble to keep secret any connection between him and this place. County records would show ownership by a limited liability corporation whose agent for service, required by law, was a company in Atlanta. Utilities, gas, and electricity were billed to the LLC at a PO box in Atlanta. Water was pumped from a well on the premises.

In spite of the meticulous precautions, Lang's enemies had found him there once. He was never quite sure how, although he suspected he or Gurt had been careless in making sure they had not been followed, a problem he was certain had been solved tonight.

The Mercedes stopped at a steel gate, and Lang got out to put a key in the padlock. What was not visually apparent were the sets of spikes concealed by a thin layer of soil, sharpened points that would shred tires to spaghetti. Unseen, Lang could hear them sink back into place as the lock clicked open.

The stop woke Manfred, who had gotten over the earlier excitement and dozed off.

"We there yet?" he asked, the perpetual question of small children in automobiles.

"Almost," Lang replied. "I'm seeing light through the trees and brush."

The house, little more than a two-room cabin, stood in the center of an area Lang had had bush hogged to give clear field of fire should that ever become necessary again. It appeared every light in the small dwelling was on, as well as those strategically placed in tree branches.

The Mercedes came to a halt behind a mud-splattered pickup. Before Lang could cut the ignition, the cabin's door burst open revealing a man who could have passed for Santa Claus had his beard been white instead of red.

"Lang!" He charged the Mercedes, open-armed to smother Lang in an embrace.

Manfred had somehow squirmed out of his seat harness and past his mother. "Uncle Larry!"

Larry turned his attention to the small boy, hoisting him above his head, a feat Lang had not attempted in years.

"The fish bitin', Uncle Larry?"

Larry set him down. "Those fish are practically jumping outta the pond. They . . ."

He stooped and ran a hand along the Mercedes's side. "Damn, Lang! You beat this thing like a borrowed mule!"

"Lot of careless drivers on the road, Larry."

"Hope you got his number."

"You might say that."

"It *was* an accident?"

"Let's just say neither party expected it to happen like it did."

Larry shook his head as he stood erect. "Damage is the same no matter what happened. A rose by any other name."

Lang wasn't surprised at the quote from *Romeo and Juliet*. Larry believed the lack of a college education did not equate ignorance. His home was lined with bookshelves. Chaucer, Shakespeare, and Milton shouldered translations of Dante, Goethe, Rousseau, and Tolstoy. Bertrand Russell competed for space with Aristotle, Plato, Nietzsche, and Jung. The Classists through the Existentialists. Nor were the historians ignored: Pliny the Younger's account of Pompeii's destruction was only a shelf above Manchester's multivolume biography of Churchill.

Lang wondered how the man found time for farming.

"Well, y'all c'mon in!" Darleen stepped out of the house.

A plump yet attractive woman, Darleen viewed Manfred as the child she and Larry had always wanted.

She ran a hand through his hair. "I just finished churnin' some ice cream for blueberry cobbler. We got more blueberries this year than ever." She shot a glance at Gurt, fully aware of her dietary regimen for her son. "'Course he got to eat his collards an' green beans first. An' the chicken I baked special."

Gurt managed a smile she didn't feel. Although Larry and Darleen were loving custodians, Gurt did not approve of the southern cuisine, food she found as bland as it was fattening. The collards, she was sure, had been seasoned with bacon fat. Darleen had made a major concession by baking the chicken rather than frying it. But she hadn't mentioned the cornbread stuffing that was as certain as death itself.

Later that evening Lang and Gurt were alone in the cabin's single bedroom after Larry and Darleen had taken Manfred and Leon across the small creek that formed the boundary between their farm and Lang's acreage.

"Don't worry, they'll take good care of him," Lang said.

"It is not the care that worries. It is the extra weight Manfred will gain."

"If he does, he'll grow into it in six months."

She had no reply. Lang's observation on his son's growth rate was accurate.

The two were silent for a few minutes before Gurt asked, "It is necessary, you believe, this trip?"

Lang nodded before he realized she couldn't see the gesture in the dark room. "You do too, if you think about it. Remember one of the first lessons the Agency taught: forgive thy enemies at thy peril. Certain people see forgiveness as weakness. And you can bet Alex Kolstas is one of them. He won't forget being made a fool of in front of his men. Besides, he's a link to getting to whoever is willing to kill for a blood sample. Also, I need to visit with that geneticist, Dr. Phoebe Kalonimos."

CHAPTER 51

Trikoupi Street
Piraeus, Greece
Two Days Later

Purse over her shoulder, she swayed on five-inch spike heels as she passed the nautical museum. The skirt was tight enough across the back to reveal the movement of every muscle in her shapely derriere. The low cut of her blouse was filled with bulging breasts like an overflowing fruit basket. The blond hair that reached her mid-back seemed to move on its own.

She did not look like the Albanian women who constituted the bulk of Greece's illegal street-walking prostitutes, nor did she resemble the one thousand or so locals who were licensed, regulated, and largely confined to legal brothels. Her jewelry — watch, ring, and bracelets — was tasteful rather than flashy.

The four dark-skinned men lounged in front of number 37. They spoke in a mixture of English and Urdu, the two official languages of their native Pakistan, but anyone who had ears had little trouble guessing the subject of the conversation. If not, doubt disappeared when the woman dug a cigarette out of her purse. Four lighters sprung to life and were proffered.

If unspoken, the men's intentions were equally clear, as the woman's above-the-knee skirt rose when she leaned against a wall while she smoked.

Among the buildings on the next block, the ones whose backs touched the rear of those on Trikoupi Street, was a small *taverna*. There was nothing to distinguish it from half a dozen others within a three- or four-block area.

Lunch customers had already departed, leaving a single elderly gentleman hunched over a small glass whose cloudy bluish contents suggested ouzo cut with water. His hands, blue-veined with age, were unsteady as he sampled, then bit into the *mezes*, the appetizers of fish, chips, olives, and feta cheese that traditionally accompanied the liqueur. His gray hair was long, touching the frayed collar of his working man's shirt. He regarded his surroundings with rheumy eyes magnified by thick glasses to resemble those of a fish.

As the establishment's staff, a father, mother, and son, busied themselves clearing tables, replacing tablecloths, and loading dishes into the sink, the sole customer rose unsteadily and made his way toward the back and the unisex toilet. Once inside, he squeezed into the small space between the sink and commode. From the pocket of his shabby jacket, he produced a small bag and laid it on the lip of the sink before turning on the water.

Touching his head, there was a swish as he tossed the white wig into the trash basket, revealing the thick brown hair of a much younger man. The spectacles followed the wig. From the bag he produced a cloth that he soaked under the faucet before running it across his face. An observer, had the tiny room been large enough to accommodate one, would have been justified in believing he had witnessed magic. Or at least a visit to the mythical Fountain of Youth. The wrinkles lining the old man's forehead were gone, as were the laugh lines around his eyes, the furrows bracketing his mouth, and the loose flesh under the chin had joined the wig and glasses as he peeled back flesh-colored plastic. He used his hands to scoop water into his eyes to dilute the drops. Bright blue eyes stared back out of the mirror.

Upstairs at nearby 37 Trikoupi Street, Alkandres Kolstas was at his desk comparing numbers provided by his army of accountants. He smiled. The world economy might be sluggish, but oil smuggling was increasingly profitable, as was the percentage he received for the transportation of narcotics on his ships. And then there were the occasional windfalls such as intimidation, strong-arm, or even murder for hire, blackmail, or kidnapping.

The thought of the latter wiped the smile from his face. The Reilly matter had gone badly, and his American customers were becoming increasingly insistent about the return of their money. Not that there was a prayer of a refund, but such things were bad for business. Hiring blacks had been a mistake, but they had been the only really organized entity he knew in the Atlanta area. He . . .

He straightened in his chair, certain he had heard something but unsure of what it had been. He paused, head cocked, before returning to the columns of numbers.

The totals on raw Afghan and Turkish heroin, opium, smuggled on behalf of the Pakistanis, were down. The brown, latex-like substance was easy enough to conceal in the false bottoms of oil barrels, mostly those headed for Marseilles, where it would be boiled in open pots, strained, reheated, and dried in the sun, thereby removing most of the toxic alkaloids. Then it was cut in exact measurements, packaged, and sent on its way throughout Europe and the West where it would be diluted or "cut" with everything from baby laxative to baking soda to dishwashing detergent before being sold on the street.

Kolstas scowled. Not for a second did he believe the demand for product was down. It was all too easy to believe the fucking Pakis were using his ships to transport more than they admitted. They . . .

That sound again, this time definitely coming from the stairs behind the tapestry. Someone had found the passage from the taverna!

Well, whoever he was, coming up those steps would be his greatest and last mistake. He reached under the desk to press a button.

At that second, the tapestry was ripped loose. The door behind it was open, and Lang Reilly, Glock in hand, stood staring at Kolstas. And he didn't look happy.

Reilly, of course! Who else knew of the door behind the tapestry? And who other than a rash American would dare come here alone?

Kolstas swallowed his surprise as he pushed his chair away from the wall to give Lang easier entry. "Well, well. Mr. Reilly. To what do I owe the pleasure?"

Lang stepped into the room, his weapon pointed at Kolstas's head. "Try guessing, Alex. Try remembering what I said would happen if you fucked with my family. Or you might guess I'm here to find out who paid you to try to snatch me."

The Greek raised both hands in mock surrender. "I never was much at guessing, but you try it: guess how many of my men are on their way up here right now. Answer: more than enough to make you regret you came back."

Lang pursed his lips, a man in thought. "Wrong answer. The correct number is zero."

For the first time there was a crack in Kolstas's confident demeanor. "They should arrive any second, along with a business associate arriving at the airport. My man should be bringing him here any moment now."

Lang sat on the far corner of the desk, the Glock pointed so the Greek was looking down the barrel. "Try again. The button under your desk. In fact, just keep it pressed."

Kolstas was making no effort at calmness now. "What have you done with my men?"

"Me? Nothing. Let's say they are being otherwise entertained while you and I discuss business. Like, for instance, who paid you to have me kidnapped?"

A shaky grin crept across Kolstas's face. "You think I will tell you so you can then kill me? Really, Mr. Reilly . . ."

Lang's gun hand moved faster than Kolstas's eyes could follow. The muzzle collided with his jaw with an audible crunch, the impact sending him sprawling onto the floor.

Shaking his head, he ran a hand across his face, glumly looking at the red streak across his palm. A second later, he felt a surge of pain along with air along his teeth. Reilly's blow had slit the cheek literally wide open.

Lang slid off the desk. "I don't get an answer, I promise you will be begging me to kill you."

Holding onto a corner of the desk, Kolstas struggled to his feet. "And if I tell you?"

"I'll forget the attempt at kidnapping. Believe me, it's the best deal anyone is giving you today."

Kolstas's mind was racing. How to tell this American something, anything, that would delay him until he could somehow summon help? Where were the Pakis who were supposed to be right outside the outside entrance?

CHAPTER 52

Yerkes National Primate Research Center
201 Dowman Drive
Emory University Campus
Atlanta, Georgia
At the Same Time

DEVINA SHASTRI, PH.D., SMILED, WHITE TEETH bright against a mocha face as she peered through the bars of a cage from which a rhesus macaque monkey returned the look. "Birbal," she said, reaching to unlatch the wire door, "come here so we may see if you are as healthy as you look."

It was strictly against the center's policy to give the animals names. To do so was to potentially humanize them, perhaps clouding the researcher's judgment. Officially the monkey was J-112-7, but when Devina selected him from the Research Center's stock of test animals at its "Main Station" some 50 miles away, she had given him a name meaning Brave Heart in her native Hindi, appropriate for the pink-faced creature whose origins were also in northern India.

Birbal was shy, cowering in the far corner of his cage. Small wonder. Contact with humans usually meant one of two things: feeding or something unpleasant like a series of shots, prodding and poking, or a rectal thermometer. He bared small but sharp teeth, screeching in his most threatening voice.

"Come now, Birbal," Devina cooed, "don't be like that. I have a treat."

She produced an orange, Birbal's favorite.

Eyes as brown as hers narrowed slightly, an expression as skeptical of the offer as a voter of a politician's promises.

She rolled the fruit around the palm of her hand, a temptation.

With a movement so quick it almost eluded the eye, Birbal snatched the orange and retreated to the limits of his cage where he began to peel it, his eyes still locked on hers.

Devina sighed. "You really must learn to play fair, Birbal," she scolded mildly. "You have your orange, but I still have my tasks to do."

If the monkey felt remorse, he didn't show it. Instead, his teeth dug into the soft pulp as orange juice drizzled from his chin.

His reaction was hardly surprising. It was a scene researcher and subject had played out before. Devina pulled up a tall stool that allowed her to watch as she consulted a thick file attached to a steel clipboard. She was not aware of the specific purpose of this experiment, but she was curious. Ordinarily, a series of tests on primates — rhesus monkeys, chimpanzees, spider monkeys, sooty mangabey — would take years. This one was being rushed. Her only real clue was the fact that rhesus monkeys were usually used in testing serums once the product had passed what Devina called "the rat test." Chimpanzees, as man's closest relative, were favored for behavioral experiments and studies, the mangabeys for observing infectious diseases such as tuberculosis, and so on.

Birbal had been on a toxic diet. Really toxic. Increasing amounts of various poisons: arsenic, strychnine, cyanide, even ricin had been mixed with his food along with the natural or herbal toxins, curare, mandrake, belladonna, henbane. At the moment, no ill effects had been noted, although the little monkey was getting enough of the stuff to kill an adult human. As if that wasn't enough, the poor animal was injected weekly with venom from nearly every snake, lizard, or scorpion available. As far as Devina could tell, the only things missing were the marine animals, the lion or scorpion fish, sea snakes, or the delectable but potentially deadly *fugu* fish so popular among the Japanese.

He also received a steady flow of other injections simply noted as X-421. As far as Devina could tell, nobody either at the Main Station or here on the Emory campus quarters of the Center knew what X-421 was. Only the prefix, the "X," designated it as experimental. When she had mentioned her curiosity to Dr. Yancey, Chief of Practical Research, he had simply shrugged his shoulders and made a very pointed suggestion that a junior research assistant was wise not to ask questions the Center obviously did not want asked, much less answered.

Birbal had finished his orange, pieces of peel littering his cage like an outbreak of spring flowers. This time he showed only token resistance as she lifted him from the cage and strapped him to the miniature examining table facedown. She placed a black bag beside him, the type doctors used for house calls in the days before medical insurance put a premium on the volume of patients seen and Medicare/Medicaid made health care a sacred right.

A diminutive stethoscope told her the monkey's heartbeat was normal. So was the pulse, blood pressure, and — through the hated thermometer — temperature. She drew a few centimeters of blood, although she was quite sure this would also produce results remarkable only in that they were normal.

Exactly what was going on? Yerkes Primate Center was trying very hard to kill Birbal and not doing a very good job of it. His invulnerability surely had something to do with the mysterious X-421. But what?

The obvious answer was that the Center, in conjunction with some bio lab, was working on an induced immunity to natural and chemical poisons.

Four years of undergraduate study, five more to get a PhD in biochemistry, and two here at Yerkes, and she was working on something that potentially had military implications. She had made her position on such things quite clear before taking this job: wars would only cease when the military no longer existed. If one major power, the United States, for example, no longer had an army, there would be no need for, say, China, to suffer that expense, either. The savings could go to world hunger, a plague her native land knew all too well.

Pacifism was a position she had thought Emory University embraced also. Over a thousand students had marched in protest at Fort Benning; the school gave a platform to a notoriously dove-ish former U.S. President, as incompetent as he was idealistic; the school paper excoriated the military with regularity; and only 9/11 had prompted the school to allow ROTC on campus after a 30-year absence.

Birbal's screeching shattered her indignation for the moment.

She released him from the straps, taking a few minutes to bounce him in her arms as she would an infant.

She would definitely have to speak to Dr. Yancey about this, seek his assurance that the project was for the common good, not for the military-industrial complex, which she regarded as a single entity, as evil and destructive as Lord Shiva's consort Kali.

Yes, she would speak to Dr. Yancey

CHAPTER 53

Trikoupi Street

THE ANSWER TO KOLSTAS'S LAST QUESTION was that his men were right where they were supposed to be. Three of the four, anyway. Perhaps not in the condition he might have preferred, but there nonetheless.

Five or six minutes earlier, the big blonde had ground out her cigarette and was smiling enticingly to the shortest of the four men, a good three or four inches shorter than the blond. Iron filings to a magnet, he sauntered over with a sheepish grin on his face.

Placing a hand on either side of his head and tilting his face upward as though to kiss him, she leaned forward. The others, snickering and making what were certainly lewd comments, came closer.

Instead of a kiss, she stomped his foot, digging in one of the spike heels. Howling with pain, he bent down only to receive a blow on the back of the neck from clasped hands. As intended, it landed at the juncture of the cervical spine and the thoracic spine, delivered with the motion and intensity of a medieval headsman performing a public execution. A little harder blow from the hammer of those hands and the disks might well have separated along with the spinal cord. As it was, the victim's knees bent, and he started what would have been a full face-plant on the sidewalk.

Instead, her own knee caught the side of his head, delivering the *coup de grace*. Instead of his face, he went over backward, the rear of his skull thumping on the concrete sidewalk.

Before he hit, his comrades overcame their astonishment enough to attempt to come to his aid. The first, a tall man missing a front tooth, grabbed the back of her blouse with one hand, the other drawn back in a fist.

In addition to hands and feet, the human body has any number of weapon-grade angles and joints, which, if employed correctly, are just as destructive as, say, a fist to the face. The Agency's physical training included the appropriate use of all of them.

Had the woman's present attacker, the one who grabbed the back of her blouse, known this, he might have chosen another stratagem. As it was, his reward for snatching the clothing from behind was the swift delivery of a well-aimed elbow into the right orbital rim, possibly fracturing its floor.

Few things are more distracting to a belligerent than possibly being blinded by the shattering of an eye socket. He forgot the woman for the moment, dropping to his knees as his hands went to his face.

Somewhere there was the sound of a cell phone ringing, or rather, buzzing. Under the circumstances, no one paid it a lot of attention despite its persistence.

The two remaining men showed a great deal more caution than the first two. There was the snick of switchblades opening as a pair of six- to nine-inch blades reflected the afternoon sun.

The woman showed more interest than fear as the two attempted to get her between them.

The closest was making slashing movements as he closed in, the sure mark of the amateur. The movement takes the participant off-balance with each move, whereas a simple stabbing movement allows an immediate return to an even weight distribution and, if successful, is much more likely to produce a lethal result.

It was a lesson the man closest to her was about to learn in the harshest terms.

Crossing his chest with his right hand, the one with the knife, he sliced empty air where the woman's throat had been milliseconds earlier. Before his swing reached its limit, she was inside the arc described by his arm. Both hands grabbed the wrist as her foot blocked his. Using his own momentum, she snatched the wrist downward, sending him airborne before she gave a final twist, turning the blade inward.

Had he had time to think, he might have dropped the weapon. Instead, he conceded to the natural impulse to hold onto it. Consequently, his contact with the sidewalk ended with a grunt and spurt of blood as he literally fell on his own blade.

The woman's back was now to the wall as her gaze darted back and forth in search of the fourth man. The only evidence of his existence was the sound of rapid footsteps rounding the near corner in a speedy retreat.

Two elderly women, each draped in a black shawl, stared at her, mouths, nearly devoid of teeth, agape. She smiled at them and they scurried away as though fearing she might turn her deadly attention to them next.

She expelled a breath loudly before leaning over the two living, moaning men. She reached inside each jacket, extracting first a Glock, then a 9mm Beretta. She removed the magazine of each, jacked the chambered rounds onto the sidewalk to be followed by the weapons themselves. She then rolled the dead man over, extracting the switchblade. Holding the bloody thing between two fingers as she might hold the tail of a dead rat, she moved toward a doorway.

She had guessed correctly. Although the four men had carried firearms, they chose to use silent if less deadly means instead. By the time they recognized a serious error in judgment, it was too late.

She looked up and down the street. Although she would have bet that any number of eyes followed her every move from behind shuttered windows, the two old women, retreating at a surprising rapid pace, were the sidewalk's only other occupants.

Turning, she opened the door of number 37 Trikoupi Street and went inside, careful to turn the dead bolt behind her.

CHAPTER 54

GURT REACHED THE TOP OF THE THIRD flight of stairs and opened an old-fashioned half-wood, half-opaque-glass door. She locked it behind her before taking in the scene in the office. An older man, Alex, she guessed, was unsuccessfully trying to staunch the blood from a wound that seemed to grin at her before she realized she was seeing teeth through an open cheek. He was trying to stand by holding the corner of a desk. His shirt, pants, and a good part of the rug beneath his feet were bathed in blood.

Lang languished on the far corner of the desk, his Glock held almost casually, pointed at the other man.

He nodded toward her. "That, Alex, my friend, is why your men weren't here to help you." He addressed Gurt. "Casualty count?"

Gurt tried not to stare at the hideous grin the slashed cheek made. "One won't be working for Alex again. Two might make it with medical attention, and the fourth is a, a *schnelles Laufer?*"

"Er, fast runner, a sprinter," Lang translated for Alex's benefit. "Apparently one of your bodyguards chose to run rather than fight. Now, Alex, if you'll give me the name of whoever hired you to kidnap . . ."

Speaking with a cheek literally spilt open gave the Greek's voice a wet lisp. "Reilly, I wouldn't last long if I gave out that sort of information."

"What makes you think your prospects are any better right now?"

Kolstas gave what might have been a snort of contempt. "You Americans have no stomach for killing in cold blood. You prosecute men who torture to get information from those who would destroy you and condemn your warriors who kill those who would kill them."

"The lady here isn't American, and she has a real specialty with that knife."

The Greek looked at the blade Gurt still held. "To do what, cut off fingers?"

Lang nodded to Gurt. "Actually, I had another appendage in mind."

Lang grabbed Kolstas from behind, locking his arms behind him. The target of Gurt's gaze made him begin to struggle frantically. She deftly sidestepped a kick as she stepped inside his legs and unzipped his fly. She stretched his flaccid organ to its limit.

"Not much of a loss, I'd say," Lang offered. "But then, it's not mine. Last chance, Alex. Oh, yeah, the balls come next. They go into your eye sockets while you choke on your own dick. Cute little trick I learned from the boys of al Qaeda."

The Greek's face was shiny with sweat. He could not take his eyes away from the hand that held his most private part. "You win Reilly, you win. But you promise if I give you what you want, you'll forgive me for trying to kidnap your son, right?"

"You have my word."

Glaring at Gurt with icy hatred, Kolstas let go of the desk long enough to zip his pants. "There's a man in the States, name of Grassley."

"Does Mr. Grassley have a first name? A place of employment perhaps?"

"He owns, or operates, a drug company."

Lang and Gurt exchanged glances. "Drugs?" Lang asked. "You mean pharmaceuticals?"

He nodded wearily. "Medicines, whatever the American word is. His company makes them. He asked me to find a place to test one of them some years ago. I didn't hear from him again until a month or so ago. He wanted something you had and had a very good idea how to go about getting it. I'm pretty sure it was him."

"You aren't sure?"

The Greek took a moment to dab at his bleeding cheek with an already bloody shirtsleeve. "Couldn't recognize the voice after all that time, but the electronic transfer came from the same account in Barclay's Bank of the Cayman Islands as before. I was curious. I checked account numbers."

"Anything else you can tell me?"

"Nothing more I needed to know. I had instructions and cash."

Gurt had put away the knife and substituted her iPad. "Dystra Pharmaceuticals. Grassley is the seeo."

"Seeo?"

"How else is C-E-O pronounced?"

"CEO, chief executive officer. Think, head of the company."

"Whatever. It is located in Atlanta."

"That should make it easy enough," Kolstas lisped, edging toward the door.

Lang brought the Glock to bear. "Where the hell you think you're going?"

"My face . . . I need medical . . ." The Greek's eyes widened as he realized what was about to happen. "You promised!"

"I promised I'd forgive you and I have. Like John Kennedy said, though, 'Forgive thy enemies but remember their names.' I remember you are the one who tried to have my son kidnapped."

Before Kolstas could speak, Lang shot him squarely between the eyes. He died with an unspoken protest on his parted lips.

Gurt and Lang watched his open eyes roll back into his head as though to examine the red spot on his forehead, as his grip on the desk relaxed and he slithered to the floor.

"It is to hope you have no regrets," Gurt said.

"I could have no regret bigger than for him to live and be successful next time," Lang responded. "Now, let's get out of here before either the cops or more of his goons come looking for us."

And they did.

CHAPTER 55

Mandraki Harbor
Rhodes Town
Island of Rhodes
The Next Morning

LANG AND GURT COULD HAVE BEEN tourists admiring the twin harbors. The smaller of the two, Mandraki, was host to yachts, sailboats, and small working craft, while cruise ships, cargo vessels, and the occasional military ship occupied the other. Across the harbor, they could see the roof of the city's old synagogue; over their right shoulders, the tower and dome of the Mosque of Suleiman. To the right was the tower of St. Paul. All testimony to the fertile soil of religion that had nurtured a variety of faiths over the ages. And why not? Asia Minor was a ghost in the northern haze; European culture as close as the next island. Here the colossus of the sun god, Helios, had supposedly straddled the entrance with a light visible to the Aegean's ancient mariners for 20 or so miles, a beacon extinguished when it tumbled into the sea as a result of an earthquake in 237 B.C.

The truth, Lang suspected, was that the 100-foot-plus stature had actually been mounted where the Palace of the Grand Masters now stood on a slight hill behind him, thereby increasing the distance at which the light could be seen. The fourteenth-century fortress itself had survived earthquake and siege only to succumb to an accidental explosion of its powder magazine in 1856. Mussolini had it carefully restored during the Italian occupation of the 1930s before the island was returned to Greece in 1947 after 700 years of foreign rule.

Although rich in both scenery and history, the harbor itself held little interest for either Lang or Gurt. Lang idly watched a ferry dock across the quay in the larger harbor. Passengers swarmed down a none-too-secure gangplank like ants sallying from a nest under attack.

Gurt turned her head, seeming to take in the entire panorama from behind oversized sunglasses. Actually, she was looking for a familiar face, anyone who might have shared the Aegean Airlines Airbus A300 from Athens. The ordinary tourist would head straight from Diagoras International Airport to his hotel; a business traveler to his destination. The purpose of anyone who traveled the eight-plus miles from the airport directly here could well be following Gurt and Lang.

Unlikely, but possible.

After wiping the knife clean of prints and finding and pocketing the single shell casing of the shot that had killed Kolstas, Gurt and Lang had left by the front entrance on the theory they would be less likely noticed than exiting through the tavern. A block away, two police cars screamed past. Someone in the neighborhood had finally noticed what had gone on in front of 37 Trikoupi Street, or one of the Greek's minions had made a grisly discovery.

Two blocks over, they had taken a cab to the Acropolis, a common tourist destination. From there, a bus to the sculpture-lined walls of the Dafni Metro Station and on to the airport. Neither Gurt nor Lang detected anything to indicate they were being followed.

The same seemed to be true here in Rhodes Town.

Doing an about-face, the pair strolled through the yellow stone, crenelated double towers of the Marine Gate to enter the walled part of the old city.

A right turn followed by a left into Odos Ippoton brought them to the slight incline that was the medieval Street of the Knights. More yellow stone, this time twin rows lining the north and south sides of the road. It was here the Knights of St. John, subsequently called the Knights of Malta, took refuge after the fall of Jerusalem in 1291. Buying the island of Rhodes from a Genoese pirate whose title was doubtful at best, they then conquered the native Greek population before fortifying their acquisition and building this series of buildings or inns, each with the crest of its residents' native land displayed in stone beside or above the door.

On the south side, below a bridge arching over the street to connect the inns of Spain and Provence, an open gate gave into a large courtyard, formed into a rectangle by the rears of buildings facing four separate streets. As a casual tourist, Gurt stepped through. Lang remained behind, ostensibly fascinated by the armorial bearings of France carved in a wall above his head. He waited until he was surrounded by a tour group of chattering, camera– and cell phone–clicking Japanese behind a woman hoisting aloft a standard consisting of a bright red bow, tied to an umbrella shaft. As she began her lecture, he slipped inside.

Again, he and Gurt were not being followed, as far as he could tell.

Once inside the square, sheltered from the sea breeze, the dry heat was debilitating, although it seemed not to adversely affect the profusion of oleander and bougainvillea that painted whitewashed walls with rainbow colors. In front of Lang a dozen or so tables were shaded by umbrellas bearing the logos of several beers. The place was full of lunching day-trippers. Gurt sat at a table with an older lady, who, despite the heat, had a shawl draped around her narrow shoulders. Her hair was in a tight steel-colored bun.

Lang stood beside her. "Dr. Kalonimos?"

She extended a hand road-mapped with blue veins and smiled with teeth that showed a lifetime lived with tobacco. "You noticed I was the only woman here with a shawl in this beastly heat, as I told you I would be. And you can call me Phoebe."

Her British accent hinted at Oxford or Cambridge.

Lang slid into a chair to her left, Gurt's right, and waved to a passing waiter. Unsurprisingly, the man looked in every direction but Lang's. Lang had long suspected some secret worldwide union of servers demanded its membership direct eyes away from customers at all times.

Realizing he was likely to perish of thirst before he got the waiter's attention, Lang stood up. "What might I get you ladies?"

Gurt wanted a beer, Phoebe a chilled glass of Argyros.

Lang went to a small bar set up in the green shade of a cedar tree, waited until he had the barkeeper's attention, and asked, "Beer? Wine?"

He was presented with a menu unreadable in Greek letters and unpronounceable in the English subtext. Must be a lunch menu, not a list of drinks.

He waived until he had the barkeep's eye again. "*Cold* beer?"

This time he had better luck. He was given a list of beers that would have done credit to any well-stocked American tavern. Budweiser, Heineken, Amstel. Everything but a Greek beer. For not the first time, Lang was puzzled. In major cities across the world — or at least the western part of it — Mythos was available. Sometimes Hellas or Athenian, too. Everywhere except Greece. The tavern at the museum had been an exception. Was Greek beer so superior that it was more profitable to sell in the sounder economies of Western Europe or America? Was there a national conspiracy to keep the golden lager of Mythos from foreigners? Was the mysterious servers' union part of it?

"You are woolgathering?" He hadn't noticed Gurt had come to stand beside him. The question was her expression for daydreaming, staring into space, or being oblivious in general to one's surroundings.

"Er, no. I was hoping to get a Greek beer."

She ran a finger down the list of international beers. "They have Lowenbrau, Pauli Girl, Becks. Why would you want Greek beer?"

Gurt could be downright chauvinistic when it came to beer. But then, she was German.

They ordered and returned to the table, bottles and a carafe of white wine sweating in their hands. Seated, Lang took a grateful pull. After the heat, he could not have enjoyed the finest champagne more. He took several more greedy gulps and was surprised to find the bottle empty.

He ordered another and turned to survey the small taverna's patrons. About an even mix of men and women, most fair-skinned and showing varying degrees of sun exposure. As at the harbor, no one seemed to be paying any attention to him.

None of that meant a lot. A true professional would blend into any gathering like a chameleon against its native backdrop. Lang noted with unease how many windows faced the small plaza, any one of which could easily conceal an observer or assassin. His and Gurt's only real defense was that he had severed the head of the snake, left Kolstas's criminal organization without its leader. He was playing this fact off against plan B — taking a time-consuming, circuitous route to Rhodes by means of an indirect path to the island, a series of ferries where no one took passengers' names.

With a little luck, the Pakistanis who manned the dead Greek's unlawful enterprises would never know he and Gurt were still in Greece, let alone Rhodes. It was also possible the removal of Kolstas would mean the disintegration of his gang or that the members of it would be too busy in-fighting for leadership to consider revenge.

Phoebe was pouring her second glass from the carafe. "From your phone call, I understand you are interested in old King Mithradates, or at least his genetics."

Lang considered the possibly debilitating effects of a third beer and decided water would combat the heat almost as well, even if he had to buy the bottled variety. "Well, I'm interested in whether his self-attained immunity to poisons was a trait that could be inherited."

Phoebe sighed, disappointed. "Always the toxins with Mithradates. No one seems to care he was the greatest Hellenic leader of the post-Classical period, that he gave the mighty Roman Republic a scare they hadn't seen since Hannibal. They pulled their greatest general, Pompey, off another campaign just to prevent Mithradates from pushing Rome out of Asia."

"By 'Asia,' you meant modern-day Turkey?" Lang asked.

"Essentially."

Lang regarded his now-empty bottle with remorse. This heat was going to make him very thirsty. "I acknowledge the man doesn't get the fame history owes him, but what I'm interested in . . ."

Phoebe nodded. "The genetics, could they be passed along like the genes that give some people blue eyes or blond hair."

Lang had not noted Gurt leaving the table. He did notice the frosty plastic bottle of Evian she placed before him.

He looked up. "How did you know?"

"That you were thinking about another cold beer and if it would be too many? You kept looking at the bar instead at Phoebe."

Maybe so, but he never got used to the way she read his mind. He turned his attention back to the professor. "We were talking about the genetics of blue eyes and blond hair."

Phoebe reached over, took the Evian bottle, and poured about a third of it into her now-empty wineglass.

"Or the possibility of inheriting them."

She paused to take a sip. "There are traits that are clearly passed along, generation to generation, and those that are not. It was once believed that the tendency to be a, say, criminal, was inherited. Today we know that criminality is more a product of environment than bloodline. The question is, where do you draw the line between the two? For example, dogs are the only members of the canine family that are domesticated. It is thought they descended from wolves man tamed. Yet puppies are born domesticated. Genetics or environment?"

"Dogs?" Lang asked skeptically.

He would have said more, but a gesture from Gurt told him to listen, not talk.

"Russian scientists are conducting an interesting experiment with *Vulpes Lagopus*, the arctic fox: dogs, the only domestic canine, wag their tails, the only canine that does. The Russians have raised a number of fox cubs as pets and those foxes' descendants, though far from completely domesticated, wag their tails."

"I'm not sure I get your point," Lang said.

Not quite true: he had not the vaguest idea of what her point might be.

"The point is, why do the pet foxes wag their tails, something no other wild canine does? Has there been some mutation of genes, or has the environment of their parents influenced the behavior of yet-unborn pups? In Mithradates' case, did his linage inherit an acquired immunity just as the fox pups inherited an acquired trait, or was it something in the environment?"

Lang was beginning to realize that, as is so often the case, this woman, an academic, was more interested in the question than the answer.

Gurt gave him a look that said to be patient.

"I was told there was an antitoxin in a young Turkish boy's blood, an immunity to snake venom among other things," Lang ventured.

Phoebe was looking covetously at the bottle of Evian. Lang gallantly poured the remaining water into her wineglass, once again empty.

When she had emptied that, she said, "Yes, but was the immunity hereditary or developed from the environment in which the child lived?"

Lang felt he was chasing his tail. "I guess it really doesn't matter how his immune system developed. The important thing is whether or not it, whatever 'it' is, can be isolated so as to be shared."

She was looking around, distracted. "If it is in his genes, so to speak, there is a process by which it can be isolated. If environmental . . ." She stood. "You would think they have a loo, a W.C., somewhere."

Gurt pointed. "On the other side of the bar."

The geneticist pushed her chair back. "Oh, thank you! Excuse me!"

Gurt and Lang watched her hurriedly pick her way between tables before Gurt observed, "She is no help. We know no more than we did an hour ago."

"A little more, maybe, including the fact we're going to be picking up her lunch tab if we stay much longer. Problem is, she has no clue if we're talking about a Mithradates gene or the effects of living on the northern Turkish coast. She . . ."

Phoebe's return interrupted the conversation. Lang stood as she seated herself.

"Well, now, where was I?"

"Isolating genes."

"Oh, yes. Gene therapy — the adding or modifying of certain genes in human cells, usually to combat a disease. Hemophilia B, for instance, has been successfully treated by gene therapy."

Whatever she had done in the ladies room had changed her personality from obtuse to informative. Both Gurt and Lang sat in amazement that they tried not to show as she continued.

"The current thinking is that some form of gene therapy might prevent contracting the HIV virus."

"Another form of immunity?" Lang asked.

"Possibly. But modified genes cannot be inherited."

"Then Mithradates' descendants could not have acquired his immunities to poisons and toxins."

Phoebe shrugged. "Mr. Reilly, science has barely scratched the surface of differentiating between environment and genetics. Just like the foxes I mentioned, no one is sure where one begins and the other ends. We know that inherited immunity is a genetic immunity to disease. An acquired immunity is like an immunity to certain diseases a person has survived. One who lived through the plague, for instance, will never have it again because certain cells of the body have a memory that activates the immune system if that particular antigen is contracted again. That, like inoculation, would be environmental immunity.

"Certain immunities are clearly inherited, the most common example being those passed from mother to child through prenatal inoculations or breast milk. How long they last varies, and it is doubtful they can be inherited a second time.

"There are racial and ethnic immunities also. Most native Africans have varying degrees of immunity to malaria, while sickle-cell anemia is uncommon among those of European linage.

"I cannot deny the possibility that certain ethnic groups can develop unique immunities such as those of the child you mentioned, quite likely through a Darwinian 'survival of the fittest' process. Many Africans who don't develop immunity to malaria die before they can pass on their genes. Perhaps a resistance to the venom of a particularly common snake was a condition of survival in the area the child lived in."

"Could the resistance to malaria, the gene that causes it, be isolated and transferred to a European?"

Phoebe shook her head. "So far, no. But then, there are a number of preventatives available. The big incentive these days is to engineer a gene that resists cancer and can be artificially transmitted."

Lang slouched back into his chair. He was getting progressively more uncomfortable as rivulets of sweat were making the back of his shirt damp. "So, basically, what you're telling us, Dr. Kalonimos, is that so far as you know, an immunity is not something that could be passed down for two millennia from family to child?"

"That is both true and not true, Mr. Reilly. I think I mentioned ethnic immunities, such as to malaria. I know of no case, though, where an acquired immunity, such as that attributed to King Mithradates, has been inherited. But that does not mean it is impossible. Only that it has not been observed. The science of gene transferal and genetic engineering is where in vitro fertilization was, say, half a century ago."

Lang leaned forward, elbows on the table. "Let me ask you a hypothetical question, Doctor. Assume that a young boy on the northern coast of Turkey is bitten by a poisonous snake. Also assume that, other than the puncture wounds, he suffers no ill effects. Assume further that he comes from a small sub-ethnic group in an area where Mithradates and his famed immunity once reigned in the first century B.C. Now, given those facts, Doctor, would you say it was possible that boy's immunity was inherited? And if so, could that trait, immunity, relate all the way back?"

The doctor looked puzzled.

"You will have to forgive him," Gurt spoke after her long silence. "He is a lawyer. They ask questions that way."

Dr. Kalonimos's lips moved without words as she composed an answer. "For what you describe to happen, there would have to have been a unique event, perhaps mutation of the DNA that would change the genes."

"Once that took place, would the gene, the one of immunity, be something that could be inherited?"

She shrugged, overawed by the number of assumptions. "I suppose so. Once the DNA mutates, I would suppose almost anything is possible."

"What causes a mutation?"

"Well, there any number of mutations, such as a point mutation in which there is a simple change in sequence, a frame shift where one or more bases are inserted or deleted, a . . ."

Lang held up a hand, stop. "Okay, okay! What causes these events?"

"A variety of things, known and unknown. A mistake a cell makes in copying itself, some environmental factors . . ."

Again the stop sign. "If environment can cause a change in DNA, then is it possible Mithradates' immunizing himself by exposure to various toxins was such a change in his environment?"

Dr. Kalonimos nodded slowly. "I suppose it is possible."

Lang leaned forward again. "And if it became part of his DNA, then it would not be surprising if his descendants have the same immunities, right?"

She nodded again. "No more than Africans' immunity to malaria."

"Then," Lang said, almost to himself, "the question becomes how does the DNA become transferrable from a blood sample?"

CHAPTER 56

Rhodes Town
Thirty Minutes Later

THE WAITER SAT A FROSTY CARAFE of white Greek wine on the table. "Semeli, from Nemea," he assured Gurt and Lang. "You will enjoy."

Lang didn't want to think how often that promise had proved hollow. Instead, he nodded knowledgeably.

"You are familiar with this wine?" Gurt asked.

"Only in that it probably would make a decent paint remover. The Greeks make great beer. Wine, not so much."

"Then why did you order it?"

"Because that was what Dr. Kalonimos was drinking, and she survived."

"Survival is your criteria for wine? Why not have another beer with your lunch?"

"Seemed we ought to at least try the local wine."

Gurt gave him her patented and-they-say-women-are-not-logical look. "You will be okay? You quit the beer hours ago?"

"With something to eat, yeah." He checked his watch. "Half past one, 13:30 local. Yeah, I'd say I'll be fine."

Lunch arrived. Gurt picked at her salad of greens, olives, and feta with vinaigrette. Lang had what could be described as Greece's national dish, moussaka, a lamb and eggplant casserole. They ate without conversation until Gurt was chasing her last olive around the bowl and Lang gave voice to what they were both thinking.

"Well, we got an answer to the question of whether an immunity can be inherited."

Gurt speared the last remnant of feta cheese. "*You* got an answer perhaps. You pushed her pretty hard, the way you might treat an enemy witness."

"Hostile witness."

"It is the same."

Lang thought about that. Maybe it was. Maybe he had pushed Dr. Kalonimos into agreement rather than scientific fact.

His thoughts would have been less academic had he been able to see behind the northeast corner of the battlements of the Palace of the Grand Masters only a block away. Built as the last line of defense of the walled city, each corner was a crenelated tower, taller than any surrounding structure. Ideal for medieval archers, the turrets now also worked to conceal a man appearing to be a photographer with a huge telephoto lens.

Most of the palace's visitors made quick note of the fortress' exterior defenses before ducking back inside, out of the relentless sun. Fifth-century mosaics of the Chamber with Colonnades and Medusa Chamber could be viewed in the relative cool of stone walls over two-feet thick.

The temperature, though, did not seem to bother the man with the camera on the northeast tower. The 90-plus-degree heat would have been considered a mild spring day in his native land when the Loo blew across the plains of northern Pakistan and the thermometer hovered in the 120s at midday. And this opportunity was heaven sent.

He was far too engrossed in making the most of the opportunity that had come from Allah himself, a chance to put himself in command of the empire of the recently deceased Alkandres Kolstas. Had it not been the hand of Allah that had sent him to the Athens airport this morning to meet a business associate of Kolstas, a tribal chief from Afghanistan whose poppy production had been slipping? Truthfully, Kolstas suspected the man had found another buyer and had intended to use whatever means necessary to ascertain if this were true.

Kolstas's man had arrived in the Athens airport yesterday afternoon ready to escort the visitor to Trikoupi Street. But right there at the airport was the American, Reilly, the man who had not only escaped a week or so ago, but made the boss look like a fool in the process. A quick phone call to the office in Piraeus informed him the boss had been killed, shot in the head like a mad dog, while a big blonde woman had somehow detained the guards posted on the street. A blonde like the one with Reilly.

The man on the palace battlements had worked for the Greek mostly as muscle, but he was not stupid. With Kolstas dead, the organization was leaderless. Whoever could step in, take charge, and demonstrate leadership abilities was likely to have the loyalty of the rest. And one way to demonstrate leadership would be to become the one who avenged the dead Greek. *Ghesasn*, the Koran's, sanctioning slaying of those who kill a relative. Either kill the murderer, accept the blood money as payment for the life, or forgive. The last two were hardly options, and Kolstas was hardly related. As a good Sunni, the man at least gave thought to the teachings of the Prophet, peace be upon him. No time now to split theological hairs.

It was divine intervention that he had seen Reilly, the will of Allah that he should note the pair waiting for the Aegean Air flight to Rhodes. It was an act from paradise itself that there was a single seat left on the aircraft, never mind the visiting Afghan chieftain whose business with Kolstas was mooted by the Greek's death. In the jumble of traffic, following their taxi to the old town unobserved had been child's play. At the inflated price offered, a passing Japanese tourist had gleefully sold him one of the multiple cameras hanging from his neck like a pagan necklace. He had, of course, chosen the one with the biggest telephoto lens. Taking pictures would draw far less attention than a pair of binoculars, and he had no intention of getting close to Reilly until he was ready to strike.

But where?

The *taverna* where Reilly and the woman were having lunch would be ideal. Reilly was seated, a position from which it would be difficult to defend himself, even if he somehow anticipated the attack at the last moment. With terrified diners scattering in all directions, escape should be easy.

He swept the open dining area with the lens.

No. Only one entrance and exit, though. With over a hundred potentially terrified people trying to get out at once, he could be trapped.

The adjacent street, the Street of the Knights?

Crowded, but a possibility. Open at both ends with several medieval alleys connecting. And that street was the only exit from where the pair were dining.

He replaced the lens cap and went inside to the double staircase that led to the first floor and outside.

CHAPTER 57

Offices of Dystra Pharmaceuticals
Atlanta, Georgia
At the Same Time (7:32 A.M.)

To WILLIAM GRASSLEY, THE PANELED BOARDROOM had become a scene from a recurrent nightmare. He knew it had been a little over a week since he and the executive committee — himself, Hassler, and Wright — had gathered here to discuss the latest failure to obtain what was now referred to as the Turkish blood sample. It seemed like yesterday.

What was anything but a dream was that the company's stock languished in the low teens, a fraction of where it had been on the NASDAQ a year ago when hopes for the feted fat pill had been high. Those hopes had been hyped by subtle "news" releases that had sent both market and shareholder expectations soaring.

When the news of FDA non-approval leaked before entering the common domain, Grassley had sold over half his shares through nominees, straw men, and empty corporations. Potential insider-trading charges paled in comparison to certain ruin if he could not maintain the high lifestyle demanded by his trophy wife, his second marriage to a woman only a year or so older than the children by his first.

Besides, they only prosecuted high-profile people for buying and selling stocks with knowledge unavailable to the average investor, like Martha Stewart, right?

What was real enough were the ugly letters and e-mail he was receiving from stockholders, and the threats of closer scrutiny of his leadership qualities at the annual shareholders' meeting this fall when his employment contract came up for renewal.

Ralph Hassler entered, opening the door to allow a woman carrying a tray with a coffee urn and cups to enter in front of him, "Morning, Bill!"

Grassley scowled at the unwarranted cheerful tone as Hassler settled into a chair.

"Thanks for joining us," he said, his voice heavy with sarcasm.

As usual, Hassler was late.

The only other man in the room, Hugh Wright, acknowledged the latecomer with a begrudging nod.

"I'll take care of that, Mindy," Grassley growled at the woman arranging sugar, cream, cups, and coffee on a heavy mahogany sideboard.

She nodded and made for the door, Grassley shutting it behind her and latching it.

Hassler was filling a cup. "I hope we're not here for more doom and gloom. Tell me there has been a positive development."

Grassley returned to his place at the head of the table. "Actually, yes. Our people at Emory tell me the Yerkes Primate Center has had some success with a serum made from the Turkish blood sample."

"Our people?" Wright wanted to know. "Hopefully more reliable than the welfare mother who alerted us to the sample in the first place."

"That welfare mother, as you call her, was right on," Hassler snarled, offended at anything remotely resembling a racial slur. "Hadn't been for her, we never would have known about the sample and its potential."

"And we wouldn't have been complicit in attempted murder and kidnapping, not to mention a home invasion and multiple conspiracies."

"I didn't hear your protest . . ."

"Gentlemen!" Grassley was standing, hands outstretched, the peacemaker. "We're pretty much all in the same boat here."

Glaring at each other, the two combatants settled in chairs on opposite sides of the table, the stretch of mahogany an armed border between belligerent nations.

Grassley settled into his chair. "As I was saying before you two got into a pissing contest, it seems that blood sample has yielded a serum with potentially positive results."

Wright's fingers were entwined, his elbows on the table. "I suppose that's good news, but unless we get our hands on it, how does it benefit Dystra?"

"That, gentlemen, is what we are here to decide."

CHAPTER 58

Rhodes Town

LANG AND GURT EXITED THE *TAVERNA* and turned left on the Avenue of the Knights, the Palace of the Grand Masters behind them. Ahead, the cobblestone road passed under a pair of Gothic arches before heading uphill as it turned onto the Soka tous Sokratous. They took Orfeos Street to St. Anthony's Gate, the newest of the city's 11 gates, having been constructed in 1512. There was little of historic interest in this, the northeast quadrant of Old Rhodes Town, and consequently, few tourists, although a number of open shops were bustling a few blocks away. Both turned to take a final look toward the harbor, searching the faces of the few pedestrians for any they might have seen earlier that day before crossing sun-seared grass, through d'Amboise Gate and onto a causeway leading to the twenty-first century.

"You notice him?" Lang asked.

Gurt was surveying the flood of traffic swirling along the streets of contemporary Rhodes Town, one more tourist competing for a taxi. "Dark-skinned, possibly Arabic, certainly Middle Eastern. Could be one of Kolstas's Pakistanis. Was pretending to take pictures."

"Pretending?"

"You saw it, too: the lens cap was on."

Lang had noticed. He simply wanted confirmation he had not been mistaken.

As one, they turned and re-entered the towering stone of St. Anthony's Gate, passing into one more cobblestone street. Although the truly medieval section of town was blocks away, there were enough twists, turns, intersections, and alleys here to confuse your average laboratory rat. Instead of stone facades of a city built with defense in mind, open shops displayed local art and products. Pottery, decorative tiles, lace, and embroidery loaded shelves and counters.

One or more cruise boats had docked in the large harbor, as evidenced by passengers in uniform white socks and sneakers, sunburns, and t-shirts from the previous island. Milling about in search of souvenirs or gifts, they screened the man with the camera.

He thanked Allah for the sudden infusion of people. Unlike the confined taverna, cross streets and alleys would provide a perfect escape route among the confusion and panic the very public execution of Reilly would cause. He let the heavy camera hang from his neck as his hand slid into a pants pocket to assure him the switchblade was still there. All he had to do was brush up against his victim, a seemingly accidental contact in a crowded area. Slide the blade upward between the top two or three ribs, and walk away. An excellent chance he would be gone before anyone realized what had happened. Easy, perhaps too easy . . .

Likewise, the new arrivals were going to provide cover for Reilly and the woman, make it more difficult to keep them in sight. One moment they were hand-in-hand, examining a string of agate, sard, and amethyst, a replica of a bead necklace pictured as being taken from an ancient tomb. In the next instant, the woman alone was admiring wood carvings hanging from the ceiling of a shop across from the dark of an intersecting alley.

Where had Reilly gone?

The man quickly stepped across the mouth of an alley, the one with the woman on the other side. Reilly wasn't to the right or left.

Which meant he had to be . . .

From the alley, an arm encircled his neck, dragging him into confines so narrow it was doubtful the sun ever dispersed the shadows. The suddenness of the attack deprived him of any chance of defense.

The arm around his neck was tightening. His ears were ringing and eyesight was dimming. His struggles to loosen the strangling grasp were weakening.

A voice, dream-like to his oxygen-starved brain, whispered, "Give it up, asshole. Keep resisting and you'll be dead in another minute, if I don't break your neck first."

He did quit resisting. Not from choice but necessity. The lack of air caused by the compression of his trachea was making the dingy alley even darker. His knees buckled, no longer willing to support him. With a fluidity that all but belied a spine, he slumped to the ground.

Behind him, Lang released the chokehold, the hold using the crook of the elbow to squeeze the neck with pressure applied by the opposite hand on the wrist, the figure four as it had been known in Agency training.

He was on the back of the man on the ground almost as soon as he fell. Hands searched pockets while the man coughed his way back from the near dead. Lang's fingers closed around the knife.

He flicked the blade open and dashed it against the stone of the alley. It took three attempts before the steel yielded, breaking off just above the handle.

Lang stood.

The would-be assassin was on hands and knees, still gasping as though each breath might well be his last.

Dropping the now-useless knife, Lang turned his attention to him. "Who sent you?"

The reply was unintelligible, either because of the speaker's panting or because Lang didn't understand the language. The tone, however, suggested an anatomical impossibility in any tongue.

Lang repeated the question with the same result.

He looked at the rectangle of sunlight that was the mouth of the alley. So far, so good. No one had noticed what was going on in the twilight. The man was still on all fours. He took a step back and delivered a kick to the man's side. Was it his imagination, or did he really hear ribs crack? There was no doubting the scream of agony.

"Okay, we'll try again. Who sent you?"

The man was curled into a fetal ball on the ground. "Nobody," he grunted.

"How did you find me?"

"Didn't." The voice was coming in gulps as if the words themselves were choking him.

Lang stepped back, beginning to swing his leg, a punter looking for no return. "Wrong answer."

"No!" the man pleaded, a hand extended in supplication.

Was that blood frothing along his lips? One of the ribs had punctured a lung.

Lang stood still. "Okay, who sent you, and how did you find me?"

"Didn't." The man was having problems speaking. "You were in Athens airport this morning. Me, too. I called Kolstas's office, heard he'd been killed. Figured you had . . ."

A woman's scream. Lang spun around to see a large woman at the alley's entrance, hands over her mouth and eyes wide with fright. Within the second, the narrow space was filled with gawking tourists. It didn't require a genius to guess they thought they were witnessing a robbery or murder, and it didn't require a Harvard PhD to know the police would soon arrive.

The man on hands and knees came to the same conclusion. He pushed himself up onto wobbly legs and staggered toward the street as the newly formed crowd parted like a human Red Sea to let him pass. Lang made it through, too. He didn't wait for some over eager soul to take his duties as a citizen too zealously and try to stop him until the authorities arrived.

Gurt was waiting a block away. She raised her eyebrows in an unasked question.

Lang took her hand. "Later. Right now we need to disappear."

CHAPTER 59

472 Lafayette Drive
Atlanta, Georgia
Two Days Later
7:08 P.M.

THE SOUND OF A LAWN MOWER and the smell of freshly cut grass flowed through an open window of the kitchen where Gurt was rinsing tomatoes and onions in the sink. To Leon's disappointment, the doctor had that morning pronounced him fit for light work such as guiding a self-propelled lawn mower. The tomatoes were the first from her garden behind the pool that had somehow survived the neighborhood squirrels.

Lang peered over her shoulder into the backyard where Leon was walking behind the mower with only minor hindrance from Manfred's efforts at assistance. "Looks like he's finally got the hang of the Toro TimeMaster."

Gurt didn't look up as she turned off the faucet. "How many times did you have to show him how to start it?"

"Every time he uses it. He's not a fast learner. He'd need help changing a lightbulb."

Gurt placed the vegetables on a wooden cutting board. "Perhaps. But he is not afraid of work. He weeds the garden weekly."

"He can tell the difference between vegetable plants and weeds?"

Gurt was chopping the onions and tomatoes. She would add olive oil, dill, and a sprinkling of sugar to make a salad to go with the chicken breasts in mustard sauce that Lang would shortly place on the charcoal already smoldering in the Weber.

In the warm months, she preferred food from the grill. It not only kept the heat of the stove out of the house, she said, but the unhealthy grease fell into the fire instead of soaking into the meat. Lang knew better than to point out the house's air conditioning was more than capable of handling the heat, and the "unhealthy" grease could easily be removed from the cooking pan. Where matters of health or the house were concerned, silence was not only golden but wise. Enduring ravenous mosquitoes, inexactly cooked meat, and an occasional grain or so of dirt should something slip off a tray and be retrieved before Grumps could get to it were small inconveniences with which he purchased domestic tranquility.

She changed the subject. "Have you called Miles?"

Lang nodded. "About an hour ago. No telling when he'll call back."

Miles Berkley, one of Lang and Gurt's few remaining contacts within the Agency. An anachronism, Miles reflected the Agency's early days when its predecessor, the World War II Office of Strategic Services' initials, OSS, were said to stand for "Oh, So Social," a commentary on the high social status of the blue-blood Harvard and Yale men who comprised the bulk of its operatives in those days. Miles's family owned a substantial portion of Alabama. He had attended a prestigious New England prep school (Lang could never remember if it was St. Paul or Groton) and done his undergraduate work at Princeton before deciding on a career in the shadows of intelligence work rather than joining the family agribusiness. His contemporaries in the Agency, including Gurt and Lang, had speculated the man carried extra pinpoint Oxford cloth shirts in his briefcase, since the one he wore at any time of day was as crisp as the creases in the trousers of his single-breasted, vented, bespoke suits.

Lang suspected Miles and Gurt might have had something going during the period Lang was married to Dawn. It was something she declined to discuss, pointing out that Lang had ended their relationship when he met Dawn.

"*Das geht dich nichts an*," she'd say with a smile. Don't go there, or mind your own business. And she was right: what she did in the years they did not see each other, the years Lang was married, was hardly his concern.

It bothered him anyway.

"It'll depend on where he is," Lang added.

Contacting Miles required calling a number with a Washington, D.C., area code and leaving a message with an operator who always announced in a bored voice, "Mr. Berkley is unavailable at the moment. Whom may I say called?"

How long it took Miles to return the call seemed to bear a direct ratio to how far he was from the United States.

Tonight, apparently not so far. The phone in Lang's office, the former broom closet under the stairs, rang.

Lang was there in less than five steps. The number shown on the receiver's screen was "unknown." Either Miles or a telemarketer ignoring the no-call list.

"Miles?"

"Good evening, Langford," Miles's mellifluous Southern accent had a faint echo, evidence it was being transmitted from its origin to multiple sources before reaching Lang, making tracing virtually impossible. "I trust you and Gurt are well. To what do I owe the pleasure?"

"I need a favor, Miles."

A short pause reinforced the fact the conversation was being re-transmitted, and then a sigh, the theatric quality of which was only slightly diminished by the electronics. "Alas, I had hoped you were calling seeking sage counseling, witty dialogue, enchanting company, or all of the above. Or better yet, that Gurt, that Aphrodite of a woman, had come to her senses and abandoned you."

"Not tonight, Miles."

Lang often wondered if Miles's reports to his superiors were as grandiloquent as the speech he enjoyed. If so, explanations for some of the Agency's worst gaffes might be at hand: by the time one got through the bullshit, whatever crisis was imminent had passed.

"Just a favor," he added.

"And what poor service might I render my good friends?"

"Information. I need to know whatever I can find out about a William Grassley, CEO of an outfit called Dystra Pharmaceuticals, based here in Atlanta."

The pause was so long Lang feared the connection had been severed. "Miles?"

This time the sigh was for real. "Lang, you know very well the Agency is specifically prohibited from any domestic activities, most especially gathering information on U.S. citizens."

"I also know the Agency is supposedly restricted to those operations likely to gather intelligence relevant to our enemies abroad, and not assume a paramilitary role executing them by drone like you're doing in Pakistan."

"Our actions there have authorization from as high as you can go," Miles said stiffly.

"I'm proud of you. Now, about that favor. You know, a gratuitous service. Like Gurt and I damn near getting killed in Haiti gathering information for you a few years ago. By the way, how 'authorized' was getting us to do the Agency's business?"

"I'll see what I can do."

The line really did go dead this time.

CHAPTER 60

Law Offices of Langford Reilly
Peachtree Center
227 Peachtree Street
Atlanta, Georgia
The Next Morning

By THE TIME SARA ARRIVED AT her desk and began taking numbers from the answering service, her employer was already in a foul mood. Her first clue was a piggish grunt when she made the routine inquiry as to his coffee choice of the day.

After an extensive Internet search a year ago, Lang had purchased a coffeemaker the size of a small refrigerator. The device was a caffeine lover's dream. The face, only slightly less complex than the instrument panel of your average Boeing 757, presented choices of mocha, espresso, hot milk, or hot chocolate in addition to sub-selections of three different blends.

All of that, and what she got was rudeness.

Being a grandmother had given her experience in dealing with truculent children — and, to her, men were nothing but oversized children. She was about to give Lang a brief but cogent tutorial on manners when addressing a lady, particularly a lady far senior to him in years. Maybe even her semimonthly threat to quit, to seek other if not greener pastures, where at least the rules of etiquette were observed.

Then the phone rang.

"Law office," Sara answered.

"Lang Reilly?"

In the spirit of general grumpiness that seemed to be prevailing this morning, Sara almost blurted out, "Do I sound like Lang Reilly?"

Instead, she politely asked, "May I tell him who is calling?"

"No. Just let me speak to him."

Should she alert the CDC of an epidemic of bad manners?

Instead, she put the mystery caller on hold. "There's a call for you. Won't say who he is," she said through the open door to Lang's inner sanctum.

He hardly looked up. "Screw him."

That was it.

Sara had had enough.

She carefully arranged the pink callback slips, locked her desk drawer and the file cabinet behind her desk, and stood.

"Where are you going?" Lang wanted to know.

"Home, or someplace where civility reigns. I do not need to be spoken to in that manner, and I won't. If you're lucky, I may look in on you tomorrow to see if you've suddenly remembered the manners your momma taught you."

Lang came from behind his desk, all apology. "I'm sorry, Sara. It's just that . . . Well, the court has scheduled a pre-trial hearing on Wipp. That guy has leeched off society all his life, and now he's leeching off me. We aren't getting paid, you know. It just piss . . . aggravates me no end, defending a criminal like that for free."

Only slightly mollified, Sara stopped halfway toward the door. "Guess you'll just have to — as those weird EST people say, 'Ride that horse the way it's going.' You're the one who took him on as a client, knowing what sort of a person he is and what a scam that EST thing was."

"Sara, we do a criminal practice. Nobody walks through that door who isn't at least suspected of doing something illegal. We don't get paid to represent choirboys."

Sara sat back down behind her desk, making moves indicating she might stay. "You ask me, we should cater to a better class of criminal."

Simultaneously, they both became aware they were not alone. In the doorway to the outside hall, a man was standing.

"Hope I'm not intruding."

Late twenties, early thirties, inexpensive suit, cheap haircut, shoes with thick rubber soles that screamed "cop."

He extended his right hand. "I just called, but it seems we got disconnected. Mr. Reilly, Langford Reilly?"

Lang shook it. "You're in the right place. Who might you be?"

The man withdrew his hand as he shot a glance toward Lang's office. "It might be better if we spoke in private."

Lang turned with a shrug. "Have it your way."

Lang stood aside to let the mysterious visitor enter before following and shutting the door behind them. As he slid behind his desk, he couldn't help but notice the man across it seemed to be taking in the furnishings, the subtle colors of the Kerman rug on which floated a Thomas Elfe breakfront with its trademark lazy eights, one of perhaps a dozen pieces by the colonial cabinetmaker still in existence. Gilt-inscribed leather bindings of first editions of both Blackstone and Coke were visible through its wavy, handblown glass. The centerpiece was the Boule desk with its ornate brass fittings and fruitwood inlays, behind which a Turner was highlighted. Two eighteenth-century French wing chairs upholstered in toile faced it, a French commode between them.

"This an office or a museum?"

It was a commentary on the criminal practice that it was the rare visitor that recognized the furnishings had not come from Walmart.

Lang smiled. "A little of both, I suppose." He sat behind the desk. "But then, I doubt you came here for a tour of European antiques, Mr . . . "

The man settled into one of the French wing chairs. "I could give you a name but it wouldn't be mine, so what's the point? Suffice it to say, Mr. Berkley is a mutual friend."

No wonder for the mystery. The Agency believed in secrecy for secrecy's sake. Believed? Worshipped would be more appropriate. And not even giving a name, albeit a fictitious one? The arrogance was typical of any number of federal agencies whose alphabet soup initials stood for names frequently paradoxical. Bureau of Army Intelligence, for instance.

Lang regarded the Man with No Name as he picked up a ballpoint pen and began to run it from finger to finger. "Okay, so we both know Miles. I assume you're here at his direction."

The nameless man looked anything but comfortable in one of the wing chairs. Lang had seen to it they were rock-hard. Cozy clients tended to linger past their time. "Assume what you wish, Mr. Reilly. I'm here because of a reference you made to an international crime kingpin, a Greek, a certain Alkandres Kolstas."

Lang said nothing. Long ago he had learned that silence often produced results conversation did not.

The Man with No Name could play the same game.

After a full minute, Lang said, "And . . .?"

"I was informed you knew Kolstas."

Lang hadn't mentioned the Greek to Miles. No Name was connected to one of the many bureaucracies whose chief function was to indiscriminately snoop on a public just awakening to the fact. "I met him."

No Name leaned forward, elbows on his knees. "And the purpose of that meeting?"

Now it was Lang's turn. "Personal business."

The man in the chair waited, obviously anticipating an explanation that wasn't forthcoming, before, "You are aware Kolstas is dead?" Lang mimed surprise.

"The Greek police think it was an intra-gang affair, someone in his own organization who wanted to be the boss."

Lang stopped moving the pen around. "And you're telling me this because . . . ?"

"Oh! I thought you knew: you mentioned one of Kolstas's associates, business partner, whatever, to Miles Berkley."

Lang had shucked oysters with more ease than getting information out of this guy. "And?"

"Exactly what do you know of the relationship between a William Grassley and Kolstas?"

Lang thought a moment. The problem with information was that it was a highly perishable commodity. Once revealed, it quickly lost value. Conversely, this particular set of facts had little value to him. "Just why do you want to know?"

"I'm not at liberty to say."

Lang stood, extending his hand. "I think our conversation is at an end."

No Name had not expected this. He motioned for Lang to sit back down. The bluff had worked. "Let's say that certain law enforcement agencies have an interest in Mr. Grassley and his company, Dystra Pharmaceuticals."

"You might tell them to look at Barclay's Bank of the Cayman Islands.

Grassley and/or Dystra have an account there from which they pay people like Kolstas for work that doesn't bear watching by law enforcement."

The Man with No Name seemed incredulous. "Kolstas told you this?"

"He did."

"I can't imagine circumstances that would cause him to reveal that sort of information."

"Then you are lucky."

No Name sat, staring at Lang for a moment, before standing. "You've been a help to your government, Mr. Reilly. By the way, this little conference never happened. You don't know who I am or for whom I work, right?"

How many times had Lang heard that? He said nothing but stood and drew a finger across his mouth, zipping his lips. "Mum's the word."

He watched his visitor depart.

"Who was that?" Sara asked as the outer door shut.

"Didn't get his name, but we have — had — an acquaintance in common."

She shook her head, muttering. She knew when her boss wasn't going to explain.

CHAPTER 61

Piedmont Driving Club South
Two Months Later

LANG WATCHED FRANCIS LINE UP HIS putt with the precision of a sniper aiming at his victim: slope of the green, windage, resistance of the immaculately cut grass. The click of the putter against ball sent it rolling left of the cup before swerving and heading straight as a homing pigeon, ending its journey with a metallic sound as it fell in the hole.

"How did you do that?" Lang asked.

"I didn't. There's a slight change in gradient that makes the ball break."

Lang wasn't so sure, but what the hell? With a score that already averaged six to seven strokes a hole, what was there to lose? He squatted to line up his shot, not because he needed to, but because the pros he had recently begun watching on the Golf Channel did it with great result. A couple of practice swings, and he thought this would determine if he broke a score of 80 for the first nine holes for the first time.

He tapped the ball.

It rolled pretty much along the line of Francis's putt until it broke right, in the opposite direction. Adding injury to insult, it continued along the all but imperceptible slope of the green back onto the fairway, where the angle of descent increased abruptly. Down the hill it went, building speed until it disappeared into the lake.

To Lang, that lake was Charlie Brown's kite-eating tree right out of the Peanuts comic strip. He was convinced that, lurking somewhere beneath its surface, there was a shark-sized bass that had reached gargantuan size feasting on his golf balls.

Both men silently watched the spreading ripples.

Lang finally spoke. "I understand why you hear God's name out here so often."

There was a muffled snicker from one of the two teenaged girls acting as caddies. Lang pretended he didn't hear.

"The rules provide you can play your ball from where it lies or take a drop with a one-shot penalty," Francis informed him with ill-concealed amusement.

Lang handed his putter to the grinning caddy. "You know, Francis, the problem with playing with you is I can't feel free to curse a priest even if he is wearing an outfit that would look better on a circus clown."

Francis's bright red trousers clashed with the electric green golf shirt.

"Delighted to hear the heathen hath some moral restraints," Francis responded amiably. "Now, drop or play? Not that it matters. *Vanitas vanitatum, omnis vanitas.*"

Lang eyed the lake. Was that his imagination, or had he glimpsed a large, triangular fin for an instant?

"I'll drop."

He still two-putted.

Followed by caddies, the two walked toward the next hole.

Seven iron in hand, Francis decapitated dandelions as they went. "You said you were no longer worried about the people who ransacked the house while I was there. What were they after, anyway?"

"A blood sample from a kid in Turkey. Turned out a pharmaceutical house was after it."

"Must have been pretty valuable to commit burglary and attempted murder."

"It was. Or the serum based on it is. One of the biggies, Merck, has contracted to pay the Foundation a couple of hundred mil for it."

Francis whistled. "*Quaerenda pecunia primum est.*"

"'*Virtus post nummos*' finishes Horace's thought," Lang added. "'Money is the first thing to be sought,' yes. But "a good reputation, after wealth.'"

"So, you can prove this pharmaceutical company was behind the break-in? I've never felt more in the hands of the Lord than while I was staring down the barrel of his gun."

Lang's mind flashed a picture of the priest with a gun to his head. Knowing the depth of his friend's faith, he could imagine the equanimity with which he faced death. "*Quod avertat Deus!* But yeah, it's provable. At least the U.S. Attorney thinks so. Company's name is Dystra Pharmaceuticals. All of its top officers are under indictment for money laundering, RICO, conspiracy, you name it. The company and its executives are also facing civil suits for patent infringement and varying degrees of industrial espionage, stealing competitors' trade secrets. All but one, that is."

"Why an exception?"

"I understand their chief operating officer, guy named Wright, swallowed his shotgun the day the indictment came down."

Francis paused long enough to cross himself, a gesture he rarely made outside of his church.

"That bad, huh?"

"Suicide is a sin. It is God's place to decide the time and circumstances of our death."

Lang smiled. "Well, it's for sure God wasn't looking at 15 to 20 in the Iron Bar Hotel."

Francis shook his head, having long decided Lang's irreverence, if not downright blasphemy, was as much his personality as his love for single malt scotch. "Speaking of jail, what about your client, Wipp, the one who belonged to that weird cult?"

"More like a cult of weirdos. Wipp bonded out. Damned if he didn't go right back to advertising seminars on the Internet, 'training,' he calls them. Of course, after the current crop of suckers, there was no seminar. I thought the judge was going to launch into outer space, he was so pissed. He revoked Wipp's bail."

"What does that mean?"

They had reached the tee. Lang stared at the limp flag dangling on its staff about 300 yards of manicured grass away. "It means Wipp is in jail until trial, either at the pre-trial detainee center out at the penitentiary or at one of the local jails where the DOP leases space."

Francis used his forearm to wipe his brow. "DOP?"

"*Department of Prisons.*"

"You don't know where exactly?"

"Only that it will be one where Wipp can't get his hands on a computer. I'm sure I'll be notified in due course."

Francis gestured to the forward part of the tee, indicating Lang should drive first. "No chance you're going to get paid?"

Lang took the driver proffered by his caddy and took a few practice swings before teeing up the ball. "About as much chance as I have of breaking par on this hole."

"*Manus e nubibus*, perhaps?"

"I'll need a hand from the clouds."

The moment club met ball, Lang knew something different was happening. The driver felt good in his hands, and the impact had the clean crack of a rifle shot. At first, he thought he was hallucinating. The white dot that was his ball sailed true toward the distant green. A 100-, 150-yard drive? Even better, a couple of decidedly favorable bounces.

There was the sound of hand-clapping. "Great! Best shot you've ever made!"

"Yeah, if I could only remember what I did different."

Lang was not a believer in omens, but he really did have a chance of breaking par on this hole. Maybe even a chance of getting paid by his client. If he could nail a drive like that, anything was possible. He began to whistle Glenn Miller's *Chattanooga Choo Choo*.

AUTHOR'S NOTE

Mithradates was an actual person. Machiavelli praised his military genius. European royalty sought his secret and Mozart wrote his first opera about him. He ruled what is now the north coast of Turkey and fought the Roman Republic twice. Only after sending their best generals, Sula and Pompey, did the Romans succeed in curbing Mithradates' ambitions to rule the Roman province of Asia (today's Turkey). Rather than be taken prisoner by his rebellious son, he took an enormous amount of poisons with no effect. Twice, he upped the dosage until he finally reached a fatal level.

Because its sure presence was difficult to ascertain, its abundance in nature plentiful, and its source obscure, poisons of varying types remained a favorite tool for ancient assassins.

Most of the material concerning Mithradates comes from Adrienne Mayor's fascinating biography of him, *The Poison King*.

A few more comments: the Black Mafia Family was a very real crime family centered in Atlanta. Although it supposedly no longer exists, snippets in the local news appear occasionally about a supposed film on the subject being in progress.

EST really existed, and yes, the people P. T. Barnum described as being born every minute paid good money to be verbally abused. See Twain's *Adventures of Huckleberry Finn*, specifically the part where the King and the

Duke put on a stage presentation so bad that none of the attendees would admit they had been flimflammed.

The Yerkes Primate Center, though owned and operated by Emory University, is miles from the school in an adjacent county. I chose to put it on campus rather than slow the story down by explaining this.

Many people believe writing is a lonely pastime. Perhaps, but not an "alone" one. Were it not for a number of people's efforts, you wouldn't be reading this. First, my wife, Suzanne, spotted the biography of Mithradates that inspired the story. Thank you! Chris Fortunato, my agent, to whom I am perpetually grateful. Without his efforts and patience, this book wouldn't exist.

Then, Christina Roth and Kelsey Reiman of Turner's editorial staff, as well as Lynn Northrup. The editorial department of a publishing house is like the offensive line of a football team: their names never get called unless something goes wrong, but without them nobody moves the ball forward. These folks do a lot more than strew commas like Johnny Appleseed. They rearrange cumbersome verbage and check facts, and note inconsistences, too. I hastily add that if there are factual errors, it's because I insisted on what was written, not because Christina, Lynn, or Kelsey didn't catch them. My fault, not theirs — thanks, ladies.

April 2013
G.L.

ABOUT THE AUTHOR

Gregg Loomis is an American author of thrillers, including the popular Lang Reilly series. He has also written several short stories and was a nominee for Writer of the Year—Fiction by the Georgia Writers Association. Born in Atlanta, Georgia, where he still resides, Loomis is a former racecar driver and is licensed as a commercial pilot. He currently works as a lawyer specializing in commercial litigation. Over half a million copies of his books are in print, and several have been translated into multiple foreign languages.

CPSIA information ca
Printed in the USA
BVOW07s234201011
381632BV00

260064